THE SNAIL ON THE SLOPE

THE
SNAIL
ON THE
SLOPE

ARKADY AND BORIS STRUGATSKY

New Translation by Olena Bormashenko

Published by Chicago Review Press Incorporated
814 North Franklin Street
Chicago, Illinois 60610
ISBN 978-0-914091-87-5 (cloth)
ISBN 978-1-61373-754-5 (paperback)

Library of Congress Cataloging-in-Publication Data
Names: Strugatskiĭ, Arkadiĭ, 1925–1991, author. | Strugatskiĭ, Boris,
    1933–2012, author. | Bormashenko, Olena, translator.
Title: The snail on the slope / Arkady and Boris Strugatsky ; translated by
    Olena Bormashenko.
Other titles: Ulitka na sklone. English
Description: Chicago : Published by Chicago Review Press Incorporated,
    2018.
Identifiers: LCCN 2018008265 (print) | LCCN 2018017211 (ebook) |
    ISBN 9781613737552 (PDF edition) | ISBN 9781613737576
    (EPUB edition) | ISBN 9781613737569 (Kindle edition) | ISBN
    9780914091875 (cloth edition) | ISBN 9781613737545
    (trade pbk. edition)
Subjects: | LCGFT: Science fiction.
Classification: LCC PG3476.S78835 (ebook) | LCC PG3476.S78835 U413 2018
    (print) | DDC 891.73/44—dc23
LC record available at https://lccn.loc.gov/2018008265

Typesetting: Nord Compo

Printed in the United States of America
5 4 3 2 1

Beyond the bend, inside
The forest deep,
My future waits,
Its vow to keep.

It won't be argued, or
Be coaxed away.
A pine wood stark
And clear as day.

—Boris Pasternak

little snail
inch by inch, climb
Mount Fuji!

—Issa

1.

PERETZ

From this height, the forest looked like dappled, fluffy foam; like a gigantic, world-encompassing porous sponge; like an animal that had once lain hidden in wait, then had dozed off, becoming overgrown with coarse moss. Like a shapeless mask, hiding a face no one had ever seen.

Peretz threw off his sandals and sat down, dangling his bare feet into the abyss. It seemed to him that his heels immediately became damp, as if he had actually dipped them into the warm lilac fog that accumulated in the shadow beneath the cliff. He took the stones that he'd gathered out of his pocket and carefully arranged them next to him, then chose the smallest one and gently tossed it down into that living silence, to be swallowed forever by its sleeping, indifferent maw. The white spark went out, but nothing happened—nobody blinked, no one's eyes opened to take a look. Then he threw another stone.

If you threw a stone every minute and a half; and if the one-legged cook nicknamed Cazalunya had been telling the truth; and if Madame Bardot, the head of the Assistance to the Locals Team, had guessed right; and if truck driver Randy and L'Estrange from the Penetration Through Engineering Team, whispering together in the cafeteria, had gotten it wrong; and if human intuition was worth a damn; and if, for once in your life, wishes were granted— then on the seventh stone, the bushes behind you would rustle and part, and the Director would emerge onto the clearing: shirt- less, wearing gray gabardine pants with purple piping, breathing loudly, glistening with sweat, yellowish-pink and hairy. Then, paying no attention to anything, neither the forest beneath him nor the sky above him, he would begin to bend, sinking his broad palms into the grass, and unbend, creating a breeze with each swing of those broad palms, and every single time, the mighty crease in his stomach would roll over his pants, and a stream of air, saturated with nicotine and carbon dioxide, would shoot out his mouth, hissing and gurgling. Like a submarine flushing out its air tanks. Like a sulfur geyser on Paramushir Island . . .

The bushes behind him rustled and parted. Peretz glanced cautiously over his shoulder, but it wasn't the Director, it was his acquaintance Claudius Octavian Bootlicherson from the Eradica- tion Team. He approached slowly and stopped two paces away, staring down at Peretz with his dark eyes. He knew or suspected something, something very important, and this knowledge or sus- picion immobilized his long face, the transfixed face of a man who had brought here, to this precipice, strange, disquieting news; no one had heard this news yet—but it was already clear that everything had changed, that the past had ceased to matter, and that everyone would finally be asked to contribute according to his or her abilities.

"Whose shoes are these?" he asked, and looked around.

"These are not shoes," Peretz said. "They are sandals."

"Oh yes?" Bootlicherson smiled sardonically and pulled a large notebook out of his pocket. "Sandals? Excellent. But whose sandals are they?" He approached the precipice, cautiously looked down, and immediately stepped back. "A man sits by a precipice," he said, "a pair of sandals by his side. The question inevitably arises: Whose sandals are they, and where is their owner?"

"These are my sandals," Peretz said.

"Yours?" Bootlicherson looked at his large notebook with uncertainty. "So you're sitting barefoot? Why?" He decisively put the large notebook away and extracted a small notebook from a back pocket.

"It's the only way," explained Peretz. "Yesterday, my right shoe fell in, and I decided that from now on I will always sit barefoot." He bent over and looked between his parted knees. "There it is. Let me just take aim . . ."

"Wait a minute!" Bootlicherson nimbly caught his arm and took the stone away. "I concede, it's just a stone," he said. "But for now, that makes no difference. I don't understand why you'd lie to me, Peretz. After all, you can't see the shoe from here— that is, if it actually is down there, and we'll have to come back to that, that's a separate discussion—and since you can't see the shoe, you therefore can't expect to hit it with the stone, even if your aim were sufficiently good and your one and only goal were to hit it . . . But we're about to sort this all out." He stuffed the small notebook into his breast pocket and took the large notebook out again. Then he hitched up his pants and crouched down. "So we conclude that you also came here yesterday," he said. "What for? Why have you repeatedly come to a precipice that the other employees of the Administration, not to mention the visiting experts, never come to except maybe to relieve themselves?"

Peretz shrank back. This is just ignorance, he thought. No, no, he isn't trying to provoke me, he isn't being malicious, and I shouldn't take it seriously. It's nothing but ignorance. There's no reason to take ignorance seriously; no one ever takes ignorance seriously. Ignorance defecates on the forest. Ignorance always defecates on something or another, and as a rule, it's not taken seriously. Ignorance never takes ignorance seriously . . .

"You probably like to sit here," Bootlicherson continued silkily. "You probably really love the forest. Do you love it? Answer me!"

"What about you?" Peretz asked.

Bootlicherson sniffed. "That's not called for," he said huffily, and opened his notebook. "You know very well whom I work for. I work for the Eradication Team, and therefore your question, or rather your counterquestion, is absolutely meaningless. You are well aware that my attitude toward the forest is determined by my official duty, whereas I'm not at all sure what determines your attitude. This is not right, Peretz. Give it some serious thought— this advice is for your benefit, not my own. It's wrong to be so mysterious. Sitting by a precipice, barefoot, throwing stones . . . Why, I ask? If I were you, I'd tell me everything. To set the record straight. You never know, there may be mitigating factors and you may ultimately have nothing to fear. Well, Peretz? After all, you're a grown man, and you must appreciate that ambiguity is unacceptable." He closed the notebook and thought for a bit. "For example, consider a stone. Lying still, it's simplicity itself; it inspires no doubts. But now a hand picks it up and throws it. You see?"

"No," Peretz replied. "I mean, yes, of course."

"There you go. It's no longer the least bit simple. 'Whose hand was it?' we ask. 'Where did it throw it? Did it throw it to someone? Did it throw it *at* someone? And why?' . . . And how can you bear sitting so close to the edge? Did it come naturally, or did you have to practice? Personally, I can't bear sitting so close to the edge. And I shudder to think what could make me practice. I get dizzy. And that's as it should be. There's no reason for a man to sit close to the edge, anyway. Especially a man without a forest pass. Please show me your pass, Peretz."

"I don't have a pass."

"Ah. You don't have one. And why not?"

"I don't know . . . They won't give me one."

"That's right, they won't give you one. We know this. But why won't they give you one? I got one, she got one, he and his grandmother got one, but for some reason, they won't give you one."

Peretz glanced at him cautiously. Bootlicherson's long, thin nose was twitching; his eyes were blinking rapidly. "It's probably because I'm an outsider," Peretz suggested. "That's probably why."

"And I'm not the only one taking an interest in you," Bootlicherson confided. "If only it were just me! Higher-ups are taking an interest, too . . . Listen, Peretz, could you move farther away from the edge so we can continue? I get dizzy looking at you."

Peretz got up. "That's because you're neurotic," he said. "Let's not continue. We should get to the cafeteria or we'll be late."

Bootlicherson looked at his watch. "You're right, we should," he said. "I got carried away today. There's something about you, Peretz, that always makes me . . . I don't even know how to put it."

Peretz began to hop on one foot, pulling on his sandal.

"Oh, do get away from the edge!" Bootlicherson shrieked in anguish, waving his notebook at Peretz. "One of these days, your shenanigans will give me a heart attack!"

"I'm all done," Peretz said, stamping his foot. "I won't do it again. Shall we?"

"Let's go," Bootlicherson said. "But I must observe that you haven't answered a single one of my questions. I'm very disappointed in you, Peretz. Is that any way to act?" He took a look at his large notebook and, shrugging, tucked it under his arm. "It's almost strange. Not a single impression, never mind any information. A complete lack of clarity."

"What's there to say?" said Peretz. "I just came here to talk to the Director."

Bootlicherson froze, as if he had gotten caught in the bushes. "Oh, so that's how you do it," he said in a new voice.

"Do what? I don't do anything."

"No, no," Bootlicherson whispered, glancing around. "Hold your tongue. No need for words. I understand. You were right."

"What do you mean, you understand? What am I right about?"

"No, no, I don't understand anything. I don't understand, and that's the end of it. You may rest assured. I don't understand, that's final. And anyway, I wasn't here and didn't see you. If you really want to know, I spent the whole morning sitting on this bench. Lots of people will confirm it. I'll talk to them, I'll ask them."

They passed the bench, climbed the weathered stairs, turned into a tree-lined walk strewn with fine red sand, and entered the gates leading to the territory of the Administration.

"Complete clarity can only exist on a certain level," Bootlicherson was saying. "And everyone should be aware of what they can pretend to. I pretended to clarity on my level—that was my right—and I have exhausted it. And where rights end, responsibilities begin, and let me assure you that I know my responsibilities just as well my rights."

They walked past the two-story villas with tulle curtains in the windows, each one subdivided into ten apartments, passed the garage with its corrugated iron roof, and crossed the athletic field, where a torn volleyball net hung abandoned between the poles. They continued past the warehouses, where the riggers were dragging a huge red container from a truck, and past the hotel, whose manager—pasty, with staring, bulging eyes—was standing in the doorway and holding a briefcase. Then they walked along a long fence, hearing the metallic grinding sounds of the machines on the other side; they walked faster and faster, because there wasn't much time left, and Bootlicherson wasn't talking anymore but only wheezing and gasping, and then they began to run. And despite all that, when they burst into the cafeteria, it was already late and all the seats were taken, and the only table that wasn't full was the attendant's table at the back, which had two empty seats. The third seat was occupied by truck driver Randy, and Randy, noticing them hovering indecisively by the door, waved them over with a fork.

Everyone was drinking buttermilk, and Peretz also got some, so there was now a row of six bottles on the worn-out tablecloth; and when Peretz wiggled his feet under the table, trying to get comfortable on his chair, which was missing its seat, there was a sound of clinking glass, and an empty brandy bottle rolled out into the space between the tables. Truck driver Randy promptly grabbed it and stuffed it back under the table, and there was again a sound of clinking glass.

"Watch your feet," he said.

"It was an accident," Peretz said. "I didn't know."

"Think I did?" Randy retorted. "There are four of 'em down there—good luck proving later they aren't yours. They can prove that two plus two makes five if they've got a mind to."

"Well, I, for one, don't drink," Bootlicherson said with dignity. "So this doesn't apply to me."

"Don't drink, huh?" said Randy. "Guess I don't drink myself, then."

"But I have liver disease!" Bootlicherson started to sound worried. "How could you? Here's a doctor's note, take a look . . ."

He conjured up a wrinkled piece of paper with a triangular seal and waved it in Peretz's face. This really was an official note, written in a doctor's illegible handwriting. Peretz could only make out a single word, "Disulfiram," and when he became interested and tried to take the paper, Bootlicherson didn't let him have it and waved it in Randy's face.

"That's the most recent note," he said. "I also have notes for last year and the year before, except they are in my safe."

Truck driver Randy didn't look at the note. He said "Cheers," slowly drained a full glass of buttermilk, and belched. Then, tearing up, he said in a hoarser voice, "Say, know what else is in the forest? Trees." He wiped his eyes with his sleeve. "But they don't stay put, they jump, OK?"

"Yeah?" Peretz said eagerly. "How do they jump?"

"Like this. It starts off standing still. Like a normal tree. Then it wriggles, it squirms, and *BOOOOM!* Crash, bang, everything's topsy-turvy. Jumps about thirty feet. Bangs up my cab. And it's standing still again."

"Why?" Peretz asked. He could imagine this very clearly. But of course, it didn't wriggle or squirm; it trembled when approached and tried to get away. Maybe it was squeamish. Maybe it was scared. "Why does it jump?" he asked.

"That's what it's called, a jumping tree," Randy explained, pouring himself some buttermilk.

"We got a new shipment of power saws yesterday," Bootlicherson informed them, licking his lips. "They are phenomenally effective. I would venture to say that these are not merely saws but sawing engines. Our sawing engines of eradication."

Meanwhile, everyone around them was drinking buttermilk—out of glasses, out of tin mugs, out of coffee cups, out of rolled-up paper bags, and straight from the bottle. Everyone had their feet tucked under their chairs. And everyone could probably show doctor's notes about diseases of the liver, stomach, or duodenum. Notes for this year, and for previous years, too.

"And then the garage foreman sends for me," Randy continued in a loud voice, "and asks why my cab is dented. 'You bastard, have you been smuggling things again?' he says. Now you, Signor Peretz, you play chess with him—put in a good word for me. He respects you, he talks about you all the time . . . Peretz, he says, is a real man! 'I won't let Peretz use a car,' he says, 'don't even ask. Can't let a man like that go. You gotta understand, morons,' he says, 'we'll miss him.' So put in a good word for me, huh?"

"A-All right," Peretz said dejectedly. "I'll try. But what's this about a car?"

"I can talk to the garage foreman," said Bootlicherson. "We were in the military together: I was a captain, and he was my lieutenant. To this day, he greets me with a military salute."

"There are also mermaids," Randy said, his glass of buttermilk in midair. "In big clear lakes. They lie there, OK? Naked."

"That's all the buttermilk making you see things, Randall," said Bootlicherson.

"Never saw 'em myself," Randy objected, bringing the glass to his lips. "But water in these lakes isn't good to drink."

"You haven't seen them because they don't exist," Bootlicherson said. "Mermaids are a myth."

"Your mom's a myth," Randy said, wiping his eyes with his sleeve.

"Wait," Peretz said. "Wait. Randy, you say they lie there . . . What else do they do? They can't just lie there and that's all." Maybe they live underwater and swim to the surface, like we go out onto a balcony from smoke-filled rooms into the moonlit night, closing our eyes and letting the cool air wash over our faces—then maybe they just lie there. Just lie there, and that's all. Relaxing. And talking languidly and smiling at each other . . .

"Don't argue with me," Randy said, staring at Bootlicherson. "Have you ever been in the forest? Never been in the forest, and you run your mouth."

"That's silly," Bootlicherson said. "What would I do in your forest? I have a pass for your forest. Whereas you, Randall, have no pass. Please show me your pass, Randall."

"I never saw these mermaids myself," Randy repeated, addressing Peretz. "But I do believe in them. Because the boys talk about them. Even Candide talked about them. And Candide, now, he knew everything about the forest. He walked through the forest like he was going on a date—he knew everything in there by feel. And he died in there, in his forest."

"If he did die," Bootlicherson said meaningfully.

"No ifs about it. A man takes off in a helicopter, and there's no word for three years. There was an obituary in the paper, there was a wake—what else do you want? Candide got smashed up, of course."

"We know too little," Bootlicherson said, "to assert anything with any degree of certainty."

Randy spat and went up to the counter to get another bottle of buttermilk. Bootlicherson bent down to Peretz's ear and, glancing around cautiously, whispered, "You should be aware that there were classified instructions regarding Candide. I consider it my prerogative to inform you, since you're an outsider . . ."

"What instructions?"

"That he's to be presumed alive," Bootlicherson said in an audible whisper, and moved away. "Nice, fresh buttermilk today," he pronounced loudly.

The cafeteria filled with noise. People who were done with breakfast were getting up, moving their chairs out of the way, and heading to the exit; they spoke loudly, lit cigarettes, and threw the matches onto the floor. Bootlicherson kept looking around balefully, and addressed everyone who walked past with "What odd behavior, ladies and gentlemen, as you can see, we're having a conversation . . ."

When Randy returned with a bottle, Peretz said, "Did the garage foreman actually say that he wouldn't let me use a car? He was probably just kidding?"

"Why would he be kidding? He's very fond of you, Signor Peretz. He'll miss you, and what's in it for him? Say he does let you go, what good does that do him? He wasn't kidding."

Peretz bit his lip. "Then how can I leave? There's nothing left for me to do here. And my visa is ending. And then I'm simply ready to leave."

"You know," said Randy, "get written up three times and you'll be out on your ass in no time. They'll get you a special bus, wake the driver up in the middle of the night—you won't even have time to pack your stuff. Know how the boys do it? First time they get written up, they get demoted. Second time they get written up, they get sent into the forest for their sins. And the third time they get written up—good-bye and good riddance. Say I wanted to quit, I'd down half a bottle and punch this guy in the face." He pointed to Bootlicherson. "Now they take my bonuses away and I'm driving a manure truck. Then I do what? I down another half a bottle, and punch him in the face again. Then they take me off the manure truck and send me to the biological research station to chase microbes. But I don't go to the biological research station, I down another half a bottle and punch him for the third time. And that's it for me. I'm fired for hooliganism and I get sent off within twenty-four hours."

Bootlicherson wagged a finger at Randy. "You're spreading misinformation, Randall, you're spreading misinformation. First of all, there has to be at least a month between the incidents, otherwise all of the aforementioned behavior will be treated as a single episode, and the offender will simply be incarcerated, with no case being initiated within the Administration. Second of all, after the second offense, the guilty party would immediately get sent into the forest accompanied by a guard, so they would be denied the opportunity to commit the third offense at their discretion. Don't listen to him, Peretz, he doesn't understand these things."

Randy drank some buttermilk, grimaced and grunted. "That's true," he admitted. "I screwed up . . . It wouldn't do. My mistake, Signor Peretz."

"Don't worry about it," Peretz said sadly. "I can't assault a man for no reason, anyway."

"Well, you don't have to, *errr* . . . assault him," said Randy. "You could, say, give him a light kick in the, *err* . . . rear. Or just shove him."

"No, I can't do it," Peretz said.

"That's too bad," said Randy. "Then you're in trouble, Signor Peretz. Here's what we'll do. Come to the garage tomorrow morning around seven, get into my cab, and wait for me. I'll drive you."

"Really?" Peretz cheered up.

"Sure thing. I gotta haul scrap metal to the Mainland tomorrow. We'll go together."

Suddenly someone in the corner shrieked in a horrible voice, *"Look what you've done! You've spilled my soup!"*

"People should be easy to understand," said Bootlicherson. "I can't figure out why you want to leave, Peretz. No one wants to leave but you."

"That's how it always is with me," Peretz said. "I always do things backwards. And anyway, why should people be easy to understand?"

"People should be nondrinkers," Randy announced, belching. "Don't you agree?"

"I don't drink," Bootlicherson said. "And the reason I don't drink is very easy to understand: I have liver disease. So you can't trap me, Randall."

"The most surprising thing in the forest," said Randy, "is the swamps. They are hot, OK? I can't stand them. Just can't get used to them. I skid off the road, get stuck, then I sit there in my cab and can't get out. It's like hot cabbage soup. Steam comes off it, and it smells like cabbage soup, I've even tried it, but it didn't taste good—maybe it wasn't salty enough. No, people don't belong in the forest. And what the hell is the point, anyway? They keep going through machines like they're throwing them in a lake— they sink, they get more, they sink, they get more . . ."

A wealth of fragrant greenery. A wealth of colors, a wealth of smells. A wealth of life. And it's all alien. It's not completely unfamiliar, it's recognizable, but it's genuinely alien. That's probably the most difficult thing to accept—that it manages to be alien and familiar at the same time. That it's a product of our world, the flesh of our flesh, but that it has cut ties with us and doesn't want to know us. That's how a *Homo erectus* would probably feel about us, his descendants—bitter and afraid.

"When the order comes," Bootlicherson proclaimed, "we won't send in your crappy bulldozers and ATVs, we'll send in something real, and in two months, we'll turn it all into, um . . . a smooth, flat paved lot."

"You would," Randy said. "You'd turn your own dear dad into a paved lot if you had half a chance. To keep things simple."

There was a loud buzzing noise. Windows rattled in their frames, and at the same time, an earsplitting bell rang above the door, the lights on the wall began to flicker, and a large neon sign saying It's Time To Go! lit up above the counter. Bootlicherson rose hurriedly, reset his watch, and ran off without saying a word.

"Well, I'm off," Peretz said. "Time to work."

"It sure is," Randy agreed. "High time." He took off his jacket, carefully rolled it up, pushed the chairs together, and lay down, putting the jacket under his head.

"So tomorrow morning at seven, then?" Peretz said.

"What?" Randy asked sleepily.

"I'll come by tomorrow morning at seven."

"Come by where?" Randy asked, tossing and turning on the chairs. "Damn things slide apart," he muttered. "How many times do I have to tell them: get a couch . . ."

"To the garage," Peretz said. "To your truck."

"Ohhh . . . Sure, sure, come along, we'll see. These things are difficult." He pulled his knees up, crossed his arms over his chest and stuck his hands into his armpits, and began to breathe heavily. His arms were hairy, and there were tattoos visible beneath the hair. The writing said THAT WHICH DESTROYS US and NEVER LOOK BACK. Peretz walked toward the exit.

He used a wooden plank to cross a huge puddle behind the building, went around the mound of empty tin cans, squeezed through a crack in the wooden fence, and went into the Administration building through the service entrance. The hallways were cold and dark, and the place smelled of tobacco, dust, and old paper. There was no one around, and he couldn't hear anything through the faux leather upholstered doors. Peretz walked up the narrow stairs to the second floor, holding on to the dingy walls since there was no railing, and walked up to a door beneath a flashing WASH YOUR HANDS BEFORE WORK sign. The door was adorned with a big black M. Peretz pushed the door open and felt a certain astonishment upon finding himself in his office. The office wasn't actually his, of course—it belonged to Kim, the head of the Scientific Guard—but that was the office in which Peretz had a desk, and this desk now stood along the tiled wall on one side of the door. As usual, half of the desk was occupied by the Mercedes arithmometer, which was still beneath its cover. Meanwhile, Kim's desk now stood by the large, clean window, and Kim himself was already working: he was sitting, hunched over, and examining a slide rule.

"I wanted to wash my hands," Peretz said, bewildered.

"Wash away, wash away," Kim said, nodding. "There's the sink. This will be very convenient. Now everyone will come visit us."

Peretz went up to the sink and began to wash his hands. He washed them with cold and hot water, two types of soap, and a special grease-absorbing paste; he scrubbed them with a loofah and with an assortment of brushes of varying stiffness. Then he turned on the electric dryer and held his damp pink hands in the whistling stream of hot air.

"At four in the morning, they announced that we were being transferred to the second floor," Kim said. "And where have you been? With Alevtina?"

"No, I was at the precipice," said Peretz, sitting down at his desk.

The door opened, and Proconsul rapidly walked into the room, gave a friendly wave of his suitcase, and disappeared behind the curtain. They heard the creak of the stall door and the click of the bolt. Peretz took the cover off the arithmometer, sat motionless for a moment, then walked over to the window and threw it open.

You couldn't see the forest from here, but the forest was present. It was always present, although you could only see it from the cliff. If you were anywhere else in the Administration, it was obscured by something. It was obscured by the cream-colored buildings of the engineering workshops, and by the four-story garage that housed employees' personal vehicles. It was obscured by the stockyards of the subsidiary farms, and by the clothes hanging by the laundromat, whose dryer was constantly broken. It was obscured by the park with its flower beds and pavilions, its Ferris wheel, and its alabaster statues of bathers, which were now completely covered in scribbled graffiti. It was obscured by the villas with their ivy-covered porches and their television antennae. And from here, a window on the second floor, you couldn't see the forest because of the brick wall—as yet unfinished, but already quite tall—that was being constructed around the flat one-story building of the Penetration Through Engineering Team. You could only see the forest from the cliff, but you could only defecate on the forest from the cliff, too.

But even a person who had never in his life seen the forest, who hadn't heard of the forest, hadn't thought about the forest, hadn't been afraid of it, and hadn't fantasized about it—even a person like that could easily guess that it existed, simply because of the existence of the Administration. I, for one, have long thought about the forest, argued about the forest, and seen it in my dreams, but I never even suspected that it actually existed. And I was convinced of its existence not when I first set foot on the cliff but when I read the sign by the door: THE ADMINISTRATION FOR FOREST AFFAIRS. I was standing in front of this sign, suitcase in hand, dusty and parched after the long trip, reading and rereading it and feeling weak in the knees, because I now knew the forest existed, and therefore, everything I had hitherto thought about it was nothing but a figment of a weak imagination, a pale and feeble lie. The forest existed, and this enormous, gloomy building concerned itself with its fate . . .

"Kim," said Peretz, "will I really never get into the forest? Because I'm leaving tomorrow."

"And you actually want to get in there?" Kim asked distractedly.

Hot green swamps, timid, nervous trees, mermaids lying on the surface of the water in the moonlight, relaxing after their mysterious activities in the depths, cautious inscrutable natives, empty villages . . . "I don't know," said Peretz.

"You shouldn't be allowed in there, Perry," Kim said. "Only people who've never thought about the forest should be allowed in there. People who've never given a damn about it. Whereas you care about it too much. The forest is dangerous for you, because it will fool you."

"Maybe," Peretz said. "But I did only come here to see it."

"Why do you want the bitter truth?" said Kim. "What are you going to do with it? And what are you going to do in the forest? Weep for a dream that has become fate? Pray for everything to be different? Or, even worse, start changing what there is into what there should be?"

"So why did I come here, then?"

"To convince yourself. Do you really not realize how important that is—convincing yourself? Others come for other reasons. To measure the number of cubic meters of firewood in the forest. Or to discover the bacteria of life. Or to write a thesis. Or to get a pass—not to go in the forest with, but just in case: it might come in handy one day, and not everybody has one. And the ultimate conceit is to shape the forest into a magnificent park, like a sculptor shapes a marble block into a statue. And then to keep pruning it. Year after year. So it doesn't become a forest again."

"I need to leave," Peretz said. "There's nothing for me here. Somebody needs to leave, either me or all of you."

"Let's do some multiplication," Kim said, and Peretz sat down at his desk, found a jury-rigged power outlet, and plugged in the arithmometer. "Seven hundred ninety-three five hundred twenty-two by two hundred sixty-six zero eleven . . ."

The arithmometer started rattling and jerking. Peretz waited until it calmed down, then haltingly read out the answer.

Kim called out more numbers and Peretz entered them in, pressing the multiplication and division keys, adding, subtracting, and taking roots. Everything went on as usual.

"Twelve by ten," Kim said. "Multiply."

"One zero zero seven," Peretz recited mechanically, then he caught himself and said, "Wait a minute, it's wrong. It should be one twenty."

"I know, I know," Kim said impatiently. "One zero zero seven," he repeated. "And now take the square root of ten zero seven."

"Just a moment," Peretz said.

The bolt behind the curtain clicked again, and Proconsul emerged looking pink, fresh, and satisfied. He started to wash his hands, simultaneously singing "Ave Maria" in a pleasant voice. Then he declared, "What a marvel the forest is, my friends! And how criminally little time we spend talking and writing about it! And yet it is worthy of being written about. It elevates us, it awakens our loftiest sentiments. It encourages progress. It is like a symbol of progress itself. And yet we still cannot curtail the spread of inappropriate stories, rumors, and jokes. We're conducting practically no pro-forest propaganda. People say and think God knows what about the forest."

"Seven eighty-five multiplied by four thirty-two," Kim said.

Proconsul raised his voice. His voice was loud and resonant—the arithmometer became inaudible. "'Can't see the forest for the trees.' 'A babe in the woods.' 'Our neck of the woods.' That is what we must struggle against! That is what we must eradicate. Take you, Monsieur Peretz, why haven't you joined the struggle? You could make a detailed and goal-oriented presentation about the forest to our club, but you haven't. I've been watching you and waiting for a long time, to no avail. What's the issue?"

"But I've never been in there," Peretz said.

"Doesn't matter. I've never been in there either, but I gave a lecture, and judging by the response I got, it was an extremely useful lecture. What matters is not whether you've been in the forest—what matters is peeling away the layers of mysticism and superstition from the facts, laying bare the crux of the matter by tearing off the garments in which it had been clad by the philistines and the opportunists."

"Two times eight divided by forty-nine minus seven times seven," said Kim.

The arithmometer started working. Proconsul raised his voice again. "I did this as a philosopher by training, and you could do it as a linguist by training. I'll suggest some propositions, and you can expand on them in the context of the latest advances in linguistics . . . By the way, what was the subject of your thesis?"

"It was 'The Characteristics of the Style and Rhythm of Female Prose in the Late Heian Period,' based on *Makura no sōshi*," Peretz said. "I'm afraid that—"

"Fan*tas*tic! That's just what we need. And make sure to emphasize that there are no swamps or bogs, only magnificent mud baths; there are no jumping trees, only the products of a highly advanced science; there are no natives or savages, only an ancient civilization of men, proud and free, with noble ideas, modest yet mighty. And please, no mermaids! No lilac fog, no purple prose—excuse the bad pun . . . This will be fantastic, Mr. Peretz, this will be wonderful. And I'm very glad you know the forest, you can share your personal impressions. My lecture was also good, but I'm afraid it was a little theoretical. I used the meeting minutes as my primary source. But you, as a forest scholar—"

"I'm not a forest scholar," Peretz said earnestly. "They won't let me in the forest. I don't know the forest."

Proconsul, nodding absentmindedly, was quickly writing something on the cuff of his shirt. "Yes," he was saying, "yes, yes. Unfortunately, that is the bitter truth. Unfortunately, we still encounter this—bureaucracy, red tape, a heuristic approach to the individual . . . You may talk about that too, by the way. You may, you may, everybody talks about it. And I'll try to get your presentation cleared with the Board of Directors. I'm damn glad, Peretz, that you are finally getting involved in our work. I've been watching you closely for a long time . . . There we go, I scheduled you for next week."

Peretz turned off the arithmometer. "I won't be here next week. My visa's expiring, and I'm leaving. Tomorrow."

"Oh, we'll figure something out. I'll talk to the Director, he's a member of our club himself, he'll understand. Count on staying another week."

"Please don't do that," Peretz said. "Please!"

"But I have to!" said Proconsul, looking into his eyes. "You know perfectly well, Peretz: I have to! Good-bye." He made a military salute and left, swinging his briefcase.

"What a tangled web," said Peretz. "Do they think I'm a fly or something? The garage foreman doesn't want me to leave, neither does Alevtina, now here's another one."

"I don't want you to leave either," said Kim.

"But I can't stand it here anymore!"

"Seven eighty-seven multiplied by four thirty-two . . ."

I'm still leaving, thought Peretz, pressing buttons. I'm still leaving. You don't want me to, but I'm still leaving. I won't play Ping-Pong with you, I won't play chess with you, I won't sleep with you or have tea and jam with you; I don't want to sing you songs anymore, do calculations on your arithmometer, help mediate your disputes, and now, on top of everything, give you lectures that you won't even understand. And I won't think for you—think for yourself—and I'm leaving. Either way, there's nothing I can do to make you realize that thinking isn't a diversion, it's a responsibility . . .

Outside, behind the unfinished wall, the pile driver was banging, the jackhammers were pounding, and bricks were clattering down. Four workers—naked from the waist up and wearing caps—were sitting side by side on top of the wall and smoking. Then a motorcycle roared and sputtered right beneath the window.

"Must be someone from the forest," said Kim. "Quick, multiply sixteen by sixteen for me—"

A man yanked open the door and rushed into the room. He was wearing a hazmat suit, and his unfastened hood dangled at his chest on the cord of his walkie-talkie. Above the shoes and below the waist, the hazmat suit bristled with pale pink young shoots, and its right leg was ensnared by an endless orange vine that was dragging on the floor. The vine was still twitching, and Peretz imagined that it was a tentacle of the forest, and that it would soon flex and drag the man back—through the corridors of the Administration, down the stairs, across the yard, past the wall, past the cafeteria and the workshops, then down again, along the dusty street, through the park, past the statues and pavilions, toward the winding road, toward the gates, but then passing them on the outside, going toward the cliff, down, down, down . . .

He was wearing motorcycle goggles, his face was caked with dust, and Peretz didn't immediately realize that this was Stoyan Stoyanov from the biological research station. There was a large paper package in his hand. He took a few steps along the tiled floor, along the mosaic of a showering woman, and stopped in front of Kim, hiding the paper package behind his back and jerking his head in a strange way, as if his neck was itchy.

"Kim," he said. "It's me."

Kim didn't answer. His pen was audibly scratching and ripping the paper.

"Kimmy," Stoyan said obsequiously. "I'm begging you."

"Get out of here," said Kim. "Lunatic."

"One last time," said Stoyan. "The very last time." He jerked his head again, and on his scrawny shaved neck, right in the groove at the nape, Peretz saw a short, pinkish shoot—very thin, sharp, already curling into a spiral, and trembling as if with greed.

"You just give it to her and say that it's from Stoyan, that's all. If she asks you to the movies, lie and say that you urgently have to work tonight. If she tries to give you tea, tell her you just had some. And refuse the wine, too, if she offers. Eh? Kimmy? The very lastest time!"

"Why are you squirming?" Kim asked maliciously. "Turn around!"

"Did I bring one in again?" Stoyan asked, turning around. "Ah well, it doesn't matter. Just give this to her, nothing else matters."

Kim, leaning across the table, was doing something to Stoyan's neck, kneading and massaging it with his elbows splayed out, grimacing in disgust and muttering curses. Stoyan was patiently shifting from foot to foot, bending his head and arching his neck.

"Hi, Perry," he was saying. "Haven't seen you in ages. How are you? And here I am with another present—what can you do? . . . The very very last time." He unfolded the paper and showed Peretz a bouquet of acid-green forest flowers. "And the smell of them! The smell!"

"Stop wriggling," snapped Kim. "Stand still! Lunatic! Nincompoop!"

"I'm a lunatic," Stoyan agreed ecstatically. "I'm a nincompoop. But! The very very last time!"

The pink shoots on his hazmat suit were already withering, shriveling, and falling onto the floor, onto the ruddy face of the showering woman.

"Done," Kim said. "Now go away." He stepped away from Stoyan and threw something writhing, half dead, and bloody into the trash can.

"I'm going away," Stoyan said. "I'm going away this instant. You know, Rita had another funny spell, now I'm almost afraid to leave the biological research station at all. Perry, you should come visit us, talk to them, maybe—"

"As if!" said Kim. "There's nothing for him to do there."

"What do you mean, nothing?" Stoyan exclaimed. "Quentin's wasting away before our eyes! You just listen: a week ago Rita ran away—well, what can you do, that's life—and during the night she came back, wet, white, and frozen. The guard went up to her unarmed—don't know what she did to him, but he's still out cold. And our entire experimental plot has overgrown with grass."

"So?" Kim said.

"And Quentin has been crying all morning—"

"I know all that," Kim interrupted him. "What I don't understand is what it has to do with Peretz."

"What do you mean? What are you saying? If not Peretz, then who? I can't do it, right? And neither can you . . . Or maybe you think we should ask Claudius Octavian Bootlicherson!"

"Enough!" Kim said, slamming a hand down on the table. "Go do your job, and don't let me see you here again during work hours. Don't make me angry."

"I'm done," Stoyan said hastily. "I'm done. I'm leaving. You'll give this to her?"

He put the bouquet on the table and ran outside, shouting in the doorway, "And the cloaca's working again!"

Kim took a broom and swept all the debris into a corner. "The crazy fool," he said. "And that Rita . . . Now we have to do the calculations all over again. Damn him and his love affair."

They heard the irritating roar of the motorcycle beneath their window, then all was quiet again, except for the pile driver behind the wall.

"Peretz," Kim said, "why were you at the cliff this morning?"

"I was hoping to see the Director. I was told that he sometimes does his morning exercises by the cliff. I wanted to ask him to let me go, but he never came. You know, Kim, I think everyone here lies. Sometimes I think that even you lie. "

"The Director," Kim said pensively. "You know, that really is a thought. Good for you. A bold move."

"I'm still leaving tomorrow," said Peretz. "Randy will take me, he promised. I'm not going to be here tomorrow, just so you know."

"I wouldn't have thought it, I wouldn't have thought it," Kim continued, not paying attention. "A very bold move . . . Maybe we really should send you in there, to sort things out?"

2.

CANDIDE

Candide woke up and thought, I'm leaving the day after tomorrow. And Nava immediately stirred in her bed in the other corner and asked, "You aren't sleeping anymore?"

"No," he answered.

"Then let's talk," she suggested. "Since we haven't talked since last night. OK?"

"OK."

"First tell me when you're leaving."

"I don't know," he said. "Soon."

"You always say that—*soon*. Sometimes you say *soon*, sometimes you say *the day after tomorrow*, you think they are the same thing, maybe, but no, you've learned how to talk by now, at first you were mixed up all the time, you'd mix up *house* and *village*, *grass* and *mushrooms*, even *men* and *deadlings* you'd mix up, or else you'd start muttering, we couldn't understand a word, no one could understand a thing . . ."

He opened his eyes and stared at the low, lime-encrusted ceiling. Worker ants were walking across it. They were moving in two straight columns: the ones going left to right were carrying things, and the ones going right to left were unencumbered. A month ago, it was the other way around: the ones going right to left had mycelium, and the ones going left to right were unencumbered. And in another month it'll be the other way around again, unless they get other instructions. Black signaling ants were stationed next to the columns at regular intervals, slowly moving their long antennae and awaiting orders.

A month ago, I also woke up and thought that I'll leave the day after tomorrow, but we didn't go anywhere, and once, long before that, I woke up and thought that the day after tomorrow we will finally leave, and of course we didn't leave, but if we don't leave the day after tomorrow, I'm leaving by myself. Of course, I'd already thought this once, but this time I'm definitely leaving. It'd be good to leave right now, without talking to anyone, without pleading with anyone, but I can't do it now, when my head isn't clear. And it'd be good to decide once and for all: as soon as I wake up with a clear head, I'm immediately getting up, going outside, and walking into the forest, without letting anyone talk to me; that's very important, not to let anyone talk to me, not to let them wear me out, not to let them talk my head off, especially those spots over my eyes, until my ears ring and I feel nauseated, until a fog fills brains and bones both. And Nava is already talking . . .

". . . and it turned out," Nava was saying, "that the deadlings were taking us somewhere at night, but at night they don't see well, they're almost blind, and anyone will tell you so, Humpy, say, would tell you, but then he's not from these parts, he's from the village that was next to our village, not the one we live in now, but the one I lived in without you, with my mom. So you couldn't know Humpy, his village got overgrown with mushrooms, the mushrooms took over, and it's not everyone who likes that, Humpy, now, he left the village immediately. There was a

Surpassment, he said, and now the village isn't fit for people . . .
Yeah. And there was no moon at the time, and they probably got
lost, everyone got crowded together, and there we were, stuck in
the middle, and it got so hot, I could barely breathe . . ."

Candide glanced at her. She was lying on her back, her hands
behind her head and her legs crossed, and she was motionless,
except for her lips, which were constantly moving, and her eyes,
which occasionally glittered in the half light. When the old man
came in, she didn't stop talking, and the old man sat down at the
table, pulled the pot toward him, smelled it, sniffling loudly, and
began to eat. Then Candide got up and wiped the night sweat
from his body. The old man sprayed spit as he slurped the food
down, keeping his eyes on the serving trough, which was covered
with a lid to protect it from mold.

Candide took the pot away from him and put it next to Nava
so she'd stop talking. The old man licked his lips and said, "Tastes
bad. Whoever you visit nowadays, it tastes bad. And that trail
I used to take has gotten completely overgrown. I walked a lot
back then, I walked to training, and I would walk to the swimming place—swam a lot in those days, I did. There was a lake
there once, now it is a swamp, and there is danger in walking
now, but someone must walk there still, else where did all the
drowned people come from? And take those reeds. I could put
it to anyone: Who made those paths through the reeds? And
nobody knows, nor should they. And what is it you have in that
trough? If it is soaked berries, say, then I would eat them, I am
fond of soaked berries, but if it is just yesterday's leftovers, scraps,
then I do not want them, eat your scraps yourself." He paused,
glancing between Candide and Nava. Without waiting for an
answer, he continued: "And there, where the reeds have sprung
up, we cannot sow there anymore. Back then, we sowed because
it was needful for the Surpassment, everyone took it to the Clay
Meadow, and they take it there still, but they no longer leave it
at the meadow, they bring it back instead. It is wrong, and so I
have told them, but they do not know what *wrong* means. The

village head asked me in front of everyone: Why is it wrong?
Big Fist was right here, like you, even closer, Hearer was right
there, say, and over there, where your Nava is, the three Baldy
brothers were standing and listening, and he asked me in front
of them all. What are you doing, I tell him, we are not alone, I
say . . . His father was the smartest of men, but maybe he was
not his father at all, I have heard it said he was not his father, and
indeed, he does not look like him . . . Why, he says, is it wrong
to ask in front of everyone, why it is wrong?"

Nava got up, handed the pot to Candide, and started to clean
up. Candide began to eat. The old man paused and watched
him for a while, making chewing motions with his mouth, then
remarked, "Your food is not fully fermented, it is wrong to eat
such things."

"Why is it wrong?" Candide asked, to tease him.

The old man snickered. "Oh, Silent Man," he said. "You would
do better to keep silent, Silent Man. You would do better to tell
me, I have long since asked: Does it hurt a lot to have your head
cut off?"

"What's it to you?" Nava shouted. "Why don't you leave us
alone?"

"She is shouting," the old man informed them. "Shouting at
me. She has not given birth once, yet she shouts at me. Why have
you not given birth? You have lived with Silent Man for a long
time, but you have not given birth. Everyone gives birth but you.
That is wrong. And do you know what *wrong* means? It means
not welcome, not approved of—and since it is not approved of,
it is wrong. What is right, that we do not yet know, but what
is wrong is wrong. Everyone ought to understand that, and you
especially, because it is a foreign village you live in, they have
given you a house, they have gotten you Silent Man here for a
husband. The head on his shoulders may not be his, it may have
been stuck on, but his body is healthy, and it is wrong to refuse
to give birth. And so we conclude that if a thing is wrong, it is
as unwelcome a thing as it possibly can be."

Nava, looking angry and sulky, grabbed the trough from the table and went into the pantry.

The old man followed her with his eyes, sniffed a few times, and continued. "What else could *wrong* mean? We can and must understand that if a thing is wrong, it is harmful . . ."

Candide finished eating, banged the empty pot down in front of the old man, and went out onto the street. The house had gotten very overgrown at night, and he couldn't see much in the surrounding dense undergrowth. He could only make out the old man's tracks, and the spot by the door where the old man had sat and fidgeted, waiting for them to wake up. The street had already been cleared. The arm-thick green creeper, which had sneaked out of the tangle of branches above the village during the night and put down roots in front of the neighboring house, had been chopped down and soaked in ferment, and was already starting to turn dark and sour. It had a sharp and appetizing smell, and the neighbor kids clustered around it, tearing off the brown flesh and stuffing juicy, succulent chunks into their mouths. When Candide walked by, the eldest shouted indistinctly with his mouth full: "Silent Man's a deadling!" But no one else joined in—they were too busy. The street, orange and red from the tall grass in which the houses were drowning, was otherwise empty; the earth was dappled with faint green spots from the sun streaming through the crowns of the trees. He could hear a discordant chorus of bored voices from the field: *"Hey, hey, sow, be merry, we have all these seeds to bury . . ."* Echoes rang in the woods. Or maybe those sounds weren't echoes. Maybe they came from the deadlings.

Of course, Crookleg was sitting at home and massaging his leg. "Sit down," he welcomed Candide. "Here's some soft grass I spread for guests. You're leaving, they say?"

Here we go again, Candide thought, we're starting all over again. "What, is it bothering you again?" he asked, sitting down.

"My leg, you mean? Nah, this just feels good. You pet it like this and it gives you a nice feeling, it does. And when are you leaving?"

"Exactly when we talked about. If you'd come with me, maybe even the day after tomorrow. But now I'll have to find someone else who knows the forest. I can tell you don't want to come anymore."

Crookleg gingerly stretched out his leg and instructed, "When you come out of my house, turn left and keep walking until the field. Walk through the field and go past the two stones, you'll see the road right away, it's not too overgrown, as it's full of rocks. Stick to the road, it'll go through two villages: the first one's empty, mushroomy, the mushrooms overgrew it, not a soul's left there, and kooks live in the second one, the blue grass went through them twice, they've been sick ever since, don't you even talk to them, no point, it's like they've lost their memories. And after the kook village, the Clay Meadow will be right there, on your right. And you don't need anyone to show you the way, you'll make it there yourself nice and easy, won't even break a sweat."

"We'll make it to the Clay Meadow," Candide agreed. "But what do we do after that?"

"After that?"

"We have to go through the swamp, where the lakes used to be. Remember, you told me about the stone road?"

"Which road would that be? The road to the Clay Meadow? That's just what I've been telling you: turn left, go until the field, past the stones . . ."

Candide let him finish and said, "I now know the way to the Clay Meadow. We'll get there. But as you know, I need to go farther than that. I have to get to the City, and you promised to show me the way."

Crookleg shook his head in sympathy. "The *Ciiity*! . . . That's where you're heading, eh? I remember, I remember . . . But, Silent Man, there's no way to get to the City. If you wanted to go to the Clay Meadow, say, that's no problem: go past the stones, through the mushroomy village, through the kook village, and the Clay Meadow will be right there, on your right. Or if you wanted to go to the Reeds, say, that's easy. When you go out, turn right, go through the open wood, past the Bread Puddle, then just follow the sun. Wherever the sun goes, you go. It'll take three days, but since you really need to go, we'll go. We used to look for pots there, before we planted our own hereabouts. You should have told me right away that you want to go to the Reeds. No point waiting for the day after tomorrow, we'll head out tomorrow morning, and we don't have to bring food, as the Bread Puddle's on the way . . . Silent Man, you talk too quick: I start to bend an ear and you've closed your mouth already. But we'll get to the Reeds. We'll go tomorrow morning . . ."

Candide heard him out and said, "You see, Crookleg, I don't need to go to the Reeds. The Reeds aren't where I need to go. They aren't where I need to go, the Reeds." Crookleg was listening attentively and nodding. "Where I need to go is the City," continued Candide. "You and I have been talking about it for a long time. I told you yesterday I need to go to the City. The day before yesterday, I told you I need to go to the City. A week ago, I told you I need to go to the City. You said you know the way to the City. You said that yesterday. And the day before yesterday, you said you know the way to the City. Not the way to the Reeds, the way to the City." Just don't let me get confused, he thought. Maybe I always get confused. Not the Reeds, the City. The City, not the Reeds. "The City, not the Reeds," he repeated out loud. "Do you understand? Tell me the way to the City. Or even better—let's go to the City together. Let's not go to the Reeds together, let's go to the City together."

He paused. Crookleg started patting his bad knee again. "Silent Man, maybe when they cut your head off, they messed something up inside. It's like my leg. It used to just be a leg, a normal leg, then one night, I was walking through the Anthills, carrying the ant queen, and this leg here got stuck in a hole, and now it's bent. Why it's bent, no one knows, but it doesn't walk well. But I can make it to the Anthills. I'll make it there myself, and I'll take you there, too. The only thing I don't understand is why you told me to get food ready for the road, the Anthills, they're a hop and a jump away." He looked at Candide, got embarrassed, and opened his mouth. "But you aren't going to the Anthills," he said. "Where are you going? You're going to the Reeds. But I can't go to the Reeds, I won't make it. My leg's bent, see? Hey, Silent Man, what do you have against the Anthills, anyways? Let's go to the Anthills, eh? I haven't been there once since that time, maybe they are gone, the Anthills. We'll look for that hole, eh?"

He's about to confuse me, thought Candide. He leaned to one side and rolled a pot toward him. "This is a very nice pot," he said. "I can't remember when I've last seen such a nice pot . . . So you'll take me to the City? You told me no one but you knows the way to the City. Let's go to the City, Crookleg. Can we make it to the City, you think?"

"Of course we can! The City? No problem! By the way, you've seen pots like these before, and I know where. It's the kooks who have pots like these. They don't grow them, you see, they make them out of clay, the Clay Meadow's right around the corner, like I've been telling you: go out and turn left, go past the stones, until you get to the mushroomy village. Not a soul in the place nowadays, no point going there. Have we never seen a mushroom before or something? When my leg was strong, I never went to the mushroomy village, I just knew that the kooks lived past it, two ravines away. Yeah. We could even leave tomorrow . . . Yeah . . . Hey, Silent Man, how about we don't go there, eh? Those mushrooms, I don't like them. See, the mushrooms in our forest, they're one thing—we can eat them, they taste good, they do. But the mushrooms there, in that village, they are kind of greenish, and they smell bad. Why go there? Might even bring spores back. We'd better go to the City. That'd be much nicer. But we can't leave tomorrow, then. Have to save up some food, have to ask around, find out the way. Or do you know the way? If you know the way, I won't ask around, as I can't think who to ask. Maybe we should ask the village head, what do you think?"

"Don't you know anything about the way to the City?" Candide asked. "You know a lot about it. You even almost made it to the City once, but you got scared of the deadlings, scared you couldn't fight them off alone—"

"I'm not scared of deadlings and never was," Crookleg objected. "I'll tell you what scares me: walking there, just the two of us, that's what scares me. Are you going to stay silent the whole way? I can't do that, I don't know how. And there's another thing I'm scared of . . . Now don't you get mad at me, Silent Man, you just tell me, and if you don't want to say it loudly, say it quietly, or maybe just nod, and if even a nod won't do, then your eye, say, it's in the shade, and you don't need to do anything but close it, I'll be the only one that sees it. Here's my question: are you maybe actually a bit of a deadling? I can't stand deadlings, you know, they give me the shakes, I can't help it."

"No, Crookleg, I'm no deadling," said Candide. "I hate them myself. And if you're scared I'll stay silent, I told you, it won't be just us two. Big Fist is coming, and Tagalong, and two guys from the Settlement."

"I won't go with Big Fist," Crookleg said firmly. "Big Fist, he took my daughter, and didn't keep her safe. Stole my daughter from him, they did. I'm not sorry he took her, I'm sorry he didn't keep her safe. They were walking to the Settlement, the two of them, the thieves ambushed them and took my daughter, and he let them take her. I looked and looked for her afterward with your Nava, but we never did find her. No, Silent Man, best take no chances with the thieves. If you and I go to the City, the thieves will give us no peace. Now the Reeds, that's another story, we could go to the Reeds without a second thought. We'll go tomorrow."

"The day after tomorrow," Candide said. "It'll be you, me, Big Fist, Tagalong, and two guys from the Settlement. And we'll make it all the way to the City."

"The six of us will make it," Crookleg said confidently. "I couldn't make it there alone, of course, but the six of us will make it. The six of us could even make it to the Devil's Mountains, but I don't know the way. Say, maybe that's where we should go, the Devil's Mountains? It's a long way away, but the six of us will make it. Or do you not need to go to the Devil's Mountains? Hey, Silent Man, let's get to the City, then we'll see. Let's just pack us plenty of food."

"All right," said Candide, getting up. "So we're leaving for the City the day after tomorrow. I'll go to the Settlement tomorrow, then I'll drop by and remind you one more time."

"Drop on by," said Crookleg. "I'd drop by and see you myself, except my leg, it hurts real bad. But drop on by, do. We'll talk. I know, it's not all folks that like talking to you, it's very hard to talk to you, Silent Man, but me, I'm not like that. I'm used to it now, I even like it. Drop by yourself, and bring your Nava, too, she's nice, your Nava, too bad she has no kids, but she'll have some one day, she's still young . . ."

Outside, Candide wiped the sweat off with his hands again. The visit had a sequel. Someone giggled and coughed nearby. Candide turned around. The old man got up out of the grass, shook a gnarled finger at him, and said, "So it is the City you are going to. An interesting plan, only no one has ever made it to the City alive, and it is wrong to go. Even if your head does not belong to your body, that is something you must understand . . ."

Candide turned right and walked down the street. The old man trailed behind him for a while, getting tangled in the grass and muttering, "If a thing is wrong, then it is always wrong, in one sense or another. For example, it is wrong to have no village head and no meetings, while on the other hand, it is right to have a village head and meetings, but again, not in every possible sense . . ." Candide walked as fast as the oppressive heat and humidity allowed, and the old man gradually fell behind.

At the village square, Candide saw Hearer. He was walking around in circles, tottering and dragging his feet, splashing handfuls of brown grasskiller from a gigantic pot that hung at his stomach. The grass behind him was smoking and withering before their eyes. Hearer had to be avoided, and Candide tried to avoid him, but Hearer changed course so adroitly that when they collided, they were nose to nose.

"Hey, Silent Man!" he yelled happily, hastily taking the strap off his neck and putting the pot down on the ground. "Where are you going, Silent Man? Heading home to your Nava, I'd think, oh, to be young again, but what you don't know, Silent Man, is that your Nava's in the field, I saw her going to the field with my own eyes, believe it or not . . . Of course, maybe she wasn't going to the field, oh, to be young again, but your Nava, she went down that lane over there, Silent Man, and that lane doesn't go anywhere but the field, and where else would she go, your Nava, I'd like to know? Unless she went looking for you, Silent Man . . ."

Candide made another attempt to pass him, and somehow wound up nose to nose with him again.

"Don't you follow her to the field, Silent Man," Hearer continued emphatically. "No need to follow her, there isn't, as I'm about to kill the grass, then I'll summon everyone here: the surveyor came by and told me that the village head ordered him to tell me to kill the grass in the square, as there's going to be a meeting here, in the square. And when there's a meeting, they all come in from the field, and your Nava will come in, too, if she went to the field, and where else could she have gone, going down that lane? Then again, now that I think about it, that lane doesn't just go to the field, so maybe—"

He suddenly paused and gave a shuddering sigh. His eyes closed, and his palms seemed to turn up of their own accord. His face spread into a saccharine smile, which turned into a teeth-baring grimace as his face drooped. A murky lilac cloud condensed around Hearer's bald head, his lips trembled, and he began to speak quickly and distinctly, in a strange, carefully enunciated voice, with unusual intonations, in a manner that wasn't of the village, possibly even in a foreign tongue, so Candide could only make out certain phrases: "On the distant periphery of the Southern Zones, new forces keep entering the battle . . .

The enemy, pushed farther and farther south . . . A victorious march . . . The Big Soil Loosening in the Northern Zones is temporarily halted due to isolated and rare . . . New waterlogging techniques are creating vast new regions in which peace reigns and the troops can . . . In all the villages . . . Great victories . . . Toil and labor . . . New squads of helpmates . . . Peace and fusion, once and for all . . ."

The old man, who had gotten there just in time, was standing behind Candide's shoulder and explaining enthusiastically, "In all the villages, did you hear that? . . . That must also mean our village . . . Great victories! I keep telling them, it is wrong . . . Peace and fusion—they ought to understand . . . If it is in all the villages, that must mean our village as well . . . New squads of helpmates, did you hear that?"

Hearer stopped talking and dropped to his haunches. The lilac cloud dissipated. The old man rapped Hearer's bald pate impatiently.

Hearer blinked and rubbed his ears. "Where were we?" he said. "Was there a broadcast or something? How's the Surpassment? Is it coming to pass? . . . Silent Man, don't you go to the field. You'd be following your Nava, I suppose, and your Nava, she . . ."

Candide stepped over the pot of grasskiller and hastily walked away. He soon stopped being able to hear the old man—either he got into an argument with Hearer, or he got winded and stepped into a house to catch his breath and have a snack while he was at it.

Big Fist's house stood right on the edge of town. An unkempt old woman, either his aunt or mother, told him, snorting ill-naturedly, that Big Fist wasn't home, Big Fist was in the field, and if he'd been home, there'd be no point looking for him in the field, but since he was in the field, then why should he, Silent Man, stand there for nothing?

They were sowing in the field. The stuffy, stagnant air was filled with a powerful mix of odors: sweat, ferment, and rotting grain. The morning harvest lay next to the furrow in deep piles, and the grain was already starting to turn. Worker flies swirled and crowded around the pots of leaven, and in the very thick of this black, glistening maelstrom stood the village head, bending his head and squinting one eye, carefully studying a drop of serum on the nail of his thumb. This wasn't an ordinary nail—it was flat, carefully polished, and scrubbed with the appropriate compounds until it gleamed. At the village head's feet, the sowers were crawling single file in the furrow, at intervals of ten feet. They no longer sang, but the *oohs* and *aahs* still rang through the forest, and it was now clear that they weren't echoes.

Candide walked along the furrow, leaning down and looking into the lowered faces. When he found Big Fist, he touched his shoulder, and Big Fist climbed out of the furrow without asking any questions. His beard was clumped with dirt.

"Keep your hands to yourself, fur and fuzz it," he rasped, looking at Candide's feet. "One guy, fur and fuzz it, he wouldn't keep his hands to himself, so they grabbed his arms and legs and tossed him up a tree, and he's up there still, and when they take him down, he'll be keeping his hands to himself, fur and fuzz it—"

"You coming?" Candide asked curtly.

"Of course I'm coming, fur and fuzz it, all the leaven stinks to high heaven, can't go in the house anymore, it reeks so bad, it's no kind of life, why wouldn't I come? The old woman can't stand it anymore, and I don't even want to look at it myself. But where are we going? Yesterday, Crookleg said the Reeds, but I won't go to the Reeds, fur and fuzz it, nobody lives in the Reeds, never mind any girls, so if you're there and you want to grab someone by the leg and toss him up a tree, then you can't, fur and fuzz it, and I can't do without a girl anymore, the village head will be the death of me. Look at him standing there, staring, and he's as blind as the heel of his foot, fur and fuzz it. One guy, he used to stand around like that, then he got socked in the eye, so he doesn't stand around anymore, fur and fuzz it, but I won't go to the Reeds, do as you like . . ."

"How about the City?" Candide said.

"The City, that's different, I'll go to the City, especially as they say there's no City at all, he's lying his head off, that old fart, comes over in the morning and eats half your pot, then he runs his mouth, fur and fuzz it: this is wrong, and that is wrong . . . I ask him: who are you to be telling me what's wrong and what's right, fur and fuzz it? Doesn't answer me, he doesn't, doesn't know himself, mumbles about some City . . ."

"We're leaving the day after tomorrow," said Candide.

"Why wait?" Big Fist said indignantly. "Why the day after tomorrow, eh? The leaven reeks to high heaven, I can't stand sleeping at home anymore, we should go tonight instead, one guy, he used to wait and wait, then they boxed his ears, so he stopped waiting, and never waited for anything again. The old woman keeps giving me hell, I can't live like this, fur and fuzz it! Hey, Silent Man, let's bring the old woman along, maybe the thieves would take her, I'd let them, eh?"

"We leave the day after tomorrow," Candide repeated patiently. "And I'm glad you prepared lots of leaven, good work. In the Settlement—"

He didn't finish, because someone screamed in the field. "Deadlings! Deadlings!" bawled the village head. "Women, go home! Run home!"

Candide looked around. The deadlings were standing between the trees at the very edge of the field—there were two blue ones a short distance away, and a yellow one farther off. Their heads, with the usual round holes for eyes and black cracks for mouths, slowly rotated from side to side, and their huge arms hung whip-like along their bodies. The earth beneath their feet was already burning, white plumes of steam mingled with the bluish smoke.

These deadlings had been around the block, and as a result, they were being extremely cautious. The yellow one's entire right side had been eaten away by grasskiller, and both the blue ones were covered from head to toe with ferment burns. Here and there, patches of their hides had died off, popped, and hung in tatters.

As they stood there and watched, the women ran shrieking to the village, while the men, muttering wordy threats, huddled together with pots of grasskiller at the ready. Then the village head said, "What are we waiting for, huh? Come on, what are we waiting for?" and everyone slowly moved at the deadlings, forming a chain.

"Get their eyes!" the village head kept shouting. "Try to splash it in their eyes! Best to aim at their eyes, it's not much use unless you hit their eyes!" The men tried to scare them off: "*Ooh ooh ooh!* Shoo, scram! *Aah aah aah!*" No one wanted to fight.

Big Fist walked next to Candide, ripping dried mud out of his beard, shouting louder than the others but reasoning between the shouts, "No, this is pointless, we should have stayed put, they won't fight us, they'll run away. Just look at them! They're all tattered, they won't fight us, no way. *Ooh ooh ooh! Boo!*" The men stopped twenty feet from the deadlings. Big Fist threw a clump of earth at the yellow one, who blocked it with extraordinary agility, knocking the clump off to the side with a broad palm.

Everyone started shouting and stomping again, and a few people showed the deadlings the pots and made threatening motions. Grasskiller was precious; no one wanted to trudge to the village to get new ferment; these were seasoned, cautious deadlings—it ought to turn out all right.

And it did turn out all right. The steam and smoke billowing from beneath their feet got thicker, and the deadlings began to back away. "That's it," the men said, "they didn't put up a fight, now they'll turn inside out." The deadlings subtly changed, as if turning inside their own hides. Their eyes and mouths vanished— they now had their backs to the villagers. A second later, they were already retreating, appearing and disappearing between the trees. In the place where they used to be, a cloud of steam was slowly sinking to the ground.

The men, chattering eagerly, began to move back toward the furrow. They suddenly realized that it was time to head to the village for the meeting. They headed there. "Off we go to the square," the village head kept telling everyone. "The meeting's at the square, so we have to walk to the square . . ."

Candide looked for Tagalong, but he couldn't see him in the crowd. He had disappeared. Big Fist trotted next to him, saying, "Remember, Silent Man, how you jumped on a deadling? You jumped right on it, fur and fuzz it, grabbed its head, like it was your Nava, then started to shriek. Remember how you shrieked, Silent Man? Got burned, you did, that's why, then you had blisters all over, they oozed, they hurt. Why did you jump on it, Silent Man? One guy, he used to jump on deadlings, then the skin on his belly all peeled off, so he doesn't jump on them anymore, fur and fuzz it, and won't let his kids jump on them either. They say, Silent Man, that you jumped on it so it'd carry you to the City, but you aren't a girl, why would it carry you? And anyway, they say there's no City at all, just that old fart making up words—the City, the Surpassment . . . And who's ever seen it, this Surpassment? Hearer stuffs himself with liquor beetles, then he runs his mouth, and that old fart's on the spot, listening, then he wanders all over, eats food that isn't his, and repeats it—"

"I'm going to the Settlement tomorrow morning," Candide said. "I'll be back in the evening, I won't be here during the day. Go see Crookleg and remind him about the day after tomorrow. I've reminded him, and I'll remind him again, but you should remind him, too, or he might wander off."

"I'll remind him," promised Big Fist. "Won't have any working legs left, he won't, when I'm done reminding him."

The entire village had come to the square. They chattered, shoved, and poured seeds onto the ground to grow soft mats to sit on. Children were underfoot, and people were dragging them about by their hair and ears so they'd stop getting in the way. The village head cursed as he chased away a column of badly trained ants about to drag the larva of a worker fly right through the square, and angrily questioned everyone: Who in the world had ordered the ants to walk there? People suspected Candide and Hearer, but there was no longer a way to make sure.

Candide found Tagalong and wanted to talk to him, but he didn't have the chance, because the meeting began, and as always the old man insisted on speaking first. It was impossible to figure out what he was talking about, but everyone sat meekly and listened, hissing at their scampering children so they would stop horsing around. A few people, who had made themselves particularly comfortable by finding spots far away from the hot sun, dozed off.

The old man spent a long time pontificating about the meaning of the word *wrong*, and the senses in which it was used, called for Surpassment for all, threatened them with victories in the North and South, and bad-mouthed the village and the Settlement along with it, because there were new squads of helpmates everywhere, but not in the village or in the Settlement either. And there was neither peace nor fusion, and it was because people forgot what *wrong* meant and imagined that nowadays everything was allowed, like Silent Man, for example—he wants to leave for the City, no less, even though no one has summoned him there. And the village is not responsible for him, because he is a foreigner, but if it turns out that he is actually a deadling, and there are those in the village who do think so, then there is no knowing what would happen, especially since Nava, for all that she's foreign herself, has no children with Silent Man, and it is wrong to put up with such things, but the village head puts up with them—

By the middle of the speech, the village head had also gotten sleepy and dozed off, but when he heard himself mentioned, he started and immediately barked, "Hey! No sleeping!

"Sleep at home," he said, "that's what homes are for, they're for sleeping, and the square, it isn't for sleeping, the square's for meetings. We've never let anyone sleep in the square, don't let them do so now, and never will." He glanced sideways at the old man. The old man nodded contentedly. "And we can all agree that it is wrong." He smoothed down his hair and announced, "A bride has turned up at the Settlement. And we have a groom, Loudmouth, who you all know well. Loudmouth, stand up and show yourself . . . Actually, you'd better not, you'd better stay seated, we all know you, we do . . . Here's the question: Should we let Loudmouth go off to the Settlement, or should the village take the bride in instead? No, no, Loudmouth, you stay seated, we'll figure it out without you . . . Those of you sitting next to him, hold on to him during the meeting, don't let him go. And let anyone who has an opinion speak up."

There turned out to be two schools of thought. Some people (mostly Loudmouth's neighbors) demanded that Loudmouth be sent off to the Settlement—let him live there, and we can stay here. But others—calm, serious people, who lived a good distance from Loudmouth—thought that no, there weren't enough women, women got stolen, so we should take the bride in: Loudmouth may be Loudmouth, but he'll still probably have kids, that's a separate thing. The argument was long, heated, and initially on topic. Then Crookleg unfortunately cried out that we're at war and no one cares. Everyone immediately forgot about Loudmouth. Hearer started explaining that there was no war and never had been, and all that there is, was, and ever would be is a Big Soil Loosening. It's not a Big Soil Loosening, someone objected in the crowd, it's a Necessary Waterlogging. The Loosening ended ages ago, it's been the Waterlogging for years, Hearer has no idea, and how could he know, anyway, since he's Hearer? The old man got up, his eyes bulging out of his head, and bellowed hoarsely that this was all wrong, that there was no war, and there was no Soil Loosening, and there was no Waterlogging, and all that there is, was, and ever would be was a Universal Struggle in the North and South. What do you mean, no war, fur and fuzz it, people answered, when there's a lake full of drowned people past the kook village?

The meeting exploded. So some people drowned, who cares? Where there's water, people will drown, everything past the kook village is strange, the kooks are no example to us, they eat off clay, they live under clay, you let the thieves take your wife, and now you talk about drowned people? They aren't actually drowned, and there's neither a struggle nor a war—there's only Peace and Fusion for the purposes of the Surpassment! Then why is Silent Man going to the City? If Silent Man's going to the City, then the City must exist, and if it exists, then how can there be a war—it must be Fusion! . . . Who cares where Silent Man's going? One guy, he was going to go somewhere, someone bonked him on the nose, now he isn't going to go anywhere . . . That's just why Silent Man's going to the City, because there is no City, we know that Silent Man, you might think he's a few leaves short of a tree, but he's a clever one, he is, you can't put one over on him, and since there's no City, how can there be Fusion? . . . There's no Fusion, there was at one time, it's true, but it's been over for a long time . . . And there's no Surpassment either! Who's that yelling there's no Surpassment? What do you mean by that? What's wrong with you? . . . Don't forget about Loudmouth! Don't let go of Loudmouth! . . . Oh no, you let Loudmouth go! How could you let him go?

Candide, who knew this would now take a while, tried to start a conversation with Tagalong, but Tagalong was in no mood for conversation. Tagalong was screaming at the top of his lungs, "Surpassment, what Surpassment? And why are there deadlings? You're quiet about the deadlings because you don't know what to make of them, that's why you scream about some Surpassment! . . ."

They spent a while screaming about the deadlings, then about the mushroomy villages, then they got tired and quieted down, wiping their faces—they now barely had enough energy to weakly wave their arms at each other in disagreement. It was soon discovered that everyone was already silent, and the only ones left arguing were Loudmouth and the old man. Then everyone came to their senses. They forced Loudmouth to sit down, piled on top of him, and stuffed leaves into his mouth. The old man kept talking for a while longer, but he'd lost his voice and wasn't audible. Then an agitated representative of the Settlement stood up and, pressing his hands to his chest and looking around ingratiatingly, started hoarsely entreating them not to send Loudmouth to the Settlement, they didn't want any Loudmouths, they'd lived for years without any Loudmouths and they'd like to live that way for many more, the village should take the bride in, and the Settlement won't skimp on the dowry, you just wait and see . . . No one had the energy to start arguing again—they promised to think about it and make up their minds later, especially since there was no hurry.

People were starting to disperse for lunch. Tagalong took Candide by the hand and dragged him under a nearby tree. "When are we going, eh?" he asked. "I'm tired of the village, I am, I want to go into the forest, I'll get sick from boredom here . . . If you aren't going, tell me, I'll go without you, I'll convince Crookleg and Big Fist and go with them."

"We're going the day after tomorrow." said Candide. "Did you get the food ready?"

"I got the food ready and ate it already, I don't have the patience to watch it sitting there for nothing, no one eating it but that old man, he makes all my insides hurt, I'll give him a good beating one day if we don't leave soon . . . What do you think, Silent Man, who is this old man, why does he eat everyone's food, and where does he live? I've been around, I've visited ten villages, I've been to the kook village, I've even spent the night with the haggard ones and almost died of fright, but an old man like that, I haven't seen that anywhere. Must be a very rare sort of old man, that's probably why we keep him around and don't beat him up, but I just don't have the patience to watch him poking his nose into my pots day and night—he eats it on the spot, and he carries it away, even though my father himself used to yell at him, before the deadlings got him . . . How does it all fit inside him, eh? All skin and bones, he is, no room in there at all, but he'll lick two pots clean and take two pots home, and he's never brought a pot back . . . You know, Silent Man, maybe there isn't just one old man, maybe there are two or three? Two of them sleep, while the other

one works. He stuffs himself, wakes another one up, and goes
to sleep himself . . ."

Tagalong walked Candide home but refused to stay for lunch
out of a sense of delicacy. He talked for another fifteen minutes
about the lake in the Reeds, which was an excellent place to fish,
you just wiggle your fingers in the water and the fish come; agreed
to drop by and see Crookleg to remind him about the trip to the
City; told Candide that Hearer doesn't hear anything at all, he's
just a very sick man, and that the deadlings catch women to eat
because men have tough meat and deadlings don't have teeth;
promised to prepare more provisions for the day after tomorrow
and to mercilessly chase the old man away; then finally left.

Candide caught his breath with difficulty and stood in the
doorway for a moment before going in, shaking his head from
side to side. Silent Man, don't you forget that you're going to
the Settlement tomorrow, going in the early morning, don't you
forget, not the Reeds, not the Clay Meadow, the Settlement . . .
And why are you going to the Settlement, Silent Man, you should
go to the Reeds instead, there's lots of fish there . . . it's fun . . .
The Settlement, don't you forget, Silent Man, don't you forget,
Candide . . . Going to the Settlement, tomorrow morning . . . to
talk those guys into coming, because the four of us won't make
it to the City . . . He went inside without realizing it.

Nava wasn't back yet, and the old man was sitting at the table,
waiting for someone to serve lunch. He gave Candide a surly
sideways glance and said, "You walk slowly, Silent Man, I have
visited two houses already, everyone is having lunch by now,
your house is the only one that is empty. That is why you have
no children, probably, because you walk so slowly, and because
you are never home when it is time for lunch."

Candide came right up to him and stood there for a bit, thinking.

The old man continued: "How long will it take you to get to
the City, if you cannot even be on time for lunch? It is said that
the City is very, very far away, I know everything about you now,
I know you intend to go to the City, there is only one thing I do

not know: How will you ever get to the City, when you spend an entire day trying to get to a pot of food, and cannot get to it still? . . . I will have to come with you, I will lead you there, I have long since needed to go to the City, but I do not know the way, and the reason I need to go to the City is this: I need to discharge a duty, and inform those concerned in it about it—"

Candide grabbed him under the arms and yanked him away from the table. The old man stopped talking in surprise. Candide carried him out of the house, holding him at arm's length, set him down on the road, and wiped his palms on the grass.

The old man recovered. "Just do not forget to bring food for me," he said to Candide's retreating back. "Bring me good food, and plenty of it, because I am discharging a duty, unlike the rest of you, who are going for your own pleasure and despite the fact that it is wrong . . ."

Candide returned to the house, sat down at the table, and rested his head on his clenched fists. I'm still leaving the day after tomorrow, he thought. That's what I have to remember: the day after tomorrow. The day after tomorrow, he thought. The day after tomorrow, the day after tomorrow.

3.

PERETZ

Peretz woke up because he felt cold fingers touching his bare
shoulder. He opened his eyes and saw a man in underclothes
standing over him. The light was off, but the man was in a
strip of moonlight, and Peretz could see a white face with
bulging eyes.

"What is it?" Peretz whispered.

"You need to vacate the premises," the man also whispered.

It's just the hotel manager, Peretz thought with relief. "Vacate
the premises?" he said loudly, and raised himself on one elbow.
"Why?"

"The hotel is full. You have to vacate the room."

Peretz looked around the room, bewildered. The room looked
the same as before, the other three cots still empty.

"Don't you peer around like that," said the hotel manager.
"We know best. And anyway, we need to change your linens and
launder them. Won't be washing them yourself, will you? Not
how you were brought up."

Peretz understood: the hotel manager was terrified, and he was being rude to work himself up. When a man was in this state, you could lay one finger on him and he'd start to shout, screech, and flail, then he'd break a window and holler for help.

"Come on, come on," said the hotel manager, and in some kind of sinister hurry started to pull the pillow out from under Peretz. "The linens, I said . . ."

"What's the matter?" Peretz forced out. "Does it have to be now? In the middle of the night?"

"It's urgent."

"My God," said Peretz. "You're out of your mind. All right . . . Take the linens, I'll manage without, I only have one night left." He climbed out of his cot onto the cold floor and started to pull the pillowcase off the pillow.

The hotel manager watched him with his bulging eyes, standing stock-still. His lips were moving. "We're renovating," he said finally. "It's time to renovate. The wallpaper is peeling, the ceiling is cracked, we need to lay new flooring . . ." His voice grew stronger. "So you still need to vacate the room. The renovations are starting now."

"You're renovating?"

"We're renovating. See the state the wallpaper's in? The workers are on their way now."

"Right now?"

"Right now. We can't possibly wait any longer. The ceiling's all cracked. You never know what could happen."

Peretz started to shake. He put the pillowcase down and picked up his pants. "What time is it?" he asked.

"It's already past midnight," the hotel manager said, whispering again, and for some reason looking around.

"But where will I go?" Peretz said, pausing with one pant leg on. "Come on, put me up somewhere. In another room—"

"We're full. And the rooms that aren't full are being renovated."

"Maybe the duty room?"

"It's full."

Peretz stared at the moon in despair. "Even the pantry would do," he said. "The pantry, the laundry, the infirmary. I only have six hours left to sleep. Or maybe I could stay with you for a bit."

The hotel manager suddenly began to rush around the room. He ran between the cots, barefoot, white, and terrible, like a ghost. Then he stopped and moaned plaintively, "What is happening here?!?! I'm a civilized man, I have two degrees, I'm not some sort of savage. I understand everything! But it can't be done, do you understand? It simply can't be done!" He ran up to Peretz and whispered into his ear, "Your visa has expired. It expired twenty-seven minutes ago, and you're still here. You can't be here. I'm begging you." He crashed onto his knees and pulled Peretz's shoes and socks out from under the bed. "I woke up at five minutes to twelve drenched in sweat," he muttered. "I'm done for, I thought. This will be the end of me. I ran over just as I was. Can't remember a thing. Clouds in the streets, nails scraping my feet . . . And my wife is about to give birth! Get dressed, get dressed, please."

Peretz got dressed in a hurry. He couldn't think straight. The hotel manager kept running between the cots, his bare feet slapping the moonlit squares, sticking his head out of the window and whispering, "My God, what is happening?"

"May I at least leave my suitcase with you?" Peretz asked.

The hotel manager snapped his teeth. "Not on your life! You will ruin me. How can you be so heartless? Oh God, oh God . . ."

Peretz hurriedly threw together his books, barely managed to close his suitcase, draped his coat over his arm, and asked, "But where will I go now?"

The hotel manager didn't answer. He was waiting, hopping up and down in impatience. Peretz picked up his suitcase and walked down the dark, quiet steps to the street. He paused on the porch, trying to quell the shaking, then he listened for a while as the hotel manager instructed the sleepy clerk: ". . . may ask to come back inside. Don't let him in! His . . . (*an indistinct ominous whisper*), do you understand? You're responsible for . . ." Peretz sat down on his suitcase and put his coat in his lap.

"No, no, excuse me," said the hotel manager from behind his back. "You have to get off the porch. You have to completely vacate the hotel premises."

He had to get off the porch and put his suitcase on the sidewalk. The hotel manager hung around for a bit, mumbling, "I beg you . . . My wife . . . Don't want any trouble . . . Consequences . . . You can't . . ." then left, his underclothes flashing white, slinking away along the fence. Peretz looked at the dark windows of the villas, at the dark windows of the Administration, at the dark windows of the hotel. Not a single light was on; even the streetlights were off. There was only a moon—round, bright, and somehow malevolent.

And he suddenly realized that he was all alone. He didn't have anyone. All around me, people are sleeping, they are all fond of me, I'm sure of that, I've seen it plenty of times. And yet I'm all alone, as if they've all suddenly died, or have become my enemies . . . Even the hotel manager—an ugly, good-natured man with an overactive thyroid, a misfit, who latched on to me from day one . . . We'd played four-handed duets on the piano and debated—I was the only person he dared to debate with, the only person who made him feel like a complete human being instead of just a father of seven. And even Kim. He came back from the chancery with a giant folder of denunciations. Ninety-two denunciations, all about me, written in the same handwriting and signed with different names. That I'm stealing the state-owned sealing wax from the post office, and that I had brought an underage lover in my suitcase and am now hiding her in the basement of the bakery, and lots more . . . And Kim kept reading these denunciations, throwing some in the garbage and laying others aside, muttering, "And this one needs a think . . ." And this was unexpected and horrible, pointless and repulsive. How he timidly glanced up at me, then immediately averted his eyes . . .

Peretz got up, picked up his suitcase, and trudged wherever his feet would take him. His feet didn't want to take him anywhere. And in any case, there was nowhere to go on these dark, empty streets. He kept stumbling, the dust made him sneeze, and it seemed that he fell several times. His suitcase was unbelievably heavy and strangely unwieldy. It rubbed heavily against his leg, then rolled ponderously off to the side, returning from the darkness only to smash into his knee. In the dark tree-lined walk in the park—where there was no light at all, and only the statues glowed dimly white, their shapes rippling in the darkness—the suitcase suddenly grabbed on to his pant leg with a loose clasp, and Peretz abandoned it in desperation. The hour of despair had come. Crying and seeing nothing through the tears, Peretz pushed his way through hedges, some dry and prickly, some green and dusty, then rolled down some steps, fell into a ditch, getting a painful blow to the back, and finally, completely worn out, suffocating in resentment and self-pity, dropped to his knees at the edge of the cliff.

But the forest remained indifferent. It was so indifferent that it wasn't even visible. There was nothing but darkness beneath the cliff. Only on the horizon did something large and layered, gray and shapeless, glow weakly in the moonlight.

"Wake up," Peretz pleaded. "Look at me just this once, now that we're all alone—don't worry, they are all asleep. Can it really be true that you don't need any of us? Or maybe you don't understand what that means, to need? It means to be unable to do without. It means to always think about. It means to always aspire toward. I don't know what you're like. No one knows that, least of all those who are absolutely certain that they know. You are the way you are, but I can still hope that you are the way I've wanted you to be my whole life: wise and good, tolerant and long-memoried, observant and maybe even grateful. We've lost all these things, we have neither the time nor the strength for them. We only build monuments, bigger, taller, cheaper monuments, but memories—we no longer have any memories. But you, you're different; that's why I've come to you from so far, without believing that you actually exist. Can it really be true that you don't need me? No, I'll be honest. I'm afraid that I don't need you either. We've seen each other, but we haven't grown closer, and that wasn't supposed to happen. Maybe they are the ones standing between us. There are a lot of them, and only one of me, but I'm one of them—you probably couldn't pick me out of a crowd, and perhaps you'd have no reason to do so. Maybe I was the one who came up with the human qualities that should appeal to you, and they don't appeal to the real you, only to my imaginary version of you."

Unexpectedly, bright blobs of white light slowly rose from below the horizon and hovered in place, swelling up. And instantly the searchlights on his right—beneath the cliff, beneath the overhanging rocks—began to swivel around in a frenzy, the searchlight beams getting stuck in layers of fog. The blobs of light above the horizon kept swelling up and stretching out, then they became whitish clouds and disappeared. In a minute, the searchlights also went off.

"They are afraid," Peretz said. "I'm also afraid. But I'm not only afraid of you, I'm also afraid for you. After all, you don't know them yet. But then, I don't know them at all well myself. I only know that they are capable of almost anything—extreme wisdom and stupidity, extreme cruelty and compassion, extreme rage and restraint. They are only missing one thing: the capacity to understand. They've always found substitutes for understanding: faith, atheism, indifference, contempt. For some reason, it has always been easiest. It is easier to believe than to understand. It is easier to be disillusioned than to understand. It is easier to give up in disgust than to understand. By the way, I'm leaving tomorrow, but that doesn't mean anything. I can't help you here—everything here is too stable, too set in its ways . . . I'm too unnecessary here, too obviously out of place. But don't worry, I'll find another focal point for my efforts. It's true, they could screw you up in some fundamental, irretrievable way, but that also takes time, and not just a bit of time. After all, they still need to find the most efficient, most economical, and—most important—easiest way. We'll keep fighting, let there only remain things worth fighting for . . . Good-bye."

Peretz rose from his knees and trudged back, through the bushes, into the park, onto the tree-lined walk. He tried to find his suitcase but couldn't. Then he returned to the main street, empty and illuminated only by the moon. It was already past one in the morning when he stopped in front of the welcomingly open door of the Administration library. The library windows were hung with heavy curtains, but inside it was as bright as day. The dried-out wood floor creaked ferociously, and there were books all around. The shelves were groaning with books, books were piled on the tables and in the corners, and other than Peretz and the books, there wasn't a soul in the library.

Peretz sank into a large old armchair, stretched his legs, leaned back, and quietly put his arms on the armrests. Don't just stand there, he told the books. Slackers! Is that what you were written for? Go on, report to me—how's the sowing progressing, how much have you sown? How much that's good, kind, eternal? And what are the prospects for the harvest? And most important, what has already sprouted? You're quiet . . . Take you, what do I call you—yes, you, the two-volume tome! How many people have read you? And how many have understood you? I really love you, old thing, you're a kind and honest friend. You've never yelled, never bragged, never beat your chest. Yes, you're kind and honest. And those who read you also become kind and honest. Even if only for a time. Even if only with themselves . . .

But you know, some people believe that we don't particularly need kindness and honesty to move forward. We need feet. And shoes. And even unwashed feet and unpolished shoes will do . . . Progress may turn out to be completely indifferent to the notions of kindness and honesty, just like it has been indifferent to them thus far. The Administration, for example, needs neither honesty nor kindness to function properly. These things are nice, they are preferable, but they are by no means necessary. Like knowing Latin for a bath attendant. Like having strong biceps for an accountant. Like respecting women for a Bootlicherson . . . But it all depends on how we understand progress. One way of understanding it results in all those infamous "buts": an alcoholic but a real professional; a womanizer but an amazing preacher; a thief, a crook, but what an administrator! A murderer, but what a disciplined and loyal man . . . Or we can understand progress to mean the process of transforming all people into kind and honest ones. Then we may live to see a day when they say, he's excellent at his job, of course, but he's scum—send him packing.

Listen, books, did you know that there are more of you than there are people? If people all disappeared, you could populate the Earth, and you'd be just like people. Some of you are good, honest, wise, and learned. But there are also the shallow airheads, the naysayers, the madmen, the murderers, the molesters, the children, the dreary preachers, the smug fools, and the hoarse rabble-rousers with bloodshot eyes. And you wouldn't know what you were for. Really, what are you for? Many of you impart knowledge, but what good is knowledge in the forest? It has nothing to do with the forest. It's as if the future architect of the cities of tomorrow were diligently taught to build fortifications, and then, no matter how much he later struggled to build a stadium or a resort, he could only ever come up with a gloomy stronghold with thick walls, a rampart, and a moat. What you've given the people who've come to the forest isn't knowledge, it's prejudice. And then there are those among you that cause people to lose faith and become discouraged. Not because they are bleak, or cruel, or counsel abandoning all hope, but because they lie. Sometimes the lies are resplendent, accompanied by upbeat songs and jaunty whistling; sometimes they are whiny, full of laments and excuses; but one way or another, they are lies. For some reason, these books are never burned and never banned—not once in human history has a lie been committed to the flames. Unless it was by

accident, out of confusion or mistaken belief. No one needs these
books in the forest. No one needs them anywhere. That's probably
why there are so many of them . . . Or rather, that's not why, it's
because people like them . . . A deception that elevates us is dearer
than a host of bitter truths— What? Who's that talking here? Oh,
that's me . . . As I was saying, there are also books that— What?

"Hush, let him sleep."

"The hell with sleeping, he oughta have a drink."

"Stop all that creaking . . . Hey, wait a minute, it's Peretz!"

"Forget Peretz, just don't fall."

"He looks so unkempt, so pitiful . . ."

"I'm not pitiful," mumbled Peretz, and woke up.

A library ladder was resting against the shelves across from
him. Alevtina from the photography lab was standing on the top
step, and the tattooed truck driver Randy was below her, holding
the ladder and looking up.

"And he always looks so lost," Alevtina said, looking at Peretz.
"He probably didn't have dinner either. We should wake him up
so he can at least have some vodka . . . I wonder what people like
that see in their dreams?"

"What I'm seeing in real life!" Randy said, looking up.

"Is it something new to you?" asked Alevtina. "Something
you've never seen before?"

"Nah," said Randy. "Can't say I've never seen it before, but
it's like some movies—you can watch 'em ten times over and
get a kick each time."

An enormous strudel, sliced into hefty chunks, was laid out on
the third step on the ladder, and cucumbers and peeled oranges
were arranged on the fourth step, while the fifth step contained
a half-empty bottle and a plastic pencil cup.

"Look all you like, just don't drop the ladder," said Alevtina,
and began to take down thick magazines and faded folders from
the top shelf. She blew dust off them, grimaced, flipped through
them, set some aside, and put the rest back.

Truck driver Randy breathed loudly through his nose.

"Do you need the year before last?" Alevtina asked.

"Right now, I only need one thing," Randy said mysteriously. "I'll go wake Peretz up."

"Don't let go of the ladder," Alevtina said.

"I'm not sleeping," said Peretz. "I've been watching you for a while."

"You can't see a thing over there," said Randy. "Come over here, Signor Peretz, we've got it all: women, wine, fruit . . ."

Peretz got up, limping on a leg that had fallen asleep, walked over to the ladder, and poured himself a drink.

"What did you dream about, Perry?" Alevtina asked from above. Peretz looked up out of habit and immediately lowered his eyes.

"What did I dream about? . . . Some nonsense . . . I was talking to books." He took a sip of his vodka and picked up a segment of the orange.

"Hold this for a second, Signor Peretz," Randy said. "I'll pour myself some, too."

"So do you need the year before last?" Alevtina asked.

"Of course!" Randy said. He splashed some vodka into his cup and began to pick out a cucumber. "The year before last, and the year before that . . . I'm always hard up. I've always been that way, I can't stand to do without it. Hell, no one can. Some can manage with less, and some can't, that's all . . . I always tell 'em: don't you preach at me, that's just how I'm made." Randy drank his vodka with relish and bit into his cucumber with a crunch. "And the way we live here is killing me. I'll be patient a bit longer, then I'll steal a car, drive it into the forest, and catch myself a mermaid . . ."

Peretz was holding the ladder and trying to think about tomorrow, while Randy took a seat on the bottom step and began relating how in his youth, he and some buddies caught a couple on the outskirts of town, beat the guy up and chased him away, and tried to force themselves on the girl. It was cold, it was damp, because of their youth and inexperience, no one could do it, the girl was frightened and kept crying, and one by one, his buddies left her alone, and only he, Randy, trailed her through the muddy alleys for a long time, grabbing her and cursing, and it kept seeming to him that he was about to pull it off, but he just couldn't do it, until he followed her all the way home, and there, in the dark lobby, he pinned her to the metal railing and finally got what he was after. In Randy's retelling, the incident sounded extraordinarily exciting and amusing.

"So those pretty little mermaids won't get away from me," Randy said. "I always know what's mine, and this time's no different. I don't believe in false advertising—what I see is what I get."

He had a dark, handsome face, thick eyebrows, bright eyes, and a mouth full of excellent teeth. He looked a lot like an Italian. If only his feet didn't smell.

"Gosh, what a mess, what a mess," said Alevtina. "The folders are all mixed up. Here, take these for now." She bent down and handed Randy a pile of folders and magazines.

Randy took the pile, flipped through a few pages, read them silently, mouthing the words, then counted the folders and said, "I need two more."

Peretz kept holding the ladder and staring at his clenched fists. This time tomorrow I won't be here anymore, he thought. I'll be sitting next to Randy in the cab, it will be hot, the metal will be just beginning to cool off. Randy will turn on the headlights, sprawl comfortably, and start to discuss world politics. I won't let him discuss anything else. He can stop at every diner, he can pick up whatever hitchhikers he likes, he can even make a detour to deliver someone a thresher from the repair shop. But I'll only let him discuss world politics. Or maybe I'll ask him about cars. About their rates of fuel consumption, about the accidents they usually get into, about the murders of corrupt inspectors. He tells a good story, and you never can tell if he's lying or telling the truth.

Randy had another drink, smacked his lips, took a lingering look at Alevtina's legs, and went on with his story, fidgeting, gesturing eloquently, and bursting into exuberant laughter.

Proceeding in meticulous chronological order, he told the story of his sex life, its progress from month to month, from year to year. The cook from the concentration camp where he did time for stealing paper during a famine (the cook kept repeating, "Come on, Randy, don't you let me down, Randy! . . ."). The daughter of a political prisoner from that same camp (she didn't care who she went with—she was sure they'd burn her no matter what she did). The wife of a sailor from a port city, who was trying to revenge herself on her horndog of a husband for his constant two-timing. A wealthy widow, whom Randy had to run away from in the middle of the night clad in nothing but his long johns, because she wanted to marry poor Randy and force him to traffic in narcotics and shameful pharmaceuticals. The women he gave rides to when he worked as a taxi driver: they paid in cash for their guests, and with their bodies at the end of the night. ("I tell her, what's all this, who'll take care of me—you've had four already, and I haven't had one . . .") Then his wife, a fifteen-year-old girl, whom he married with special permission from the state; she gave him twins, and eventually left him when he tried to pay with her body for the use of his buddies' lovers . . . Women . . . babes . . . bitches . . . dolls . . . snakes . . . sluts . . .

"So I'm no womanizer," he concluded. "I'm just a hot-blooded man, not some limp dick." He finished his vodka, took away the folders, and left without saying good-bye, whistling and creaking the wooden floor, hunching strangely, suddenly resembling either a spider or a prehistoric man.

Peretz was helplessly watching him go when Alevtina said, "Give me your hand, Perry." She sat down on the top step, put her hands on his shoulders, and jumped down with a soft yelp. He caught her under her arms and lowered her onto the floor, and they stood this way for some time, close together and face to face. She kept her hands on his shoulders, and he held her under the arms.

"I got kicked out of the hotel," he said.

"I know," she said. "Come with me, if you'd like?"

She was kind and warm, and she was looking calmly but not particularly confidently into his eyes. Looking at her, it was easy to imagine lots of kind, warm, and blissful images, and Peretz greedily flipped through them and tried to imagine himself next to her, but he suddenly realized that he couldn't do it; instead of himself he saw Randy—handsome, insolent, precise in his movements, and smelling of feet.

"Thank you, but there's no need," he said, and pulled his hands away. "I'll manage."

She immediately turned around and started to gather the remaining food onto a sheet of newspaper. "Why should you manage?" she said. "I can make you a bed on the couch. You can get some sleep, and in the morning we'll find you a place to stay. You can't spend every night in the library."

"Thank you," said Peretz. "But I'm leaving tomorrow."

She looked at him in astonishment. "Leaving? For the forest?"

"No, I'm going home."

"Home . . ." She was slowly wrapping the food in the newspaper. "But you've always wanted to get into the forest, I've heard you say it myself."

"You see, I did want to . . . But they won't let me in. I don't even know why. And there's nothing left for me to do in the Administration. So I arranged something . . . Randy will drive me tomorrow. It's already past three. I'll go to the garage, climb into Randy's truck, and wait there until morning. So you don't need to worry about me."

"That means we should say good-bye . . . Or maybe do come with me?"

"Thank you, but I'd rather sleep in the truck . . . I'm afraid to oversleep. Randy won't wait, you see."

They went out onto the street and walked to the garage arm in arm. "So you didn't like Randy's stories?"

"No," said Peretz. "I didn't like them at all. I don't like stories about that. What's the point? It's embarrassing, that's all . . . I was embarrassed for him, and embarrassed for you, and embarrassed for myself. I was embarrassed for everyone. It's all so meaning-less. Like they only do it out of intense boredom."

"Most of the time, intense boredom really is why they do it," said Alevtina. "And don't be embarrassed for me, I don't care about that. It doesn't matter to me in the least. All right, here's where we part ways. Kiss me good-bye."

Peretz kissed her, feeling some vague regret.

"Thank you," she said, turned around, and quickly walked in the opposite direction. For some reason, Peretz waved at her retreating back.

Then he walked into the garage, which was illuminated by blue lights, stepped over the guard, who was snoring peacefully on a seat that he had dragged out of some vehicle, found Randy's truck, and climbed into the cab. Here it smelled of rubber, gaso-line, and dust. A Mickey Mouse, his arms and legs outstretched, swayed in front of the windshield. This is nice, thought Peretz. It's cozy. I should have come here from the beginning. The guard was snoring loudly. The cars were sleeping, the guard was sleep-ing, and the whole Administration was sleeping. And Alevtina was getting undressed in front of the mirror in her room, next to her unmade bed—her large, king-sized, soft, hot bed . . . No, let's not think about that. Because during the day, we're distracted by the idle chatter, by the rattle of the arithmometer, by the meaningless chaos of working life, whereas now there's no eradication, no engineering-based penetration, no scientific guard, and no other sinister nonsense, there's only a sleepy world on a cliff, ghostlike in the way of all sleepy worlds, invisible and inaudible, and no more real than the forest. Actually, right now the forest is more real—after all, the forest never sleeps. Or maybe it's sleeping and seeing us all in its dreams. We're the forest's dream. An atavistic dream. The coarse ghosts of its diminished sexuality . . .

Peretz lay down, contorting himself, and put his crumpled-up coat under his head. Mickey Mouse swayed gently on the string. Whenever girls saw this toy, they would squeal "What a cutie!" and truck driver Randy would answer, "It ain't no false advertising." The gearshift pressed into Peretz's side, and Peretz didn't know how to move it. Or whether it was a good idea to move it. Maybe if he moved it, the truck would go forward. At first slowly, then faster and faster, heading straight for the sleeping guard, and Peretz would flail around the cab and press anything within reach of his hands or his feet, and the guard would get closer and closer—you would already be able to see his open, snoring mouth. Then the truck would jump, make a sharp turn, crash into the garage wall, and blue sky would appear in the breach—

Peretz woke up and saw that it was already morning. Mechanics were smoking in the open doors of the garage, and he could see the ground in front of the building, which was yellow in the sun. It was seven o'clock. Peretz sat up, rubbed his face, and looked at himself in the rearview mirror. I could use a shave, he thought, but he didn't get out of the car. Randy wasn't here yet, and he had to wait for him right there, in the truck, because drivers were all forgetful and they would always leave without him. There were two rules for dealing with drivers: first of all, never get out of the vehicle when you can bear to stay inside and wait, and second, never argue with a driver who's giving you a ride. If worse comes to worst, pretend to be asleep.

The mechanics standing in the doorway threw their cigarette butts on the ground, smeared them meticulously into the pavement with the toes of their boots, and came into the garage. Peretz didn't know the first mechanic, and it turned out that the second one wasn't a mechanic at all but the garage foreman. They walked right by Peretz, and the foreman actually paused by the cab, put a hand on the fender, and for some mysterious reason looked under the truck. Then Peretz heard him order the other one around: "Hey, you, get a move on, get me the jack." "Where is it?" asked the unfamiliar mechanic. "#$@%!" the foreman calmly replied. "Look under the seat." "How the hell should I know?" the mechanic asked, irritated. "I did warn you that I'm a waiter . . ." For a while it was quiet, then the driver's side door of the cab opened, revealing the glum, disappointed face of the mechanic-waiter. He glanced at Peretz, looked around the cab, tugged on the steering wheel for some reason, then stuck both hands under the seat and began to clank around.

"Is this thing the jack?" he asked softly.

"N-No," Peretz said. "I think that's an adjustable wrench."

The mechanic brought the adjustable wrench close to his face, examined it, pursing his lips, put it on the running board, and reached underneath the seat again.

"Is this it?" he asked.

"No," Peretz said. "I'm absolutely certain of that. This is an arithmometer. A jack doesn't look like this."

The mechanic-waiter, his low forehead wrinkled, was examining the arithmometer. "What does a jack look like?"

"*Uhhh* . . . It's a sort of metal rod . . . There's more than one kind. They have these cranks . . ."

"This thing has a crank. Like on a cash register."

"No, it's a completely different kind of crank."

"And what happens if I turn this crank?"

Peretz was now completely stumped. The mechanic waited a bit, sighed, put the arithmometer on the running board, and looked under the seat again.

"Could this be it?" he asked.

"It's possible. Looks a lot like it. Except there should be another metal stick. A thick one."

The mechanic found this stick, too. He rocked it in the palm of his hand, said, "All right, that'll do for a start," and left, leaving the door open. Peretz lit a cigarette. Curses and sounds of clanking metal came from somewhere behind him. Then the truck began to shake and groan.

There was still no sign of Randy, but Peretz wasn't worried. He was imagining how they'd drive down the main street of the Administration, no one paying any attention to them. Then they'd turn down a dirt road, raising clouds of yellow dust, and the sun would keep rising higher and higher on their right, and the cab would soon get hot, and they would turn off the dirt road onto the highway, which would be long, flat, smooth, and boring, and mirages resembling large pools of water would shimmer on the horizon . . .

The mechanic walked past the cab again, rolling a truck's heavy rear wheel in front of him. The wheel had gathered speed as it rolled on the concrete floor, and you could tell that the mechanic was trying to stop it and lean it against the wall, but the wheel only changed course slightly and rolled heavily outside, the mechanic running clumsily after it, falling farther and farther behind. They both disappeared from view, then the mechanic screamed loudly and desperately outside. Peretz heard the pounding of many feet, then a number of people rushed past the door, shouting, "Grab hold! Get on its right side!"

Peretz noticed that the vehicle wasn't as level as before, and stuck his head out of the cab. The garage foreman was doing something by the rear wheel.

"Morning," said Peretz. "What are you—"

"Peretz, my friend!" the foreman shouted joyfully, continuing to work. "You just sit, you sit, no need to get out! You aren't in our way. Damn thing is stuck . . . One came off without a hitch, but this one's stuck."

"What do you mean, it's stuck? Did something break?"

"Doubt it," said the garage foreman, standing up and wiping his forehead with the back of the hand holding the wrench. "Just a bit rusty, I'd guess. I'll deal with it quick . . . Then the two of us can go play some chess. What do you say?"

"Chess?" Peretz said. "But where's Randy?"

"Randy? You mean Randall? Randall is now a senior lab technician. He was sent to the forest. Randall doesn't work for us anymore. What do you want him for?"

"Oh, nothing," Peretz said quietly. "I just thought . . ." He opened the door and jumped onto the cement floor.

"You didn't need to get out, you know," said the foreman. "Should have stayed where you were—you weren't in the way."

"What's the point?" Peretz said. "This truck isn't going any-where, right?"

"No, it's not going anywhere. Can't go anywhere without wheels, you know, and the wheels need to come off . . . Stuck right on, the piece of shit! Ah, damn you . . . Forget it, the mechanics will do it. Let's go play a game instead."

He took Peretz by the arm and led him to his office. They sat down at his desk; the foreman pushed a pile of papers aside, took out the chessboard, and unplugged the phone.

"Should we use a clock?" he asked.

"I don't even know," said Peretz.

The office was dimly lit and cold, bluish tobacco smoke drifted between the cabinets like gelatinous seaweed, and the foreman—warty, bloated, covered in varicolored spots, resembling a giant octopus—opened the lacquered shell of the chessboard with two hairy tentacles and began to fussily extract its wooden innards. His round eyes glistened dully; the glass right eye kept pointing at the ceiling, while the left eye, lively like dusty mercury, rolled freely around its socket, constantly shifting between Peretz, the door, and the chessboard.

"Let's use a clock," the garage foreman finally decided. He took the clock out of the cabinet, wound it up, pressed his button, and made the first move.

The sun continued to rise. Outside, people were shouting "Get on its right side!" At eight, the foreman was deep in thought over a difficult position, then suddenly demanded breakfast for two. Vehicles kept rumbling out of the garage. The foreman lost a game and proposed another one. They had hearty breakfasts: each drank two bottles of buttermilk and ate a stale strudel. The foreman lost another game, looked at Peretz with devotion and admiration with his real eye, and proposed a third game. He kept opening with the same exact Queen's Gambit, never deviating by a single move from his once- and forever-chosen losing variation. It was as if he were fulfilling a quota of defeats, and Peretz moved the chess pieces completely automatically, feeling like a piece of training equipment: there was nothing either inside or outside him other than the chessboard, the button on the clock, and the rigidly specified plan of action.

At five to nine, the internal broadcasting system grunted and announced in a genderless voice, "All Administration workers report to your phones. The Director will be addressing the employees." The garage foreman became very serious, plugged in his phone, picked up the receiver, and put it to his ear. Both his eyes were now pointing at the ceiling. "Can I go?" asked Peretz. The garage foreman gave a terrible frown, put a finger to his lips, then waved Peretz away. A nasal squawking sounded from the receiver. Peretz tiptoed out.

The garage was full of people. Their faces were all stern, serious, and even solemn. No one was working; they were all pressing phones to their ears. Only the mechanic-waiter—sweaty, red, disheveled, and gasping for breath—was still chasing the wheel in the brightly lit yard. Something very important was happening. This isn't right, thought Peretz. This isn't right, I'm always on the sidelines, I never know anything—maybe that's the whole problem, maybe everything's exactly the way it should be, but I don't know what's what, and that's why I'm always left out.

He jumped into the nearest phone booth, picked up the receiver, and listened greedily, but there was only a busy signal. Then he felt a sudden apprehension, a nagging anxiety that he was again late for something, that someone somewhere was giving things away, and that he'd be left empty handed as always. Leaping over ditches and potholes, he cut across the construction site, recoiled from the guard with a gun in one hand and a phone in the other who tried to block his way, and clambered up a ladder to the top of the unfinished wall. He had just enough time to glance into each window, seeing concentrating, frozen people with phones in every single one, when there was a piercing screech in his ear, and a moment later a revolver went off behind his back. He jumped down onto a pile of garbage and ran to a service entrance. The door was locked. He yanked on the handle a few times and the handle broke off. He tossed it aside and took a moment to figure out what to do. The narrow window next to the door was open, so he climbed through it, getting completely covered in dust and tearing his nails.

The room he found himself in had two desks. Bootlicherson was sitting at one of the desks, holding a phone receiver. His face was as still as a statue's, and his eyes were closed. He was pressing the receiver to his ear with his shoulder, and he was rapidly writing something down in his large notebook with a pencil. The second desk was empty, and there was a phone on the desk. Peretz greedily grabbed the receiver and started to listen.

Rustling. Crackling. An unfamiliar high-pitched voice: ". . . The Administration can realistically only manage an insignificant portion of the territory in the ocean of forest that envelops the continent. There is no meaning of life, nor is there any meaning to our acts. We can do a great many things, but we still haven't figured out which of these things we actually ought to do. It doesn't even resist, it simply doesn't notice. If an act has brought you pleasure, it was good; if it didn't—it was meaningless." More rustling and crackling. "We resist with millions of horsepower, with dozens of ATVs, airships, and helicopters, with medical science and with the best theory of logistics in the world. The Administration has revealed itself to have at least two serious flaws. Currently, deeds of this sort can have far-reaching encrypted messages in the name of Herostratus, so that he remains our most beloved friend. It is completely incapable of creating without undermining authority or showing ingratitude." Beeps, whistles, something that sounded like a bad cough. "It is very fond of the so-called simple solutions: libraries, internal communications, geographical and other maps. The paths it deems shortest, in order to think about the meaning of life for all people at once, but people don't like that. Employees sit there, dangling their feet over the abyss, everyone in his or her place, shoving each other, cracking jokes and throwing stones, the heavier the better, while the consumption of buttermilk helps neither cultivate nor eradicate nor even sufficiently conceal the forest. I'm afraid we haven't even figured out what it is that we want, and nerves do need to be trained, after all, just like we train our ability to perceive, and the intellect does not blush nor does it feel remorse, because the question morphs from a correctly posed, scientific one into a question of morals. It's deceitful, shifty, fickle, and it's always pretending. But someone does need to be the irritating one, and instead of telling tales, thoroughly preparing for a trial exit. I will see you again tomorrow and see how well you've prepared. At twenty-two hundred hours, there will be a radiological alarm and an earthquake; at eighteen hundred hours, I will call a meeting with the off-duty personnel on, how do you say it, the carpet; at twenty-four hundred hours, there will be a general evacuation."

A sound like running water came from the receiver. Then everything went quiet, and Peretz noticed Bootlicherson watching him with stern, accusing eyes.

"What is he talking about?" Peretz whispered. "I don't understand a thing."

"That is not surprising," Bootlicherson said frigidly. "This is not your phone." He looked down, wrote something down in his notebook, and continued: "By the way, this is an absolutely unacceptable violation of the rules. I insist you put down the phone and leave. Otherwise I'll have to call the authorities."

"Fine," said Peretz. "I'll leave. But where's my phone? This is not my phone. Then where is my phone?"

Bootlicherson didn't answer. His eyes were closed again, and the phone was again pressed to his ear. Peretz heard more squawking.

"I'm asking you, where's my phone?" Peretz screamed. He could no longer hear anything in his receiver. There was more rustling and crackling, then he heard the series of short beeps that indicated he'd been disconnected. He dropped the receiver and ran out into the hallway. He threw open office doors, finding a mix of familiar and unfamiliar employees everywhere. Some were frozen completely still, resembling sitting or standing wax figures with glass eyes; others were pacing their offices, stepping over the telephone cords that dragged behind them; still others frantically wrote in thick notebooks, on scraps of paper, in newspaper margins. There were no free phones. Peretz tried to take a phone away from one of the employees frozen in a trance, a young man in coveralls, but he immediately came to life, started squealing and kicking, then everyone else began to shush them and wave their arms, and someone shouted hysterically, "This is an outrage! Call security!"

"Where's my phone?" shouted Peretz. "I'm human, just like you—I have the right to know. Let me listen! Let me have my phone!"

They kept throwing him out of rooms and locking the door behind him. He made it all the way to the top floor, where by the entrance to the attic, next to the machine room of the perpetually broken elevator, two on-duty mechanics were sitting and playing tic-tac-toe. Peretz leaned against the wall, out of breath. The mechanics glanced at him, smiled vaguely, and bent over the paper again.

"You don't have phones either?" asked Peretz.

"We do," one of the mechanics said. "Not have phones? We haven't sunk that low."

"So why aren't you listening?"

"Can't hear a thing, why bother?"

"Why can't you hear a thing?"

"'Cause we cut the line."

Peretz wiped his face and neck with a balled-up handkerchief, waited until one of the mechanics won the game, and went downstairs. The hallways had gotten noisy. Doors were opening; employees were coming out for a smoke. There was a buzz of lively, excited, agitated voices: "I'm telling you, it's a fact: licorice is made out of liquor. What? But, after all, I read it in this book . . . Can't you hear it yourself? *Li-co-rice. Li-quor.* What?" "I checked the Yvert catalog: one hundred and fifty thousand francs, and that was in 1956. Can you imagine how much it must cost now?" "These cigarettes are a bit odd. They say they don't put any tobacco in cigarettes nowadays, they take special paper, shred it, and saturate it with nicotine . . ." "Tomatoes can also give you cancer. Tomatoes, pipes, eggs, silk gloves . . ." "How did you sleep? Just think, I couldn't fall asleep all night—that pile driver simply wouldn't stop. Hear that? It was like that all night . . . Good morning, Peretz! They were saying you left. I'm glad you stayed . . ." "They finally found the thief, remember how things kept going missing? Turns out, it was the discus thrower from the park, you know, the statue by the fountain. The one with an obscene inscription on his leg . . ." "Perry, do me a favor, lend me five bucks till payday. Till tomorrow, that is . . ." "And he wasn't flirting with her at all. She was throwing herself at him. Right in front of her husband. You don't believe me, but I saw it with my own eyes . . ."

Peretz went down to his office, said hello to Kim, and washed his face. Kim wasn't working. He was sitting still, his hands resting on top of his desk, staring at the tiled wall. Peretz took the cover off the arithmometer, plugged it in, and looked expectantly at Kim.

"Can't work today," Kim said. "Some idiot keeps going around fixing everything. I've been sitting here, not knowing what to do."

Then Peretz noticed a note on his desk: "For Peretz. This is to inform you that your phone is located in office 771." Peretz sighed.

"You've got no call to sigh," Kim said. "You should have come to work on time."

"But I didn't know," Peretz said. "I was planning to leave today."

"Serves you right," Kim said drily.

"I still listened for a bit. And you know, Kim, I didn't under-stand a thing. Why is that?"

"You listened for a bit! You silly man. You fool. The chance you missed . . . I don't even want to talk to you. Now I'll have to introduce you to the Director. Just out of pity."

"Please do," said Peretz. "You know," he continued, "it occasionally felt like I was getting it, like I was grasping certain fragments of ideas, very interesting ones at that, but I'm now trying to remember them—and there's nothing there."

"Whose phone was it?"

"I don't know. It was in Bootlicherson's office."

"*Ahh* . . . That's right, she's on maternity leave. Bootlicherson has no luck. He hires a new woman, she works for him half a year, then always—maternity leave. Yes, Perry, you got a woman's phone. So I might not even be able to help you . . . Besides, no one listens to it all in a row, probably not women either. You see, the Director is addressing everyone at once, but at the same time, he's speaking to each person individually. Do you understand?"

"I'm afraid that—"

"For example, here's how I'd recommend you listen. Write out the Director's speech in a single line, excluding punctuation, and select words at random by throwing down imaginary dominoes. If two domino halves agree, the word is selected and written down on a separate piece of paper. If they do not agree, they word is temporarily rejected, but it's left on the page. There are a few subtleties, associated with the frequency of vowels and consonants, but that's a second-order effect. Do you understand?"

"No," said Peretz. "I mean, yes. I wish I had known about this method. So what did he say today?"

"It's not the only possible method. There's also, say, the variable-stroke spiral method. This method is fairly crude, but if only basic economic issues are under discussion, then it's very convenient due to its simplicity. There's the Stevenson-Zade method, but it requires the use of electronic devices. So I'd say that in the majority of cases, the domino method is best, while the spiral method is preferred in situations with a limited and specialized vocabulary."

"Thank you," Peretz said. "And what did the Director talk about today?"

"What do you mean?"

"What? . . . *Uhhh* . . . What did he talk about? W-What did he . . . say?"

"To whom?"

"To whom? To you, say."

"Unfortunately, I can't tell you that. That's classified information, and you are, after all, a visiting employee. So don't be angry."

"I'm not angry," said Peretz. "I'd just like to find out what . . . He was saying something about the forest, about free will . . . The other day, I was throwing stones into the abyss, just for fun, for no particular reason, and he said something about that, too."

"Don't tell me about that," Kim said nervously. "That's none of my business. Or yours either, since it wasn't your phone."

"Come on, wait, did he talk about the forest at all?"

Kim shrugged. "Well, of course. He never talks about anything else. That's enough about that. Tell me how you tried to leave instead."

Peretz told him.

"You shouldn't beat him all the time," Kim said pensively.

"I can't help it. I am a fairly strong chess player, and he's just an amateur. And then he plays in an odd sort of way."

"It doesn't matter. If I were you, I'd give it some serious thought. Something's been off about you lately . . . People write denunciations about you . . . You know what, I'll set up a meeting with the Director for you tomorrow. I think he'll let you go. Just make sure to emphasize that you're a linguist, a philologist, that you came here by accident, and mention as if in passing that you had really wanted to get into the forest, but that you've now changed your mind, because you consider yourself unqualified."

"All right."

They were silent for a bit. Peretz imagined himself face to face with the Director and blanched. The domino method, he thought. The Stevenson-Zade method . . .

"And most important, don't be afraid to cry," Kim said. "He likes it."

Peretz jumped up and walked around the room in agitation. "My God," he said. "If I just knew what he looks like. What he's like."

"What he's like? Not very tall, red-haired . . ."

"Bootlicherson says that he's a real giant."

"Bootlicherson is an idiot. A show-off and a liar. The Director is a red-haired man, on the heavy side, with a small scar on his right cheek. He's a little pigeon-toed when he walks, like a sailor. In fact, he actually used to be a sailor."

"And Randy said that he's lean and wears his hair long, because he's missing an ear."

"Who's this Randy?"

"A truck driver, I've told you about him."

Kim laughed sardonically. "How could truck driver Randy know all that? Listen, Perry, you shouldn't be so gullible."

"Randy says that he'd driven him and seen him a few times."

"So what? He's probably lying. I was his personal secretary, and I haven't seen him once."

"Haven't seen who?"

"The Director. I was his secretary for a while, before I defended my thesis."

"And you haven't seen him once?"

"Of course not! You really think it's that simple?"

"Wait, so how do you know he's red-haired, etcetera?"

Kim shook his head. "Perry," he said gently. "Dear heart. No one has ever seen a hydrogen atom, but everybody knows that it has a single electron shell with specific characteristics, and a nucleus which in the simplest case consists of a single proton."

"That's true," Peretz said weakly. He could feel that he'd gotten tired. "Then I'll see him tomorrow."

"No, no, ask me something simpler," said Kim. "I'll set up a meeting for you, I can guarantee you that much. But I can't tell you who or what you'll see there. And I don't know what you'll hear there either. After all, you aren't asking me whether the Director will let you go, and you're right not to ask. Because I can't know that, right?"

"But this is different," said Peretz.

"It's the same thing, Perry," Kim said. "It's the same thing, I assure you."

"I probably seem very obtuse," Peretz said sadly.

"Maybe a tiny bit."

"It's just that I didn't sleep well today."

"No, you're just impractical. Why didn't you sleep well, anyway?"

Peretz explained. And he got scared. Kim's good-natured face suddenly turned beet red; his hair stood on end. He snarled, grabbed the phone, dialed the number in a frenzy and roared, "Hotel manager? What's the meaning of this? How dare you evict Peretz? Siiilence! I didn't ask you what ended, I asked you how dare you evict Peretz! What? Siiilence! Don't you dare! What? Nonsense, bullshit! Siiilence! I'll crucify you! You and your Claudius Octavian Bootlicherson! You'll be scrubbing toilets, you'll be sent into the forest within twenty-four hours, within sixty minutes! What? Yes . . . Yes . . . What? Yes . . . All right. That's better. And only the best linen . . . That's your business, on the street if you have to . . . What? Good. OK. OK. Thank you. I apologize for the trouble . . . Well, of course . . . Thank you very much. Good-bye."

He put down the receiver. "It's all settled," he said. "He's a wonderful man. Go rest. You'll live in his apartment, and his family will move into your old hotel room—there's no other way, unfortunately . . . And don't argue, I beg you, don't argue, it's absolutely none of our business. It was his choice. Go, go, that's an order. I'll give you a call about the Director later."

Peretz staggered out onto the street, stood still for a bit, squinting in the sun, then headed to the park to look for his suitcase. He didn't find it immediately, because the suitcase was tightly gripped in the strong alabaster hand of the thieving fountain-side discus-thrower, the one with an obscene inscription on his left thigh. Actually, the inscription wasn't even that obscene. Someone had written in indelible pencil GIRLS, BEWARE OF SYPHILIS.

4.

CANDIDE

Candide left before dawn so he could get back in time for lunch. It was about six miles to the Settlement; the road was familiar and footworn, covered in bald patches from all the splashed grasskiller. It was considered safe for walking. Warm, bottomless swamps lay to the left and right: rotting black branches stuck out of the fragrant rust-colored grass, giant swamp toadstools poked out their sticky caps, looking like shiny, round domes, and occasionally he'd come across abandoned, crushed houses of water spiders right next to the road. It was difficult to tell what was happening in the swamp from the trail; the densely interwoven treetops above his head emanated a myriad of thick green columns, ropes, and gauzy, weblike threads, their impatient roots reaching into the bog. The greedy, insolent greenery created a wall that looked like fog, and that hid everything but the smells and sounds. From time to time, something would snap off in the yellow-green gloom and slowly tumble down, the noise lingering, then there'd be a thick, greasy splash, the swamp would sigh, rumble, and squelch, and there'd be silence again—then a minute later, the fetid stink of the disturbed abyss would worm its way onto the road through the green curtain. It was said that no man could walk across these bottomless places, but the deadlings walked everywhere; they weren't deadlings for nothing—the swamp didn't accept them. Candide fashioned himself a cudgel just in case, not because he was afraid of the deadlings—as a rule, deadlings didn't pose a threat to men—but because rumors abounded about swamp and forest life, and for all their absurdity, some could turn out to be true.

He had walked about a quarter mile from the village when Nava caught up with him. He stopped.

"Why did you leave without me?" Nava asked, sounding slightly out of breath. "Told you I'd go with you, I did, I don't want to stay in that village by myself, there's nothing for me to do there by myself, no one loves me there, and you're my husband, you have to take me with you, it doesn't matter that we don't have kids, you're still my husband, and I'm your wife, and the kids, they'll still come. Only I'll be honest with you, I don't want kids yet, I have no idea what they are for or what we'd do with them. I don't care what the village head says, or that old man of yours, in my village it was completely different: if you wanted to have kids, you had them, and if you didn't want to have kids, you didn't."

"Go home right now," said Candide. "Where did you get the idea that I was leaving? I'm just going to the Settlement, I'll be home for lunch."

"Good, then I'll come with you, we'll go home for lunch together, I made lunch yesterday, and I hid it so well that even that old man of yours, he won't find it . . ."

Candide walked on. Arguing was pointless; may as well let her come. He even cheered up, feeling the urge to pick a fight, to swing his cudgel, to take out the many years' worth of accumulated despair, anger, and helplessness on someone. On the thieves. Or on the deadlings—what difference did it make? Let the girl come. Thinks she's a real wife, talking about not wanting kids . . . He swung as hard as he could and whacked a tree stump by the side of the road with his cudgel, then almost fell over: the stump disintegrated into dust and the cudgel flew through it as if it were a shadow. Several nimble gray animals jumped out, plopped into the dark water, and disappeared.

Nava bounded next to him, now running ahead, now falling behind. Once in a while, she'd grab Candide's hand and hang on him, looking very pleased with herself. She talked about lunch, which she had hidden so cleverly from the old man, about how the lunch might have been eaten by wild ants, if she hadn't done something so the ants would never ever find it, about how some annoying fly woke her up, and about how yesterday, when she was falling asleep, he, Silent Man, was already snoring, and he was muttering strange words in his sleep, and how do you know words like that, Silent Man, it's really amazing, no one in our village knows words like that, only you know them, and you always knew them, even when you were very sick, you knew them . . .

Candide both listened and didn't, the familiar tedious droning echoing in his brain. He was walking and thinking dull, rambling thoughts about why he couldn't think about anything, it was probably from the constant vaccines, the most popular village pastime besides mindless chatter, or maybe it was from something else . . . Maybe it was the effect of this drowsy way of life—not even primitive but downright vegetative—that he'd been forced to lead ever since that distant time when his helicopter crashed full speed into an invisible barrier, warped, broke its propellers, and fell into the swamp like a ton of bricks. That's probably when I got thrown out of the cabin, he thought. That's when I was thrown out of the cabin, he thought for the thousandth time. I hit my head on something, and I never recovered . . . And if I hadn't been thrown out, I would have drowned in the swamp along with my helicopter, so it was actually a good thing that I was thrown out . . . It suddenly dawned on him that these were deductions, and he was delighted. He had thought that he'd long since lost the capacity for deductive reasoning and only knew how to say the same thing over and over again: the day after tomorrow, the day after tomorrow . . .

He took a look at Nava. The girl was hanging on his left arm, looking up at him, and was eagerly telling him, "So then they all huddled together, and it became really hot, you know how hot they are, and there was no moon that night at all. Then my mom, she started nudging me gently, so I crawled on all fours under everyone's legs, and that was the last time I saw her, my mom—"

"Nava," Candide said, "you're telling me this story again. You've told me this story two hundred times already."

"So what?" Nava said, surprised. "You're a strange one, Silent Man. What else is there to tell you? There's nothing else I know or remember. It's not like I'm going to tell you about how you and I dug out the cellar last week, you were there, you saw it yourself. Now if I'd dug out the cellar with someone else, Crookleg, say, or Loudmouth—" She suddenly became animated. "You know, Silent Man, that might even be interesting. Why don't you tell me about the cellar, how you and I dug it out last week, no one told me about that yet, because no one saw us do it . . ."

Candide got distracted again. Yellow-green vegetation drifted past them, swaying gently; something was sighing and breathing loudly in the water; a swarm of the soft, whitish beetles used for intoxicating liqueurs rushed past them with a high-pitched whine; the road beneath their feet kept changing, turning soft from tall grass, then hard from broken stone. Yellow, gray, green patches— there was nothing to catch the eye and nothing to remember. Then the path turned sharply left. Candide walked a few more steps and stopped with a start. Nava broke off midsentence.

A large deadling lay by the side of the road, its head in the swamp. Its arms and legs were splayed out and twisted in an unpleasant way, and it was completely motionless. It was lying on the trampled, heat-yellowed grass, pale and wide, and even at this distance you could tell how savagely it had been beaten. It was like jelly. Candide carefully walked around it. He started to feel anxious. The fight was very recent: the bent blades of yellow grass were straightening out as they watched. Candide carefully inspected the road. There were lots of tracks, but he couldn't make heads or tails of them, and there was another bend in the road just a short distance away, and he couldn't guess what was beyond it. Nava kept looking back at the deadling.

"That wasn't our kind," she said very softly. "Our kind don't know how. Big Fist keeps threatening to, but he doesn't know how either, he just waves his arms . . . And people in the Settlement don't know how either . . . Silent Man, how about we head back, eh? What if it's the freaks? They say they walk here, not often, but they do walk here. We better head back . . . Why are you taking me to the Settlement, anyway? Not like I've never been to the Settlement before."

Candide got angry. What the hell? He'd walked this road a hundred times and he'd never come across anything worth remembering or thinking about. And now, when he needed to leave tomorrow—not even the day after tomorrow, but tomorrow, finally!—the one safe road becomes unsafe . . . Because the only way to the City is through the Settlement. If it's even possible to get to the City, if the City even exists, then the road to it goes through the Settlement . . .

He came back to the deadling. He imagined how Crookleg, Big Fist, and Tagalong, constantly chattering, bragging, and threatening, would mill about this deadling and then, continuing to threaten and brag, would turn back toward the village, out of harm's way. He bent down and grabbed the deadling by the legs, which were still hot but no longer burned. He shoved the heavy body hard into the swamp. The bog squelched, wheezed, and gave way. The dark water rippled, then it was still again.

"Nava," Candide said, "go back to the village."

"How can I go back to the village," Nava said reasonably, "if you don't go back? Now if you go back to the village, too—"

"Stop chattering," said Candide. "Run back to the village right now and wait for me. And don't talk to anyone there."

"What about you?"

"I'm a man," Candide said. "No one will do anything to me."

"Sure they will," objected Nava. "I'm telling you: What if it's the freaks? They don't care if it's man, woman, or deadling, they'll make you a freak yourself, you'll be walking here, frightening people, and at night, you'll have to stick yourself to a tree . . . How can I go alone, if they might be over there, behind us?"

"There's no such thing as a freak," Candide said, not very confidently. "It's all lies."

He looked back. There was a bend in the road there, too, and he couldn't guess what was around that bend either. Nava was talking to him, saying lots of things in a rapid whisper, and this felt especially unpleasant. He got a better grip on his cudgel. "All right. You can come along. Only stay close, and if I order you to do something, do it immediately. And keep quiet—close your mouth and keep quiet all the way until the Settlement. Let's go."

She didn't know how to keep quiet, of course. She really did stay close—she stopped running ahead and falling behind—but she kept muttering things under her breath: first about the freaks, then about Crookleg, how they had walked here together and he made her a whistle . . . They went around the dangerous bend, then around another dangerous bend, and Candide was just starting to relax when some people silently stepped out from the tall grass, coming toward them out of the swamp.

That does it, Candide thought wearily. I have no luck. I never have any luck. He glanced at Nava. Nava was shaking her head; her face had puckered.

"Don't you give me away, Silent Man," she muttered, "I don't want to go with them. I want to stay with you, don't give me away . . ."

He looked at the people. There were seven of them—all men, all with beards up to their eyes, and all holding enormous gnarled cudgels. They didn't look local, and they didn't dress in local fashion—they were wearing completely different plants. They were thieves.

"What are you stopping for?" the head thief said in a deep, resonant voice. "Come here, we won't hurt you . . . If you were deadlings, then of course it'd be a different story, except then there wouldn't be much of a story, we'd be greeting you with our sticks and clubs, that'd be the end of that story . . . Where are you two going? To the Settlement, is that right? That's fine, that's allowed. Pops, you go on by yourself. And leave your daughter with us, of course. And don't be sorry, she'll be better off with us, she will."

"No," said Nava, "I don't want to go with them. Silent Man, I mean it, I don't want to go with them, they are thieves."

The thieves laughed—not maliciously, like they were used to it.

"Maybe you'll let us both go?" Candide asked.

"No," said the head thief, "you can't both go. There are deadlings all around, your daughter would perish, she'd become a fine helpmate or something nasty like that, and we don't want that, and you don't want it either, Pops, just think about it, if you're a man and not a deadling, and you don't look like a deadling, though you're a strange-looking one, of course."

"She's just a girl," said Candide. "Why would you hurt her?"

The head thief was surprised. "Who says we'll hurt her? She won't be a girl forever, when the time comes, she'll be a woman, not some fine helpmate, but a woman."

"It's all lies," Nava said, "don't you believe him, Silent Man, do something quick, since you brought me here, or they'll take me away, like they took Crookleg's daughter away, and no one has ever seen her since, I don't want to go with them, I'd rather be that fine helpmate thing . . . Look how wild and skinny they are, they probably don't even have anything to eat."

Candide looked around helplessly, then he suddenly had what appeared to him to be a very good idea. "Listen, men," he said pleadingly, "take us both."

The thieves came closer. The head thief carefully examined Candide from head to toe. "No," he said. "What would we do with your kind? You villagers, you're good for nothing, you have no daring to you, I don't know what your lives are for, we can come and take you barehanded. We don't need you, Pops, you don't talk right, not like everyone else, no telling what kind of man you are, go on to your Settlement, and leave us your daughter."

Candide sighed deeply, gripped his cudgel with both hands, and told Nava softly, "Run, Nava! Run and don't look back, I'll slow them down."

How stupid, he thought. My goodness, how very stupid. He remembered the deadling lying with its head in the dark water, looking like jelly, and raised his cudgel above his head.

"Go, go, go!" the leader shouted.

All seven of them piled forward, elbowing each other and slipping. Candide listened to the staccato drumming of Nava's heels, then he had other things to think about. He felt ashamed and afraid, but the fear soon passed, because it unexpectedly turned out that the only decent fighter among the thieves was the head thief. Parrying his blows, Candide watched the remaining thieves menacingly and pointlessly shake their cudgels, accidentally hitting each other, staggering from their own herculean swings, and frequently stopping to spit on their hands. One of them suddenly screamed hysterically "I'm drowning!" and loudly crashed into the swamp, then another two immediately abandoned their cudgels and began to drag him out. The head thief pressed on, grunting and stomping his feet, until Candide accidentally hit him in the kneecap. The head thief dropped his cudgel, hissed, and crouched down. Candide sprang back.

Two thieves were dragging the drowning one out of the swamp. He had gotten badly stuck—his face had turned blue. The head thief was still crouching, anxiously examining his injury. The remaining three thieves were huddling behind him with their cudgels raised, looking over his head and also contemplating the injury.

"Pops, you fool," the head thief said reproachfully. "What a thing to do, you stupid villager. What hole did you crawl out of? Don't know what's good for you, you woodenhead, you numb-skull . . ."

Candide didn't wait any longer. He turned around and ran after Nava as fast as he could. The thieves yelled after them in anger and derision; the head thief whooped and roared, "Stop him! Don't let him get away!" They weren't chasing him, and Candide didn't like that. He felt vexed and disappointed, and as he ran he tried to figure out how these clumsy, bumbling, and not unkind people could strike terror into whole villages, and also somehow destroy deadlings—clever and ruthless fighters.

He soon saw Nava: the girl was running about eighty feet ahead of him, hitting the ground firmly with her bare heels. He watched as she disappeared around a bend, then suddenly leaped back out—this time coming toward him—paused for a moment, and shot off to the side, right through the swamp, jumping from stump to stump, water spraying from under her feet.

Candide's heart sank. "Stop!" he bawled, out of breath. "You're crazy! Stop!"

Nava immediately stopped, grabbed on to a hanging vine, and turned to look at him. Then he saw three more thieves come out toward him from around the bend. They also stopped, looking between him and Nava.

"Silent Man!" Nava shrieked. "Beat them up and run this way! Don't worry, you won't drown! Beat them up, beat them up! With the stick! *Ooh-ooh-ooh! Oh-ho-ho* them!"

"Now, now," one of the thieves said solicitously. "Hold on tight and don't shout, hold on real tight, or we'll have to drag you out . . ."

He heard feet pounding the ground behind him and people shouting "*Ooh-ooh-ooh!*" The three thieves in front of him were waiting. Then Candide grabbed the two ends of the cudgel, held it out in front of his chest, took a running start, and crashed into them, taking all three of them down and falling down himself. He got a nasty bump from crashing into someone, but he immediately jumped up. His head was swimming. There was another frightened wail of "I'm drowning!" Someone's bearded face appeared in front of him, and Candide hit it with the cudgel without looking.

The cudgel broke. Candide tossed the remaining piece away and jumped into the swamp.

The stump slid out from under his feet and he almost fell off, but he immediately leaped to the next one and began to jump heavily from stump to stump, sending the stinky black mud flying. Nava was squealing triumphantly and whistling at him. Irritated voices were buzzing behind him: "What was that? You got two left hands?" "What about you, eh?" "The girl got away from us, now she's doomed . . ." "The man's gone crazy, fighting like that!" "Damn it, he ripped my clothes, my fine clothes, they were irreplaceable, those clothes of mine, and it wasn't even him who ripped them, it was you . . ." "Come on, that's enough talk—we should catch them, not talk. Look, they're running away, and all you do is talk!" "What about you, eh?" "He hurt my leg, see? He messed up my knee, I can't understand how he messed up my knee, I was just taking a swing and . . ." "Where's Seven Eyes? Guys, Seven Eyes is drowning!" "Drowning! So he is . . . Seven Eyes is drowning and all they do is talk!"

Candide stopped next to Nava and also grabbed on to some vines, then he listened and watched, breathing heavily, as the strange men, huddling together and waving their arms, dragged their Seven Eyes from the swamp by the head and feet. He could hear snorts and sounds of gurgling water. Then again, two thieves were already walking toward Candide, testing the depth of the bog with their cudgels, knee-deep in the black muck. They walked around the stumps. It's all lies again, thought Candide. People can wade through the swamp, and they told me there was no way to go but the road. They tried to scare me with the thieves, and just look at them . . .

Nava tugged on his arm. "Let's go, Silent Man," she said. "What are you standing around for? Come along quick. Or do you maybe want to fight more? Then wait, I'll find you a good stick, you can beat those two up, then the others, they'll probably be scared off . . . But if they aren't scared off, they'll overpower you, I think, since there's one of you, and there are . . . one . . . two, three . . . four . . ."

"Where should we go?" Candide asked. "Can we make it to the Settlement?"

"Probably," said Nava. "I don't see why we couldn't make it to the Settlement . . ."

"Then go in front," said Candide. He had already mostly caught his breath. "Show me the way."

Nava began leaping toward the forest, light on her feet, heading into the thicket, into the green haze of vegetation. "Actually, I don't know how or where to go," she said as she ran. "But I've already been here once, or maybe more than once, maybe many times. I walked here with Crookleg, before you came to us . . . Actually, no, you had already come to us, but you couldn't think straight, didn't understand anything, couldn't talk, looked at everyone like a fish, you did, then they gave you to me, and I nursed you back to health, but you don't remember any of it, probably . . ."

Candide jumped after her, trying to keep his breathing regular and follow precisely in her footsteps. From time to time, he looked around. The thieves were close behind.

"And I walked here with Crookleg," Nava continued, "when the thieves took Big Fist's wife, Crookleg's daughter. He always took me with him then, he might have wanted to trade me for her, or maybe he wanted me to be like a daughter to him, so he came to the forest with me, since he was so broken up about his daughter . . ."

The vines stuck to his hands and whipped him in the face, and tangled balls of dead vines kept catching on his clothes and getting underfoot. Insects and other trash would fall on them from above; from time to time, heavy, shapeless masses would sink down, fall through the tangled greenery, and swing right over their heads. Sticky purple clusters kept flickering through the curtain of vines on both sides of them—they might have been mushrooms, or fruit, or the nests of some nasty forest creature.

"Crookleg, he said there's a village around here"—Nava spoke effortlessly as she ran, as if she weren't running at all but lounging in bed; you could immediately tell that she wasn't a local, locals didn't know how to run—"not our village, not the Settlement, but some other village, Crookleg told me its name, but I don't remember, it was a long time ago, after all—you hadn't come to us yet . . . No, wait, you had already come to us, but you couldn't think straight, and they still hadn't given you to me . . . By the way, breathe through your mouth when you run, not your nose, it makes it easier to talk, too, else you'll run out of breath soon, and we still have a long way to go, we haven't passed the wasps yet, that's where we better run real fast, although they might have gone away since then, the wasps . . . The wasps were over there, in that very same village, and no one's lived in that village for a long time, Crookleg said, the Surpassment happened there already, he said, so there isn't a soul left . . . No, Silent Man, I'm wrong about that, I am, he said that about some other village . . ."

Candide got a second wind and running became easier. They were now deep in the thicket, in the very midst of the greenery. Candide had only gone in this far once, the time he had mounted a deadling, hoping to be taken to its masters—the deadling had broken into a gallop, it was scorching hot, like a boiling kettle, and Candide eventually fainted from the pain and fell off its back into the mud. For a long time after, he was tormented by the burns on his palms and chest.

It was getting darker and darker. He could no longer see the sky at all, and the humidity kept rising. On the plus side, there was less and less open water, and enormous carpets of white and red moss had appeared underfoot. The moss was soft, cool, and very springy, and it was pleasant to run on.

"Let's . . . rest . . ." wheezed Candide.

"No, no, Silent Man," said Nava. "This is no place to rest. Hurry up, we need to quickly get away from this moss, this is dangerous moss. It's not really moss, Crookleg said, it's an animal lying here, sort of like a spider, and if you fall asleep on it, you'll never wake up, that's the kind of moss it is, let those thieves rest here instead—but then, they probably know not to, too bad, I wish they would . . ."

She took a look at Candide and slowed down to a walk after all. Candide dragged himself to the nearest tree, leaned his back, head, and whole body against it, and closed his eyes. He really wanted to sit down, to collapse, but he was afraid to. He kept repeating silently, like a mantra: it's lies, it's all lies, it's a lie about the moss, too. But he was still afraid. His heart was pounding wildly, his legs didn't seem to be there at all, his lungs kept exploding and flowing painfully through his chest with each breath, and the entire world was slippery and salty with sweat.

"What if they catch us?" He heard Nava's voice like through cotton wool. "What are we going to do when they catch us, Silent Man? Looks like you aren't good for much right now, you probably can't fight anymore, eh?"

He wanted to say, I can fight, but he only managed to move his lips without making a sound. He was no longer afraid of the thieves. He was no longer afraid of anything at all. He was only afraid to move and afraid to lie down in the moss. This was the forest, whatever lies they had told, this was still the forest, he always remembered that, he never forgot that, even when he had forgotten everything else.

"You don't even have a stick anymore," Nava was saying. "Should I maybe find you a stick, Silent Man? Should I find you one?"

"No," he mumbled. "Don't . . . Too heavy . . ."

He opened his eyes and pricked up his ears. The thieves were close; he could hear them clomping through the thicket, huffing and puffing, and they didn't sound the least bit lively—the thieves were also having a hard time.

"Let's keep going," said Candide.

They passed the region of the dangerous white moss, then the region of the dangerous red moss, then they were again surrounded by the wet swamp with its thick, still water. The surface of the water was plastered with humongous pale flowers smelling unpleasantly of meat, and there was a mottled gray animal peeking out of every flower, following them with its eyes on stalks.

"Splash the water harder, Silent Man," Nava said matter of factly, "or something will latch on to you, you'll never be able to get it off, don't think that being vaccinated means it won't latch on to you, it will, too. Then it'll die, of course, but much good will that do you . . ."

The swamp suddenly ended, and the terrain rose steeply. Tall, striped grass with sharp knifelike edges now made an appearance. Candide looked back and saw the thieves. For some reason, they'd stopped. For some reason, they were standing knee-deep in the swamp, leaning on their cudgels and watching them go. They must have run out of breath, thought Candide—they must have also run out of breath. One of the thieves raised his hand, gestured for them to return, and yelled, "What are you doing? Come back!"

Candide turned away and followed Nava. After the swamp, it was a big relief to walk on solid ground, even going uphill. The thieves were yelling something—at first two thieves yelled in unison, then three. Candide glanced back one last time. The thieves were still standing in the swamp, in the leech-filled mud; they hadn't even come out onto dry ground. Seeing him turn around, they started frantically waving their arms and shouting over each other. It was hard to make out the words.

"Come back!" they seemed to be yelling. "Come *baaack*! . . . We won't touch *yoooou*! . . . You idiots are *dooomed*! . . ."

We aren't that stupid, Candide thought with malicious delight, takes one to know one, like I'll believe you. I'm sick and tired of believing people . . . Nava had already disappeared behind the trees, and he hurried after her.

"Come *baaack*! . . . We'll let you *gooo*! . . ." the leader bellowed.

How out of breath can they be if they can yell that loud? Candide thought in passing. Then he immediately started thinking that now was a good time to get a bit farther away, then to sit down for a rest and check his body for ticks and leeches.

5.

PERETZ

Peretz showed up at the Director's waiting room at precisely 10:00 in the morning. There were already about twenty people there. Peretz was assigned to be fourth in line. He sat down in a chair between Beatrice Wah, an employee of the Assistance to the Locals Team, and a sullen employee of the Penetration Through Engineering Team. The sullen employee, according to the name tag on his chest and the inscription on his white cardboard mask, was to be addressed as "Brandskugel." The waiting room was painted pale pink, a sign saying No Smoking, No Littering, No Noise hung on one wall, and there was a painting on another wall depicting the heroic feat of Selivan the forest explorer: before the eyes of his astonished companions, Selivan was raising his arms and transforming into a jumping tree. The pink curtains on the windows were completely drawn, and a giant chandelier blazed beneath the ceiling. Besides the front door, which said Exit, the waiting room also had a huge door upholstered with yellow leather, which said No Exit. These words were written in fluorescent paint and had the appearance of a grim warning. The secretary's desk, which contained an electric typewriter and four colorful phones, was immediately beneath these words. The secretary, a stout older woman wearing pince-nez, was haughtily studying a textbook on atomic physics. The visitors were talking in hushed voices. Many were obviously nervous and were feverishly leafing through old picture magazines. This was all precisely like the waiting room at the dentist's, and Peretz again felt an unpleasant chill, a trembling in his jaws, and the desire to immediately go somewhere else.

"They aren't even lazy," said Beatrice Wah, turning her handsome head slightly toward Peretz. "However, they do not tolerate systematic work. For example, how would you explain their singular readiness to abandon their settlements?"

"Are you talking to me?" Peretz asked timidly. He had no idea how to explain this singular readiness.

"No. I'm talking to *mon cher* Brandskugel."

Mon cher Brandskugel fixed the left side of his mustache, which was coming unglued, and mumbled in a strangled voice, "I don't know."

"We don't know either," Beatrice said sadly. "As soon as our people appear near a village, they desert their houses and all their possessions and leave. This creates the impression that they have absolutely no interest in us. That they don't need anything from us. What do you think, is this actually the case?"

For some time, *mon cher* Brandskugel was silent, as if pondering this, looking at Beatrice through the strange cruciform portholes in his mask; then he said in the same exact tone, "I don't know."

"It's very unfortunate," Beatrice continued, "that our team consists entirely of women. I understand that this is full of deep meaning, but all too often, we sorely feel the lack of masculine firmness, decisiveness—I would even say focus. Unfortunately, women have a tendency to spread themselves too thin; you may have noticed this yourself."

"I don't know," said Brandskugel, and his mustache suddenly fell off and glided gently to the floor. He picked it up, inspected it carefully, raising the edge of his mask, then spat on it in a businesslike manner and stuck it back in its place.

A bell rang musically on the secretary's desk. She put away the textbook, looked through her list, gracefully holding her pince-nez, and announced, "Professor Cockatoo, please enter."

Professor Cockatoo dropped his picture magazine, jumped up, sat back down, looked around, and turned white before their eyes. Then, biting his lip, his face utterly contorted, he launched himself out of his chair and disappeared behind the door that said No Exit. There were a few seconds of strained silence in the waiting room. Then voices began to drone and pages began to rustle again.

"We simply can't figure out," said Beatrice, "what to interest them in, what to get them excited about. We've built them comfortable, dry dwellings on stilts. They fill them with peat and populate them with insects. We've tried to offer them tasty food instead of that sour muck they eat. No use. We've tried to dress them like human beings. One died, two got sick. But we keep experimenting. Yesterday we scattered a truckful of mirrors and gold-plated buttons around the forest . . . Movies don't interest them, and neither does music. Immortal works of art evoke something resembling a giggle . . . No, we need to start with the children. I, for one, would propose catching their children and organizing special schools. Unfortunately, this is fraught with technical difficulties—you can't catch them by hand, this would require special machines . . . But then, you know that as well as I do."

"I don't know," *mon cher* Brandskugel said drearily.

The ball rang again, and the secretary said, "Beatrice, it's your turn now. Please enter."

Beatrice began to bustle around. She was about to rush through the door when she stopped, glancing around her with a bewildered look. She came back, looked under the chair, whispered, "Where did it go? Where is it?" scanned the waiting room with huge eyes, tugged on her hair, shouted loudly, "Where did it go?!"—then suddenly grabbed Peretz by the lapels and dumped him out of his chair onto the floor. It turned out that Peretz had been sitting on a brown folder, and Beatrice snatched it up, stood there for a few seconds hugging the folder to her chest, her eyes closed and an immeasurably happy expression on her face, then slowly walked toward the yellow leather–upholstered door and disappeared behind it. There was complete silence as Peretz got up and brushed off his pants, trying not to look at anyone. Then again, no one was paying any attention to him; everyone was looking at the yellow door.

What will I say to him? thought Peretz. I'll say that I'm a philologist and can't be of use to the Administration; let me go, I'll leave and never come back, I swear. Then why exactly did you come here? I've always been very interested in the forest, but then they don't let me into the forest. And in any case, I came here totally by accident—I'm a philologist, you know. There's nothing for philologists, writers, philosophers to do in the Administration. So they are right not to let me in, I acknowledge it, I admit it . . . I can't stand to be in an Administration where people defecate onto the forest, nor in a forest where they catch children with machines. I'd rather leave and do something simpler. I know that people here are fond of me, but they are fond of me like children are fond of their toys. I'm here for their amusement; I can't teach anyone here what I know . . . No, I shouldn't say that, of course. I ought to try to squeeze out a tear, but where am I supposed to find it, this tear? I'll trash the whole damn place, let him only try not to let me go. I'll trash it and go on foot. Peretz imagined walking along the dusty road beneath the scorching sun, mile after mile, his suitcase getting more and more willful. And with each step, he'd be getting farther and farther away from the forest, from his dream, from the angst that had long since become the meaning of his existence . . .

It's been a while since they've called anyone in there, he thought. The Director must have taken a real interest in the child-capturing project. And why does no one ever come out of that office? There must be another way out.

"Excuse me, please," he said, addressing *mon cher* Brandskugel. "What time is it?"

Mon cher Brandskugel looked at his wristwatch, thought about it, and said, "I don't know."

Then Peretz bent down to his ear and whispered, "I won't tell a soul. Not. A. Soul."

Mon cher Brandskugel wavered. He indecisively fingered the plastic tag with his name, furtively looked around, yawned nervously, looked around again, and, pressing the mask closer to his face, replied in a whisper, "I don't know." Then he got up and quickly decamped to another corner of the waiting room.

The secretary said, "Peretz, it's your turn."

"Why me?" Peretz was surprised. "I thought I was fourth."

"Visiting employee Peretz," the secretary said, raising her voice. "It's your turn."

"This one's a philosopher," someone grumbled.

"His sort need to be drummed out," came loudly from his left. "On their asses!"

Peretz got up. His legs were wobbly. For no particular reason, he ran his hands up and down his body, making his clothes rustle. The secretary was staring at him.

"A guilty conscience needs no accuser," he heard from the waiting room.

"The truth will out."

"And this is the kind of person we've been tolerating!"

"Excuse me, but you're the one who's been tolerating him. I've never seen him before."

"What, you think I have?"

"Hush!" said the secretary, raising her voice. "Be quiet! And you over there—no littering . . . Yes, I mean you. Employee Peretz, are you coming or not? Or do I need I call security?"

"Yes," said Peretz. "Yes, I'm coming."

The last person he saw in the waiting room was *mon cher* Brandskugel, who had barricaded himself into a corner with a chair: he was crouching down, his teeth bared, with a hand in the back pocket of his pants. Then he saw the Director.

The Director turned out to be a slender, well-built man of about thirty-five, in an immaculately fitting expensive suit. He was standing in front of an open window and scattering bread crumbs for the pigeons that crowded on the windowsill. The office was completely empty; there were no chairs, not even a table, only a small copy of *The Heroic Feat of Forest Explorer Selivan* on the wall across from the window.

"Peretz, visiting employee of the Administration?" the Director said in a clear, ringing voice, turning the fresh face of an athlete toward Peretz.

"Y-Yes . . . That's right . . ." Peretz stammered out.

"A pleasure, a real pleasure. So glad to finally meet you. Hello. My name is Ahti. I've heard a lot about you. Let's get acquainted."

Peretz, hunching with shyness, shook his hand, which was dry and strong.

"As you can see, I'm feeding the pigeons. Such curious birds. I sense that they have enormous potential. How do you feel about pigeons, Monsieur Peretz?"

Peretz hesitated, because he couldn't stand pigeons. But the Director's face radiated such joy, such keen interest, such eager anticipation of the answer, that Peretz mastered himself and lied: "I like them a lot, Monsieur Ahti."

"Do you like them fried? Or stewed? Personally, I like them in a pie. A pigeon pie and a glass of a good semi-dry wine—what could be better? What do you think?" And once again, a look of keen interest and eager anticipation appeared on Monsieur Ahti's face.

"An amazing thing," said Peretz. He decided to give up and agree with everything.

"Then take Picasso's *Dove of Peace!*" said Monsieur Ahti. "It always brings to mind: 'All inedible, nonpotable, unkissable. Time comes, time goes . . .' What a clear articulation of our inability to capture beauty and give it material form!"

"An excellent poem," Peretz said dully.

"When I first saw the *Dove of Peace*, I, like probably many others, thought that the picture must be incorrect or at least unnatural. But since then, my job has given me the opportunity to take a closer look at pigeons, and I suddenly realized that Picasso, that wizard, had captured the precise moment a dove folds its wings before landing! Its feet are already touching the ground, but it's still in air, still midflight. It is the instant when motion becomes stillness, flight becomes rest."

"Picasso has some strange pictures that I don't understand," Peretz said, showing an independence of judgment.

"Oh, you just haven't looked at them long enough. To understand true art, it isn't enough to walk through a museum two or three times a year. Pictures need to be looked at for hours. As often as possible. And they have to be originals. Not reproductions. Not copies . . . Here, take a look at this picture. Your face tells me exactly what you think of it. And you're right: this is a bad copy. But if you'd ever had the opportunity to study the original, you would have appreciated the artist's vision."

"And what exactly is it?"

"I'll try to explain it to you," the Director offered readily. "What do you see in this picture? Strictly speaking, it's a half human, half tree. The picture is static. There's no way to see or sense the transition from one form to the other. The picture is missing the most important thing: the direction of time. But if you'd ever had the opportunity to study the original, you would have understood that the artist was able to imbue the image with profound symbolic meaning, that it wasn't a human tree he captured, nor even the transformation of a human into a tree, but nothing other than the transformation of a tree into a human. The artist used the idea from the old legend to depict the creation of a new being. The new from the old. The living from the dead. Intelligence from inanimate matter. The copy is completely static, and everything represented in it exists outside of the current of time. Whereas the original contains the motion of time! Its vector! The arrow of time, as Eddington would put it."

"And where is the original?" Peretz asked politely.

The Director smiled. "The original was destroyed, of course, as befits a work of art that cannot be allowed to have ambiguous interpretations. The first and second copies were also destroyed as a precautionary measure."

Monsieur Ahti went back to the window and shoved the pigeons off the windowsill with his elbow.

"OK. We've chatted about the pigeons," he said in a new, strangely bureaucratic voice. "Name?"

"What?"

"Name? Your name?"

"Pe- . . . Peretz."

"When were you born?"

"Nineteen thirty."

"Be more precise!"

"March 5 of 1930."

"Why are you here?"

"I'm a visiting employee. Assigned to the Scientific Guard Team."

"I'm asking: Why you are here?" said the Director, turning unseeing eyes toward Peretz.

"I . . . I don't know. I want to leave."

"Your opinion of the forest. Briefly."

"The forest—it's . . . I've always . . . I'm . . . afraid of it. And I love it."

"Your opinion of the Administration?"

"There are lots of good people here, but—"

"That's enough." The Director came up to Peretz, hugged him around the shoulders, and, looking into his eyes, said, "Listen, buddy! Quit it! How about we go out for drinks, huh? We'll bring the secretary along—did you check out that broad? That's no broad, that's a garden of delights! *Open the coveted quart, boys! . . .*'"

he sang in a hoarse, strained voice. "Huh? Are we gonna open it? Quit it, I don't like it. Got it? How about it?" He suddenly gave off an odor of alcohol and garlic salami; his eyes crossed. "We'll take Brandskugel, my *mon cher*," he continued, pressing Peretz to his chest. "The stories he tells, we won't need any grub . . . You coming?"

"We could, I guess," Peretz said. "But I . . ."

"You what?"

"Monsieur Ahti, I—"

"Cut it out! I'm no monsieur. I'm your comrade, get it? Your bosom buddy!"

"Comrade Ahti, I came to ask you . . ."

"*Aaask* away! Whatever your soul desires! Need money? Here you go! Don't like someone? We'll look into it! Well?"

"N-No, I just want to leave. I can't seem to figure out how to leave—I came here by accident, Comrade Ahti, and there's no longer anything for me to do here. Please let me leave. No one wants to help me, and I'm asking you, in your capacity as director . . ."

Ahti let go of Peretz, fixed his tie, and smiled drily. "You're mistaken, Peretz," he said. "I'm not the Director. I'm the Assistant Director of Human Resources. I apologize for keeping you. Please go through this door. The Director will see you."

He opened a low door at the back of his empty office in front of Peretz and gestured for him to come through. Peretz coughed, gave a distant nod, bent down, and squeezed into the next room. As he did so, he thought he felt a light smack on the rear. Then again, he probably just imagined it, or Monsieur Ahti may have been in too much of a hurry to close the door.

The room he found himself in was a precise copy of the waiting room; even the secretary was a precise copy of the first secretary, except that she was reading a book titled *The Sublimation of Genius*. Just like before, gray-faced people were sitting in chairs and perusing magazines and newspapers. Professor Cockatoo was here, suffering from a bad case of nerves and compulsively scratching himself. Beatrice Wah was also in the room, holding the brown folder in her lap. However, the remaining visitors were strangers to him, and beneath *The Heroic Feat of Forest Explorer Selivan*, the single stern word SILENCE! flashed on and off at regular intervals. As a result, no one here was talking. Peretz carefully lowered himself onto the edge of a chair. Beatrice gave him a somewhat guarded but overall friendly smile.

After a minute of strained silence, the bell rang, and the secretary put down her book and said, "Reverend Luke, you're next."

Reverend Luke was awful to behold, and Peretz looked away. Never mind, he thought, closing his eyes. I can handle it. He remembered that rainy autumn evening when they brought Esther into the apartment, stabbed to death by a drunk hoodlum at the entrance to the building . . . and the neighbors hanging on his neck, and the glass crumbs in his mouth—he had bitten into a glass when they'd brought him water . . . Yes, he thought, the worst is behind me . . .

Rapid scratching sounds caught his attention. He opened his eyes and looked around. One chair away from him, Professor Cockatoo was furiously scratching under his armpits with both hands. Like an ape.

"What do you think, should we separate the boys from the girls?" Beatrice asked in a shaky whisper.

"I don't know," Peretz answered caustically.

"Integrated education does, of course, have its advantages," Beatrice continued mumbling, "but this is a special case . . . My God!" she suddenly whined. "Is he really going to fire me? Where would I go? I've already been fired everywhere else, I don't have a single decent pair of shoes left. All my pantyhose have runs, my powder's gone lumpy . . ."

The secretary put down her book and said sternly, "Don't get distracted."

Beatrice froze in fear. Then the low door opened and a man with a shaved head squeezed into the waiting room. "Is there a Peretz here?" he boomed.

"I'm Peretz," Peretz said, leaping up.

"Gather your things and go! Your ride is leaving in ten minutes—get a move on!"

"What ride? Why?"

"You're Peretz?"

"Yes."

"Did you want to leave or not?"

"I did, but—"

"Well, up to you," the man barked irately. "My job was to tell you."

He disappeared and the door slammed shut. Peretz rushed after him.

"Get back!" the secretary yelled, and several hands grabbed his clothes. Peretz desperately tried to break free; his jacket started to rip.

"But my ride is over there!" he groaned.

"Have you gone insane!" said the irritated secretary. "Why are you breaking down the door? Here's a door, it says EXIT, and where are you going?"

Firm hands directed Peretz toward the EXIT sign. There turned out to be a spacious polygonal hall behind the door, with many other doors leading out of it, and he started darting around, trying them one by one.

Bright sunlight, sterile white walls, people in white coats. A naked back smeared with iodine. The smell of medicine. Not it.

Darkness, the crackling of a film projector. A person on-screen being pulled in two different directions by his ears. White blobs of faces turned toward him in displeasure. "The door! Close the door!" Not it either . . .

Peretz crossed the hall, slipping and sliding on the polished wood floor.

The smell of a bakery, a short line of people holding bags. Cakes, pastries, and gleaming buttermilk bottles in a glass case.

"Ladies and gentlemen!" shouted Peretz. "Where's the exit?"

"Exit from where?" asked the stout clerk in a chef's hat.

"From here . . ."

"It's the door you're standing in."

"Don't listen to him," a frail old man in line told the clerk. "We have one joker around here, all he does is hold up the line . . . Do your job, don't pay attention."

"I'm not joking," said Peretz. "My ride is about to leave."

"No, it's not him," said the fair-minded old man. "That one always asks about the lavatory. Where did you say your ride was, sir?"

"Out on the street."

"Which street?" the clerk asked. "There are lots of streets."

"I don't care which street, I just need to go outside!"

"No," said the astute old man. "It's still the same guy. He just has a new routine. Don't pay attention to him."

Peretz looked around in despair, leaped back into the hall, and tried the next door. It was locked. A gruff voice inquired, "Who's there?"

"I need to get out!" Peretz shouted. "Where's the exit?"

"Wait a minute."

A variety of sounds came from behind the door: water splashed, drawers banged shut. The voice asked, "What do you want?"

"I need the exit! I want to get out!"

"One minute."

He heard a key turn in the lock, then the door opened. The room was dark. "Go ahead," said the voice.

It smelled of photographic developer. Peretz, arms held out in front of him, took a few uncertain steps.

"I can't see anything," he said.

"You'll get used to it soon," the voice promised. "Well, go on, what are you stopping for?"

Someone took Peretz by the sleeve and led him along. "Sign here," said the voice.

A pencil appeared in Peretz's fingers. He now saw a piece of paper in front of him, glowing dimly in the dark.

"Did you sign it?"

"No. What am I signing?"

"Don't worry, it's not a death sentence. Sign that you didn't see anything."

Peretz signed somewhere at random.

Someone took him firmly by the sleeve again and guided him between some curtains, then the voice asked, "How many of you are there?"

"There are four of us." The words sounded as if they came from behind a door.

"Are you lined up? Be advised, I'm about to open the door and let a man out. Come in single file, no pushing, and no goofing around. Got it?"

"Got it. Not our first time."

"Everyone brought their clothes?"

"We did, we did. Let him out."

He heard a key turning in a lock again. Peretz was nearly blinded by the bright light, then he was shoved outside. He slid down a bunch of stairs without opening his eyes, and only then did he realize he was in the inner courtyard of the Administration. Irritated voices began to shout, "Peretz, what's going on? Hurry up! How long are we supposed to wait for you?"

A truck stood in the middle of the courtyard, filled with employees of the Scientific Guard. Kim was sticking his head out of the cab and waving angrily. Peretz ran up to the vehicle and clambered up onto the side of the truck, then he was grabbed, scooped up, and dumped into the back with the others. The truck immediately roared and lurched forward, someone stepped on Peretz's hand, someone sat down hard on him, everyone began to laugh and shout, and they were off.

"Perry, here's your suitcase," someone said.

"Peretz, is it true that you're leaving?"

"Signor Peretz, do you wish to have a cigarette?"

Peretz lit a cigarette, sat down on his suitcase, and raised the collar of his suit jacket. Someone gave him his coat, and he wrapped himself in it, smiling gratefully. The truck was going faster and faster, and despite the hot day, the oncoming wind felt rather brisk. Peretz smoked, covering the cigarette with his hand, and looked around. I'm leaving, he thought. I'm leaving. This is the last time I'll see you, wall. This is the last time I'll see you, villas. Good-bye, dump, I lost my galoshes around here once. Good-bye, puddle; good-bye, chess; good-bye, buttermilk. How nice this is, how easy! I'll never drink buttermilk again. I'll never sit down at a chessboard again . . .

Employees, huddling by the cab, holding on to each another, and hiding behind each other from the wind, conversed on a variety of unrelated topics. "It's been calculated, I've calculated it myself. If we keep going at this rate, then in a hundred years, there will be ten employees for each square meter of land, and the total weight will be such that the cliff will collapse. We will need so much food and water that to transport it all we'll need a continuous chain of vehicles between the Administration and the Mainland—they'll need to move at thirty miles an hour and be one meter apart, and they'll have to unload on the go . . . No, no, I'm completely sure that the Board of Directors is already considering regulating the influx of new employees. Judge for yourself: there's the hotel manager, for example, seven kids and another on the way—it's not right. And all of them healthy. Bootlicherson says we have to do something about it. It doesn't have to be sterilization, like he proposes—"

"Bootlicherson shouldn't talk."

"That's why I said that it doesn't have to be sterilization."

"They say that annual leave will be increased to six months."

They passed the park, and Peretz suddenly realized that the truck was going the wrong way. They were about to go through the gates and drive down the winding road that went beneath the cliff.

"Listen, where are we going?" he asked anxiously.

"What do you mean, where? To get our salaries."

"Not to the Mainland, then?"

"Why would we go to the Mainland? The pay clerk has arrived at the biological research station."

"So you're going to the biological research station? To the forest?"

"Well, yeah. We're the Scientific Guard, and we get paid at the biological research station."

"What about me?" Peretz asked in bewilderment.

"You'll get paid, too. You're supposed to get a bonus . . . By the way, did everyone fill out their forms?"

There was a flurry of activity: the employees took multicolored, variously formatted documents with official seals out of their pockets and carefully looked them over.

"Peretz, did you fill out the questionnaire?"

"What questionnaire?"

"Excuse me, what in the world do you mean? Form eighty-four."

"I didn't fill anything out," said Peretz.

"Kind sirs! What is going on here? Peretz has no documents!"

"Oh, it doesn't matter. He probably has a pass."

"I don't have a pass," said Peretz. "I don't have anything. Just a suitcase and this coat . . . You see, I wasn't planning to go into the forest, I was going to leave . . ."

"Did you get a physical? Vaccines?"

Peretz shook his head. The truck was already rolling along the winding road, and Peretz was watching the forest with detachment, seeing the porous, flat layers on the horizon, the motionless seething of its thunderstorm, and the sticky spiderweb of fog in the shadow of the cliff.

"You can't get away with a thing like that," someone said.

"Then again, the road itself doesn't contain classified material."

"What about Bootlicherson?"

"What does Bootlicherson have to do with it, if there's no classified material on the road?"

"You don't know that, I assume. And neither does anyone else. Last year, Candide flew off without documents, the reckless fellow, and where is he now?"

"First of all, it wasn't last year, it was a long time ago. And second, he was killed, that's all. In the line of duty."

"Yeah? And you've seen the order about it?"

"That's true, there was no order."

"Then there's nothing to argue about. They've stuck him in the bunker by the checkpoint, and there he sits ever since. Filling out questionnaires . . ."

"Perry, why in the world didn't you fill out the questionnaire? Do you have something to hide?"

"One minute, gentlemen! This is a serious matter. To be on the safe side, I propose examining employee Peretz in democratic fashion, as it were. Who will be chairman?"

"Bootlicherson for chairman!"

"A very good proposal. We elect the highly respected Bootlicherson as honorary chairman. Your faces tell me it's unanimous. And who will be deputy chairman?"

"Vanderbilt for deputy chairman!"

"Vanderbilt? . . . Well . . . There is a proposal to elect Vanderbilt as deputy chairman. Are there any other proposals? Who's for? Who's against? Anyone abstaining? Hmm . . . Two abstained. Why did you abstain?"

"Me?"

"Yes, you."

"I don't see the point. Why crucify the man? He feels bad as is."

"Got it. And you?"

"None of your damn business."

"As you wish . . . Deputy Chairman, take that down: two abstained. Let us begin. Who wants to go first? No volunteers? Then allow me. Employee Peretz, please answer the following question. How many total miles did you travel between the ages of twenty-five and thirty, a) on foot, b) using ground transportation, and c) by air. Take your time—think about it. Here's a pencil and paper."

Peretz obediently took the pencil and paper and started trying to remember. The truck lurched and jolted. At first everyone was looking at him, then they got tired of looking at him and someone began to drone, "Overpopulation doesn't scare me. But have you noticed all the machinery standing around? Seen the stuff on the wasteland behind the workshops? And what kind of machinery is it, do you know that? That's right, it's all in boxes, boarded up. And no one has had the time to open them up and take a look. You want to know what I saw there the night before last? I stopped to have a smoke, and suddenly I heard a cracking noise. I turned around and saw: the side of one of the boxes—a huge box, as big as a house—was being pushed out and swinging open, like a door. And a mechanism crawled out of the box. I won't describe it to you, I don't need to tell you why. But it was one hell of a sight . . . It stood there a few seconds, produced a long tube with a whirligig on the end from its innards, stuck it up into the sky, almost seemed to be looking around, then it climbed back into the box and closed it. I wasn't feeling well at the time, so I simply didn't believe my eyes. But this morning I thought: I may as well take a look. I got there, and my skin crawled. The box looked completely normal, not a single gap or crack, but that side was nailed in from the *inside*! And the pointy ends of the nails were sticking out, shiny, as long as your finger. So now I've been thinking: what did it climb out for? And are there others like it? Maybe every night they . . . look around like this. So for now there's overpopulation, there's this, there's that, but one day they'll massacre us wholesale, and our bones will rain down from the cliff . . . And we'll be lucky if it's bones and not bone powder . . . What? No way, pal, thanks a lot, tell the engineers yourself if you like. I *saw* this machine, you know, and how am I supposed to know whether I was allowed to see it? The boxes don't say whether their contents are classified . . ."

"Well, Peretz, are you ready?"

"No," said Peretz. "I can't remember a thing. It was a very long time ago."

"That's strange. Now I, for example, remember perfectly well. I traveled six thousand seven hundred and one miles by rail, seventeen thousand one hundred fifty-three miles by air (of which three thousand two hundred and fifteen miles were for personal reasons), and fifteen thousand and seven miles on foot. And I'm older than you. Strange, Peretz, very strange . . . All right, then. Let's try another question. What were your favorite toys when you were of preschool age?"

"Wind-up tanks," said Peretz, and wiped the sweat off his brow. "And armored vehicles."

"Aha! This you remember! And this was back when you were in preschool, in far more distant times, as it were. But less crucial times, eh, Peretz? All right. So, tanks and armored vehicles. Next question. At what age did you first feel attracted to a woman—in parentheses, toward a man? The sentence in parentheses is usually addressed to a woman. You may answer now."

"A long time ago," said Peretz. "It was a very long time ago."

"Be more precise."

"How about you?" asked Peretz. "You tell me first, then I'll answer."

The chairman shrugged. "I have nothing to hide. This first happened to me when I was nine years old, when I was being bathed with my cousin . . . And now answer me, please."

"I can't," said Peretz. "I refuse to answer questions like that."

"You idiot," someone whispered in his ear. "Just tell a lie with a straight face, and that'll be the end of it. What are you torturing yourself for? You think someone will check?"

"All right," Peretz said meekly. "When I was ten years old. When I was being washed with our dog Daisy."

"Very good!" the chairman exclaimed. "So you can do it if you want to! And now list all the foot diseases you've ever suffered from."

"Rheumatism."

"Any others?"

"Intermittent claudication."

"Very good. Any others?"

"Colds," said Peretz.

"That's not a foot disease."

"I don't know about that. Maybe for you it isn't. It certainly is for me. My feet get wet, and presto, a cold."

"*Weeell*, all right. Any others?"

"Isn't that enough?"

"Do as you please. But you should know—the more, the better."

"Spontaneous gangrene," said Peretz. "Followed by amputation. That was my very last foot disease."

"That will probably suffice. One last question. Briefly state your worldview."

"I'm a materialist," said Peretz.

"What kind of materialist?"

"An emotional one."

"I don't have any more questions. How about you, gentlemen?"

There were no more questions. Some of the employees were dozing and some were chatting, their backs turned to the chairman. The truck was now going slowly. It was getting hot, and humid air with a whiff of forest was starting to waft toward them—an unpleasant, pungent odor that didn't usually reach the Administration. The truck's engine had been turned off, and in the distance, in the most distant of distances, they could hear the faint rumbling of thunder.

"I can't believe what I'm hearing," the deputy chairman was saying, his back also turned to the chairman. "This must be some kind of unhealthy pessimism. First of all, man is by nature an optimist. And second—and most important—do you really think that the Director spends less time thinking about these things than you do? That's almost funny. During his last speech, while speaking to me, the Director revealed majestic prospects. It took my breath away, and I'm not ashamed to admit it. I've always been an optimist, but this vision . . . If you care to know, everything here will be knocked down, all these walls, these villas . . . In their place, we will have dazzlingly beautiful structures made out of transparent and translucent materials—swimming pools, air parks, crystalline bars and diners! Stairs into the sky! Slender, lithe women with supple, tanned skin! Libraries! Muscles! Laboratories! Soaked through with sunshine and light! Flexible schedules! Cars, gliders, airships . . . Public debates, sleep-learning, stereoscopic cinema . . . After work, employees will spend hours in the library, reflecting, composing music, playing guitars and other musical instruments, carving wood, reciting poetry to each other!"

"And what will you do?"

"I'll carve wood."

"And what else?"

"I'll write poetry, too. They'll teach me to write poetry, I have good handwriting."

"And what will I do?"

"Whatever you like!" the deputy chairman said magnanimously. "You could carve wood, you could write poetry . . . Whatever you like."

"I don't want to carve wood. I'm a mathematician."

"And that's great! Do mathematics to your heart's content!"

"I do mathematics to my heart's content as it is."

"Now you get paid for it. It's silly. You'll take up diving off a high board."

"Why?"

"What do you mean, why? Aren't you curious?"

"I'm not curious."

"What exactly are you trying to say? That you aren't interested in anything but mathematics?"

"You know, I'm probably not . . . After a day's work, I'm too tired to be interested in much of anything."

"You're just limited. That's all right, they'll develop you. They'll find your hidden talents—you'll compose music, carve things . . ."

"Composing music—that's no problem. Finding an audience, on the other hand . . ."

"I'd be happy to listen to you . . . Peretz here . . ."

"You just think you would. You wouldn't listen to me. And you wouldn't write poetry. You'd hack a bit at your wood, then go chase skirt. Or you'd go on a bender. I know you. And I know everyone else here. You'd slouch between the crystalline bar and the diamond diner. Especially if you had a flexible schedule. I shudder to think what would happen if everyone here had a flexible schedule."

"Everyone is a genius in one way or another," the deputy chairman countered. "We just need to bring this genius to light. We don't even suspect it, but maybe I'm a culinary genius, and you're, say, a pharmaceutical genius, and we spend our time on all the wrong things and never discover our true natures. The Director said that in the future this will be handled by experts, who will search for our secret potentialities."

"Well, you know, potentialities are a funny thing. I'm not arguing with you, exactly—it's possible that everyone really does have some hidden genius, but what are we going to do if it turns out that someone's genius is only of use in either the distant past or the distant future? And in the present, no one would think of it as genius, whether it's been exhibited or not. Of course it'd be wonderful if it turns that you're a culinary genius. But we might instead learn that you're a brilliant coachman, and Peretz is a magnificent arrowhead polisher, and my unique talent lies in detecting a certain Z-field that hasn't been discovered yet and won't be discovered for another two centuries . . . And that's when, as the poet said, leisure will turn its grim visage toward us . . ."

"Guys," someone said, "you know, we didn't bring any food. By the time we get there, then get our salaries . . ."

"Stoyan will feed us."

"Yeah, right, Stoyan will feed us. They have a ration system."

"Damn it, my wife even packed me sandwiches!"

"Don't worry, we'll manage—look, there's the barrier."

Peretz craned his neck. There was a yellow-green wall of forest in front of them, and the road disappeared into it, like a thread disappears into a multicolored rug. The truck drove past a plywood sign that exclaimed, Attention! Slow Down! Get Your Documents Ready! They could already see the guard's booth with the lowered black-and-white-striped barrier next to it, and the barbed wire, white pinecones of insulators, and latticework searchlight towers to the right of the booth. The truck stopped. Everyone began staring at the guard, who was dozing standing up, his legs crossed and his carbine under his arm. An extinguished cigarette was stuck to his lower lip, and the ground beneath him was littered with cigarette butts. Warning signs were nailed to a post next to the barrier: ATTENTION! FOREST! . . . UNFOLD YOUR PASS BEFORE PRESENTING IT! . . . DON'T BRING DISEASE IN! The driver honked tactfully. The guard opened his eyes, stared in front of him blearily, then detached himself from the booth and went around the vehicle.

"Why are there so many of you?" he said hoarsely. "Coming to get paid?"

"Precisely," the former chairman said ingratiatingly.

"A fine mission," said the guard. He walked around the truck, stepped onto the running board, and peered into the back. "My goodness, what a lot of you there are," he said reproachfully. "And your hands? Are your hands clean?"

"They're clean!" the employees said in unison. Some showed their palms.

"Everyone's hands are clean?"

"Everyone's!"

"Okeydokey," said the guard, leaning so far into the cab that his whole upper body disappeared. Peretz heard voices coming from within. "Who's boss here? You are? How many have you brought? Uh-huh . . . You aren't lying to me, are you? Your last name? Kim? You'd better watch it, Kim, I'm writing that down . . . Hey, Waldemar! Still driving? . . . And I'm still guarding. Let me see your driver's license. Now, now, don't bite my head off, let me see . . . Your license is in order or I'd bust your ass . . . Why in the world are you writing phone numbers on your license? Wait a minute . . . Who's this Charlotte chick? Ah, I remember. Let me copy that down real quick . . . Thanks a lot. Off you go. You may go now."

He jumped off the running board, raising dust with his boots, walked up to the barrier, and leaned hard on the counterweight. The barrier went up slowly; the long johns that had been hanging on it slid into the dust. The truck began to move.

There was a hubbub in the cargo area, but Peretz didn't hear a thing. He was entering the forest. It was coming closer, towering over him, looming higher and higher, like an ocean wave, then it suddenly swallowed him. The sun and the sky were gone, space and time were gone—the forest had taken their place. Nothing existed but the somber colors flashing by, the dense humid air, the strange smoky smells, and the tart taste in his mouth. The forest touched all of his senses but one: the sounds of the forest were drowned out by the roar of the engine and the chatter of the other employees. This is the forest, Peretz repeated. I'm in the forest, he repeated inanely. Not above it but inside it; not an observer but a participant. I'm in the forest. Something cool and damp touched his face, tickled him, then broke off and slowly sank onto his knees. He looked at it: it was a long, thin fiber from some plant, or possibly some animal, or perhaps this was simply the forest making contact—either greeting him amicably or examining him suspiciously. He didn't touch the fiber.

Meanwhile, the truck sped along, following the path of the glorious human incursion—yellow, green, brown splotches disappeared obediently behind them, while columns of the long-forgotten, deserted veterans of the advancing army stretched alongside the road: the bucking bulldozers with their fiercely lifted rusty shields; the tractors buried in the ground up to their cabs, their torn-off treads snaking behind them; the trucks without wheels or windows—they were all dead, forever abandoned, yet they still looked fearlessly forward with their mangled radiators and broken headlights. And the forest rippled around them, trembling and writhing, changing color, blazing up and shimmering, deceiving the eye, approaching and retreating; the forest mocked you, scared you, teased you, and it was utterly unusual, and it was impossible to describe, and it made you dizzy.

6.

PERETZ

Peretz had opened the door of the ATV and was looking into the thicket. He didn't know what he was supposed to see. Something that looked like nauseating jelly. Something extraordinary that couldn't be described. But the most extraordinary, most unimaginable, most impossible objects in this thicket were people, and that was why Peretz saw only them. They were walking toward the ATV, slim and graceful, confident and elegant; they walked with ease, never stumbling, instantly finding where to step, and they pretended not to notice the forest, to be at home in the forest—and they probably weren't even pretending; they really did feel that way. Meanwhile, the forest loomed over them, shaking with silent laughter, pointing at them with myriad mocking fingers, cleverly pretending to be familiar, obedient, and simple—completely tame. For now. For the time being . . .

"That Rita sure is a looker," said the erstwhile truck driver Randy to Peretz. He was standing next to the ATV, his slightly crooked legs spread wide, holding the grunting and vibrating motorcycle with his thighs. "I definitely would have had a go at her, but that Quentin . . . He's one observant man."

Quentin and Rita came right up to them, and Stoyan climbed out from behind the wheel to meet them. "How's it doing?"

"It's breathing," Quentin said, studying Peretz closely. "What, have they brought the money or something?"

"This is Peretz," said Stoyan. "I've told you about him."

Rita and Quentin smiled at Peretz. He didn't have the chance to get a good look, and merely thought in passing that Rita was the strangest woman and Quentin the most profoundly unhappy man he had ever met.

"Hello, Peretz," said Quentin, continuing to smile pitifully. "Did you come to have a look? Have you never seen it before?"

"I still don't see it," said Peretz. It was obvious that the strangeness and the unhappiness were elusively but inextricably linked.

Rita turned her back to him and lit a cigarette.

"You are just looking the wrong direction," said Quentin. "Look over there, right in front of you! Don't you see it?"

And then Peretz saw it and immediately forgot about the people. It appeared, like a picture emerges on photographic paper, like the main character appears in a child's "Where's the bunny?" puzzle—and once you saw it, it was impossible to unsee. It was very close, about ten yards away from the trail and from the wheels of the ATV. Peretz swallowed hard.

A living pillar rose toward the tree crowns, a sheaf of extremely thin transparent threads, sticky and shiny, taut and writhing; this sheaf pierced the dense foliage and continued still higher, into the sky. And it originated in a cloaca, a greasy, seething cloaca filled with protoplasm—a living, active cloaca swelling with bubbles of primitive flesh, busily organizing and then instantly decomposing itself, spilling the products of decomposition onto its flat banks, spitting out sticky foam . . . And at the same time, the cloaca's voice became distinct from the grunting of the motorcycle, as if someone had turned on invisible audio filters; he heard gurgling and burbling, splashing, sobbing, and prolonged swampy moans. A wall of oppressive smells bore down on them: odors of oozing raw meat, lymph, fresh bile, serum, hot, starchy paste—and only then did Peretz notice that there were oxygen masks dangling at Rita's and Quentin's chests, and that Stoyan, grimacing squeamishly, was lifting a respirator toward his face. But Peretz didn't put on a respirator himself, as if hoping that the smells would tell him the story that his eyes and ears were failing to tell him . . .

"It stinks here," Randy was saying with disgust. "Like in a morgue . . ."

And Quentin was saying to Stoyan, "You should talk to Kim, have him do something about the rations. We have a dangerous work environment, after all. We deserve milk, chocolate . . ."

Rita was smoking pensively, blowing smoke out of her thin, flexible nostrils.

The trees surrounding the cloaca were quivering, bending over it solicitously, all their branches pointing the same direction, hanging over the bubbling mass, and there were thick, fuzzy vines streaming along the branches and falling into the cloaca, and the cloaca accepted them into itself, and the protoplasm gnawed at them and turned them into yet more protoplasm, in the same way that it could dissolve everything surrounding it and turn it into its own flesh . . .

"Perry," said Stoyan. "If you goggle like that, your eyes will pop out." Peretz smiled, but he knew the smile looked fake.

"Why did you bring the motorcycle?" asked Quentin.

"In case we get stuck. They'll crawl along the path, I'll drive with two wheels on the path and the other two on the grass, and the motorcycle will take up the rear. If we get stuck, Randy will go fetch a tow truck on the motorcycle."

"You're bound to get stuck," said Quentin.

"Of course we are," said Randy. "This is a stupid idea—I told you so from the first."

"Be quiet," Stoyan told him. "Did anyone ask for your opinion? . . . Are they coming out soon?" he asked Quentin.

Quentin looked at his watch. "Well . . ." he said. "It's currently having a litter every eighty-seven minutes. Therefore, it's going to be another . . . another . . . Hold on, we don't have to wait at all—look, it started already."

The cloaca was having a litter. Blobs of rippling, quivering white dough were being extruded onto its flat banks with impatient jerks; they rolled blindly and helplessly along the ground, then they paused, flattened out, extended a number of cautious pseudopods, and began to move in a deliberate manner—they continued to wiggle and root, but they were now all heading the same direction, one particular direction, wandering off then bumping into one another, but continuing to go the same way, following the same ray away from the womb, streaming into the thickets in a single white column, looking like giant, pouchy, slug-like ants . . .

"We're surrounded by quicksand," Randy was saying. "We'll get stuck so fast that no tow truck will do—we'll just snap its cables."

"Maybe you'd like to come with us?" Stoyan asked Quentin. "Rita is tired."

"Well, maybe Rita could go home and we'll go for a ride."

Quentin was hesitating. "How are you feeling, darling?" he asked.

"Yes, I'll go home," said Rita.

"Oh, good," said Quentin. "And we'll go take a look, all right? We'll probably be back soon. We won't be gone long, right, Stoyan?"

Rita threw her cigarette butt on the ground and left without saying good-bye, setting out along the path leading to the biological research station. Quentin lingered indecisively for a bit, then said to Peretz softly, "Excuse me . . . May I get by?"

He climbed into the backseat, and at the same time the motorcycle let out a horrible roar, broke free from Randy, and, jumping high into the air, headed right for the cloaca. "Stop!" shouted Randy, dropping to his haunches. Everyone stopped in their tracks. The motorcycle hit a hummock, screeched wildly, stood upright on its rear wheel, then fell into the cloaca. It seemed to Peretz that the protoplasm yielded beneath the motorcycle, as if to soften the blow. Then it silently and effortlessly let the motorcycle inside and closed over it. The engine went quiet.

"You clumsy bastard," Stoyan told Randy. "What the hell did you just do?"

The cloaca became a maw—a sucking, savoring, relishing maw. It was rolling the motorcycle around like a little boy rolls a large candy from cheek to cheek with his tongue. The motorcycle kept circling the foaming mass, appearing and disappearing again, impotently wiggling its handlebars and getting smaller and smaller with each reappearance—the metal skin was thinning, it became as translucent as tissue paper, they could see the engine through it, then the skin came apart at the seams, the tires disappeared, and finally, the motorcycle took one last dip and never emerged again.

"It ate it," Randy said with imbecilic delight.

"You clumsy bastard," Stoyan repeated. "You're going to pay for this. You're going to spend your whole damn life paying for this."

"Yeah, yeah," Randy said. "I'll pay for this, sure. What did I do, really? All I did was turn the throttle the wrong way," he told Peretz. "That's how it got away from me. See, Signor Peretz, I wanted to throttle down so it wouldn't make such a racket, and I turned the throttle the wrong way. Could have happened to anyone. And anyway, it was just an old bike . . . Then I'm off," he told Stoyan. "There's nothing left for me to do here. I'll head home."

"What are you looking at?" Quentin suddenly said, in a tone that made Peretz involuntarily recoil.

"Huh?" said Randy. "I'll look wherever I please." He was looking over his shoulder, watching the path, where Rita's orange shawl was flickering beneath the lime green canopy of branches, receding into the distance.

"Let me get by," Quentin told Peretz. "I need to have a talk with him."

"Wait, wait," Stoyan began to mutter. "Calm down, Quentin—"

"Calm down, sure—I've been watching him a long time, I know what he's after!"

"Come on, don't be an idiot . . . Get a grip! Calm down!"

"Let me go, I'm not kidding, let go of my hand!"

They were tussling noisily, shoving Peretz on both sides. Stoyan was holding Quentin's sleeve and the flap of his jacket, while Quentin, suddenly red and sweaty, refusing to take his eyes off Randy, was pushing Stoyan away with one arm and trying as hard as he could to bend Peretz in half with the other so he could step over him. He was moving in jerks, and with each jerk, he left more and more of his jacket behind. Peretz waited for his chance and rolled out of the ATV. Randy was still looking in Rita's direction—his lips parted, his eyes lascivious and tender.

"Why do they wear pants?" he asked Peretz. "That's the style nowadays, pants . . ."

"Don't defend him!" Quentin screamed from the ATV. "He's not a sexual neurotic, he's just an asshole! Let me go, or I'll let you have it, too!"

"They used to have these skirts," Randy was saying dreamily. "They'd wrap a piece of cloth around themselves and secure it with a safety pin. And I'd go ahead and open it . . ."

If this had been a park . . . If this had been a hotel, or a library, in an auditorium . . . And this actually had happened before—in parks, in libraries, even in an auditorium, during Kim's presentation "The Statistical Methods Each Administration Employee Needs to Know." And now the forest was witnessing it all: the salacious gleam in Randy's eyes, and Quentin's purple face bobbing in the ATV doors, looking strangely stupid and bovine, and Stoyan's tormented muttering—something about work, about responsibility, about stupidity—and the sound of buttons popping off and cracking against the windshield . . . And it was impossible to know what it thought about all this, whether it was horrified, amused, or grimacing in disgust . . .

"$%#@!" Randy said with relish.

And then Peretz punched him. He punched Randy in the face, hitting what felt like his cheekbone with a crunch, and he dislocated his finger. Everyone immediately stopped talking. Randy grabbed his cheekbone and looked at Peretz with astonishment.

"We can't have this," Peretz said firmly. "We can't have this here. Stop."

"Fine by me," Randy said, shrugging his shoulders. "I was just saying that there's no reason for me to be here anymore—see for yourself, there's no motorcycle . . . What am I doing here?"

Quentin inquired loudly, "You punched him in the face?"

"Yeah," Randy said with vexation. "He got my cheek, right on the bone . . . Lucky it wasn't my eye."

"No, really, you punched him in the face?"

"Yes," Peretz said firmly. "Because we can't have this here."

"Then let's go," Quentin said, leaning back in his seat.

"Randall," said Stoyan, "get in. You can help push if we get stuck."

"I'm wearing new pants," Randy objected. "How about I take the wheel?"

No one answered him, so he climbed into the backseat and sat down next to Quentin, who had scooted over. Peretz got in next to Stoyan, and they were off.

The pups had already covered a good distance, but Stoyan, maneuvering with a lot of precision, his right wheels on the path and his left wheels on the lush moss, caught up to them, then slowly crept behind them, carefully adjusting the speed with the clutch. "You'll burn the clutch," said Randy, then he turned to Quentin and started to explain that he didn't mean anything by it, that one way or another, he no longer had a motorcycle, and that a man was always a man, and if everything was working right, he always would be a man, whether he was in a forest or someplace else . . . "Didn't you already get punched in the face?" Quentin would ask.

"Come on, give it to me straight—did you or did you not already get punched in the face?" he would insert occasionally. "Come on," Randy would reply, "come on, wait, hear me out first . . ."

Peretz stroked his swelling finger and watched the pups. The children of the forest. Or maybe the servants of the forest. Or maybe the excrement of the forest . . . They moved slowly and tirelessly in a single file, seeming to flow along the ground, streaming over the rotten tree trunks, over the ditches, across the stagnant puddles, through the tall grass, and through the thornbushes. The trail would disappear, plunging into the fragrant mud or hiding beneath the layers of hard gray mushrooms that crunched under their wheels, then it would appear again, and the pups kept to the trail and managed to remain white, clean, and smooth—no dust clung to them, no thorn left a mark on them, and they didn't get covered in the sticky black mud. They flowed forward with dull, unreflecting confidence, as if following a familiar road, one they knew well. There were forty-three of them.

I was dying to get here, and now I'm here, and I'm finally seeing the forest from within, and I don't see a thing. I could have thought all this up without leaving the hotel, in my bare room with its three empty cots, late at night, when I'm suffering from insomnia and all is silence, and then suddenly the pile driver begins to bang as it hammers in the piles at the construction site. I could have probably thought up everything in this forest: the mermaids, and the wandering trees, and these pups, and how they suddenly turn into forest explorer Selivan—I could have come up with all the most absurd, all the most sacred things. And I could have thought up everything in the Administration without leaving my house; I could have thought it all up lying on the sofa next to the radio, listening to symphonic jazz and to voices speaking in foreign tongues. But that doesn't mean anything. If you see something without understanding it, you may as well have thought it all up. I'm living it, seeing it, and not understanding it; I'm living in a world that someone else has thought up without bothering to explain it to me, or maybe even to themselves . . . I'm longing to understand, Peretz thought suddenly. That's what I'm sick with: the longing to understand.

He leaned out of the window and pressed his aching finger to the vehicle's cold side. The pups paid no attention to the ATV. They probably didn't even realize it existed. They emanated a strong, unpleasant odor, their skin now looked transparent, and waves of something shadowlike moved beneath it.

"Let's catch one," suggested Quentin. "It'd be a piece of cake—just wrap it in my coat and bring it back to the lab."

"It's not worth it," said Stoyan.

"Why not?" asked Quentin. "We'll need to catch one someday anyway."

"I'm scared to," said Stoyan. "First and foremost, if it dies, God forbid, then we'd have to write a report for Bootlicherson . . ."

"We used to cook them," Randy suddenly informed them. "I didn't like the taste, but the guys said it wasn't bad. It tasted like rabbit, and I never touch the stuff—to my mind, a rabbit's no better than a cat. I'm too squeamish."

"I've noticed one thing," said Quentin. "The size of the litter is always a prime: thirteen, forty-three, forty-seven . . ."

"Nonsense," objected Stoyan. "I've met groups of six and twelve in the forest."

"That's in the forest," said Quentin. "After a while, they split off in different directions. But the number of pups in a litter is always prime—you can check the logbook, I recorded every number . . ."

"And one time," said Randy, "me and my pals caught one of the local girls—that was a hoot!"

"Well, then, write a paper," said Stoyan.

"I've already written it," said Quentin. "It'll be my fifteenth."

"I've published seventeen," said Stoyan, "and I have another one due to appear. And who's going to be your coauthor?"

"I don't know yet," said Quentin. "Kim recommends the garage foreman—he says that transportation is essential nowadays—and Rita suggests the hotel manager."

"Anyone but the hotel manager," said Stoyan.

"Why?" asked Quentin.

"Not the hotel manager," Stoyan repeated. "I won't say another word, but be advised."

"The hotel manager used to water down the buttermilk with brake fluid," said Randy. "That was back when he ran the barbershop. So the guys and I tossed some bedbugs into his apartment."

"They say that there's an order in the works," said Stoyan. "Anyone who's published fewer than fifteen papers will be required to undergo a special treatment."

"Oh yeah?" said Quentin. "Bummer, I know those special treatments—your hair stops growing and your breath stinks for a year . . ."

I need to go home, Peretz thought. I need to hurry on home. Now there's really nothing left for me to do here. Then he saw the pups break formation. Peretz counted: thirty-two pups went straight, while the remaining eleven, lining up single file like before, turned left and began to descend toward the body of dark, motionless water that had suddenly appeared between the trees not far from the ATV. Peretz saw a low, foggy sky and the dim outline of the Administration's cliff on the horizon. The eleven pups were confidently proceeding toward the lake. Stoyan turned off the engine and everyone got out, watching as the pups flowed over the crooked tree stump right on the shore, then plopped heavily into the lake, one by one. Oily ripples spread through the dark water.

"They're going in the water," Quentin said in surprise. "Drowning themselves."

Stoyan took out the map and spread it on the hood of the ATV. "I knew it," he said. "This lake isn't on here. It shows a village, not a lake . . . It says, *Nat. vill. seventeen point eleven.*"

"That's how it always goes," said Randy. "Who the hell uses a map here? First of all, the maps are all crap, and second, you don't need them. When it comes to the forest, one day something's a road, the next it's a river; one day something's a swamp, the next it's surrounded by barbed wire and has a watchtower in the middle. Or you suddenly find a brand-new repository."

"For some reason I don't feel like going farther," Stoyan said, stretching. "Maybe that's enough for today?"

"Of course it's enough," said Quentin. "Peretz still has to get his money. Let's get back in the ATV."

"What I'd give for a pair of binoculars," said Randy suddenly, avidly peering into the lake, a hand shading his eyes. "I think I see a girl swimming."

Quentin stopped in his tracks. "Where?"

"All naked," said Randy. "All naked, honest to God. Without a stitch on."

Quentin suddenly turned white and sprinted to the ATV. "Where do you see her?"

"Over there, on the other shore."

"There's nothing there," Quentin said hoarsely. He was standing on the running board, sweeping the distant shore with his binoculars. His hands were shaking. "The fucking liar . . . Begging to be punched in the face again . . . There's nothing there!" he repeated, passing the binoculars to Stoyan.

"What do you mean, nothing?" said Randy. "I'm not some near-sighted egghead, I have the eyes of an eagle—"

"Patience, patience, don't grab," Stoyan said to him. "Didn't your mother teach you to wait your turn?"

"There's nothing there," Quentin was mumbling. "It's all lies. Nothing but tall tales."

"I know what it is," said Randy. "It's a mermaid. I'm telling you."

Peretz started. "Let me have the binoculars," he said hurriedly.

"Like you can believe a word he says," Quentin kept mumbling, slowly calming down.

"I saw her, I swear," said Randy. "She must have gone underwater. She's about to come up . . ."

Peretz adjusted the binoculars. He didn't expect to see anything—that would be too easy. And he didn't see anything. Only the smooth surface of a lake, a distant, thickly forested shore, and the outline of a cliff above the jagged tree line. "What did she look like?" he asked.

Randy started to describe what she looked like, giving lots of detail and gesturing expressively. He was giving a highly appetizing description with great gusto, but this wasn't at all what Peretz had wanted.

"Yes, of course . . ." he said. "Yes . . . Uh-huh."

Maybe she had come out to meet the pups, he thought, bouncing up and down next to the morose Quentin in the backseat, and watching Randy's ears moving rhythmically as he chewed something. She had come out of the thicket, pale, cold, and confident, and she had stepped into the water, into the familiar water; she had walked into the lake like I walk into a library; she plunged into the murky green depths and swam out toward the pups. And by now, she has met them midway, at the bottom of the lake, and she's taking them somewhere, to someone, for some reason, and another tangle of events will form in the forest, and something else might happen or start to happen many miles away: clouds of lilac fog, which isn't actually fog, will began to swirl between the trees, or another cloaca will open up in some peaceful meadow. Or maybe a group of colorfully dressed natives, who have just been sitting quietly, watching educational films and patiently listening to a lecture by Beatrice Wah, whose voice has gone hoarse from the zealous effort, will suddenly get up and go into the forest, never to return again . . . And everything will be full of deep meaning, in the same way that the behavior of any complicated system is full of deep meaning, and it will all be strange, and it will therefore be meaningless to us, at least to those of us who still haven't gotten used to the meaninglessness and accepted it as the norm. And he felt the significance of every event, every phenomenon around them: the fact that there couldn't be forty-two or forty-five pups in a litter; the fact that the trunk of this tree was covered in red moss and not something else; the fact that the overhanging branches were blocking his view of the sky . . .

The ATV was bouncing up and down, Stoyan was driving very slowly, and Peretz saw the sign on the rickety post from a good distance away. Rain had partially washed away the writing and the sun had faded it, it was very old writing on a very old dirty-gray sign, and it was nailed to the pole with two huge rusty nails: IN MEMORY OF FOREST EXPLORER GUSTAV, WHO TRAGICALLY DROWNED HERE TWO YEARS AGO. A MONUMENT WILL BE ERECTED HERE IN HIS HONOR. The ATV went past the pole, lurching from side to side.

Gustav, Gustav, thought Peretz. How in the world did you manage to drown here? You were probably a big guy, Gustav, with a shaved head, a stubbly square jaw, and a gold tooth, and you were covered in tattoos from head to toe, and your arms hung down past your knees, and there was a finger missing on your right hand, which had been bitten off in a drunken brawl. And it wasn't in response to an inner calling that you had become a forest explorer, of course, it had just worked out that way: you were serving your time on the cliff that currently houses the Administration, and there was nowhere to run but the forest. And you didn't write papers in the forest, and never even thought about them—the laws of nature weren't your thing; the only laws you ever cared about had been written before your time and had always been against you. And you had been building a strategic road, laying down concrete slabs and felling trees on both sides of the road, clearing a wide swath, in order to make it possible for eight-engine bombers to land on the road if the situation required it. And you thought the forest would put up with it? So it went ahead and drowned you in a dry place. But in ten years they'll put up a statue in your honor, and they'll name a diner after you. The diner will be called Gustav's, and truck driver Randy will drink his buttermilk here and pet the blowzy girls from the local choir . . .

I think Randy has two convictions on his record, and for some reason, neither is for the right kind of thing. The first time he wound up behind bars was for stealing a company's business stationery, and the second time was for breaking passport laws.

Stoyan, on the other hand, doesn't have a record. He doesn't drink buttermilk; he doesn't drink anything at all. He loves Alevtina with a pure and tender love—Alevtina, who has never been loved with a pure and tender love in her life. When his twentieth paper comes out, he will offer his heart and hand to Alevtina, and he will be rejected, despite his publications, despite his broad shoulders and his handsome Roman nose, because Alevtina can't stand prigs, suspecting them (not without reason) of being impossibly refined degenerates. Stoyan lives in the forest, and he came here voluntarily, unlike Gustav, although for him the forest is nothing more than a gigantic heap of untapped material for papers that will save him from special treatments . . . You can remain endlessly surprised that there exist people who can get used to the forest, but this is actually true of the vast majority of people. At first the forest attracts them as a romantic spot, or as a place to make a buck, or as a community where much is allowed, or as a refuge. Then it frightens them a bit, and then they suddenly discover for themselves that "things are just as fucked up here as anywhere else," and this allows them to come to terms with the forest's strangeness, but none of them intend to spend their lives here . . . Now, Quentin, rumor has it, only stays here because he's afraid to leave his Rita unsupervised, whereas Rita refuses to leave for any price and won't tell anyone why . . . And now I've come to Rita. Rita can go into the forest and not return for weeks. Rita swims in the forest lakes. Rita breaks all the rules and no one dares reprimand her. Rita doesn't write papers; Rita doesn't write anything at all, even letters. It's very well known that Quentin cries at night and never sleeps at home—he always spends the night with the cafeteria girl, unless she's busy with someone else.

Everyone knows everything at the biological station . . . My God, in the evenings, they turn on the lights in the clubhouse, they turn on the stereo, they drink buttermilk—they drink ridiculous quantities of buttermilk—and at night, by the light of the moon, they toss the bottles into lakes, to see who can throw the farthest. They dance, they play truth or dare and spin the bottle, they play cards and they shoot pool, they swap women, and during the day they toil in their laboratories, they pour the forest from one test tube to another, they examine the forest under a microscope, and they count the forest on their arithmometers. Meanwhile, the forest surrounds them, hangs over them, sends shoots through their bedrooms, and in the stuffy hours before a thunderstorm, it appears at their windows, taking the form of hordes of roaming trees, and it probably also can't understand what they are and why they are here and what they are for . . .

It's a good thing I'm leaving, he thought. I've been here, I didn't understand a thing, I didn't find any of the things I wanted to find, but now I know for sure that I will never understand anything and I will never find anything, that things have to happen in their own time. I have nothing in common with the forest; I'm no closer to the forest than I am to the Administration. But at least I won't be disgracing myself here. I'll leave, I'll do my work, and I'll wait. And I'll hope that the time comes . . .

The courtyard of the biological research station was empty. There was neither a truck nor a line at the pay office window. There was only Peretz's suitcase, which was standing on the porch and blocking the way, and Peretz's coat, which was draped over the railings. Peretz climbed out of the ATV and looked around in bewilderment. He could smell the food and hear the clinking dishes in the cafeteria, and he saw that Randy and Quentin were already walking toward it, arm in arm. Stoyan said, "Let's go have dinner, Perry," and went off to park the ATV in the garage. Peretz suddenly realized, horrified, what all this meant: the wailing stereo, the meaningless chatter, the buttermilk, buttermilk, and more buttermilk, and how about another round? And the same thing every night, many, many nights in a row . . .

The pay office window banged and the angry pay clerk leaned out and shouted, "Come on, Peretz! How long am I supposed to wait for you? Come over here and sign this."

Peretz approached the window on unbending legs.

"Write the amount in words right here," said the pay clerk. "No, not over there—right here. Why are your hands shaking? Here you go . . ." He began to count out the bills.

"Where are the others?" asked Peretz.

"Be patient . . . The others are here, in this envelope."

"No, I mean—"

"Nobody cares what you mean. I can't change established protocol for you. Here you go. Tell me, did you get paid?"

"I wanted to know—"

"I asked whether you got paid. Yes or no?"

"Yes."

"Thank God. Here's your bonus. Did you get your bonus?"

"Yes."

"That's all. Allow me to shake your hand—I'm in a hurry. I need to be in the Administration before seven."

"I just wanted to ask," Peretz said hastily, "where the other people are . . . Kim, the truck . . . They promised to drive me, you see . . . To the Mainland."

"I can't drive you to the Mainland, I'm needed in the Administration. Excuse me, I'm closing the window."

"I won't take up much room," Peretz said.

"It doesn't matter. You're a grown man, you have to understand. I'm a pay clerk. I am in charge of employee records. What if something happened to them? Please remove your elbow."

Peretz removed his elbow and the window slammed shut. Through the blurry, fingerprint-smudged window, Peretz watched as the pay clerk gathered the employee records, crumpled them haphazardly, and stuffed them into his briefcase; then a door in the pay office opened and two enormous security guards came in, tied the pay clerk's hands, and threw a noose around his neck. One security guard started pulling the pay clerk along, using the rope as a leash, while the other one picked up the briefcase, scanned the room, and suddenly noticed Peretz. For a while, they stared at each other through the dirty glass, then the security guard very slowly and carefully placed the briefcase on a chair, as if afraid of

scaring someone off, and, without taking his eyes off Peretz, began
to reach for the rifle leaning against the wall, his motions just as
slow and careful as before. Peretz waited, cold shivers running
down his spine, unable to believe it, while the guard grabbed his
rifle and, walking backward, went outside, closing the door behind
him. The light went off.

Then Peretz sprang back from the window, ran to his suitcase
on tiptoe, grabbed it, and ran away as fast as he could. Hiding
behind the garage, he watched as the security guard went out
onto the porch, his rifle at the ready, and looked right, then left,
then under his feet. Then he took Peretz's coat off the railings,
held it in his hand as if to gauge its weight, went through its
pockets, looked around once, and went inside. Peretz sat down
on his suitcase.

It was chilly and getting dark. Peretz sat there, vacantly watching the brightly lit windows, which were covered halfway up with
chalk. Shadows were moving on the other side of the glass; the
mesh radar antenna on the roof was spinning silently. Dishes were
clanging; night animals were screeching in the forest. Then a searchlight went on somewhere and started to swivel around, and a dump
truck came around the corner, rolled into the searchlight beam,
clattered loudly as it bounced over a pothole, and headed toward
the gate, followed by the light. The security guard with the rifle was
sitting in the back of the truck. He was lighting a cigarette, hiding
from the wind, and you could see the thick, fuzzy rope wrapped
around his wrist disappearing into the half-open cab window.

The dump truck left and the searchlight went off. The other
security guard crossed the courtyard like a dark shadow, shuf-
fling his booted feet, holding his rifle under his arm. From time
to time he bent down and felt around on the ground—he was
probably looking for footprints. Peretz pressed his sweaty back
against the wall and followed the security guard with his eyes,
keeping very still.

Something in the forest was letting out protracted, bone-
chilling screams. Doors were slamming. On the second floor,

a light went on, and a loud voice said, "Is it ever stuffy in here." Some round, shiny object fell into the grass and rolled up to Peretz's feet. He froze again, but then he realized that it was an empty buttermilk bottle. I should walk back to the Administration, thought Peretz. I have to walk back. Through twelve miles of forest. It's too bad it's through the forest. Now the forest will get the chance to see a pitiful, trembling man, sweating in fear and exhaustion, perishing beneath his suitcase but for some reason not abandoning it. I'll be dragging myself along and the forest will be hooting and screaming at me from both sides . . .

The security guard reappeared in the courtyard. He wasn't alone; he was accompanied by somebody, a panting and snorting somebody who seemed to be on all fours. They stopped in the middle of the courtyard, and Peretz heard the guard muttering, "Take it, take it . . . Don't eat it, stupid, smell it . . . That's not food, that's a coat, you have to smell it . . . Well? Come on, go *cherchez* . . ." The somebody on all fours was yelping and whimpering. "Damn it!" said the security guard in vexation. "Fleas, that's all you know how to find . . . Beat it!" They melted into the darkness. He heard the guard's boots pounding on the porch and the door slamming. Then something cold and wet nudged Peretz in the cheek. He started and almost fell over. It was a huge wolfhound. It yelped softly, gave a deep sigh, and put its heavy head onto Peretz's knees. Peretz scratched it behind the ear. The wolfhound yawned and began to make itself comfortable. It had almost settled in when a stereo began to blare from the second floor. The wolfhound silently recoiled and galloped away.

The stereo was going wild; for many miles around, the world contained nothing but the stereo. And then, just like in a thriller, the gates were suddenly silently bathed in blue light and swung open, letting in a huge truck that sailed into the courtyard like a colossal ship, decked out in whole constellations of flashing lights. The truck stopped and turned off its headlights, which slowly dimmed to darkness, as if a forest monster were drawing its last breath. Truck driver Waldemar leaned out of the cab and started yelling something, opening his mouth wide—he yelled for a long time, growing hoarse and becoming enraged before Peretz's eyes, then he gave up and disappeared back into the cab. He leaned out again and wrote an upside-down "Peretz!!!" on the door with chalk. Then Peretz realized that the truck had come for him, grabbed his suitcase, and dashed across the yard, afraid to look back, afraid that he'd hear shots behind him. He barely managed to clamber up the two sets of steps leading up to the cab, which was as spacious as a bedroom; as he was finding a place for his suitcase, as he was sitting down and looking for his cigarettes, Waldemar kept talking, growing hoarse, gesturing and shoving Peretz in the shoulder with an open palm, but only when the stereo suddenly went silent did Peretz finally hear his voice: Waldemar wasn't saying anything important, he was simply swearing up a blue streak.

The truck hadn't even made it through the gates when Peretz fell asleep, as if someone had pressed a chloroform-soaked rag to his face.

7.

CANDIDE

It was a very strange village. When they had come out of the forest and seen it in the basin below, they had been struck by the silence. It was so silent that they weren't even glad to see it. The village was shaped like a triangle, and the big clearing in which it was situated was also triangular—a spacious clay meadow without a single bush, without a single blade of grass, as if everything on it had been burned away then trampled down. It was completely in the shade: the fused crowns of the mighty trees entirely obscured the sky.

"I have a bad feeling about this village," Nava declared. "They probably won't even give us food. How could they have any food, when they don't even have a field, only bare clay? They are probably hunters, they probably catch animals and eat them, it makes me sick just to think about it, it does . . ."

"Maybe we're in the kook village?" asked Candide. "And this is the Clay Meadow?"

"This is no kook village. The kook village, it's a normal sort of village, it's just like our village, except it's full of kooks . . . And this place, it's different—look how quiet it is, and there's no one around, not even kids, although maybe the kids are already in bed . . . Why is there no one around, Silent Man? Let's not go to this village, I have a really bad feeling about it . . ."

The sun was setting, and the village below was sinking into the twilight. It seemed very empty—not neglected, not abandoned and left behind, but empty, as if it weren't a village but a stage set. No, thought Candide, we probably shouldn't go there, but my feet hurt and I want a roof over my head. And I'm hungry. And night is coming . . . My goodness, we've been wandering through the forest all day; even Nava's tired, clinging to my arm and not letting go.

"All right," he said hesitantly. "Let's not go there."

"Let's not go there, let's not go there," mimicked Nava. "What if I'm hungry? How long are we supposed to go without eating? I haven't eaten a thing since morning . . . And those thieves of yours . . . Do you have any idea how hungry they make you? No, how about we go down there, have some food, and if we don't like it there, we'll just leave. It's going to be a warm night, it's not going to rain . . . Come on, what are you waiting for?"

They were hailed as soon as they got to the periphery of the village. A gray, almost fully naked man was sitting on the gray ground by the first house. It was hard to see him in the half light; he almost blended into the ground, and Candide could only make out his silhouette against the white backdrop of the wall.

"Where are you going?" the man said weakly.

"We need a place to spend the night," said Candide. "We're going to the Settlement in the morning. We've lost our way. We ran away from the thieves and lost our way."

"So you're alone, then?" the man said limply. "Good for you . . . I'm glad you've come . . . Come in, come in, there's a lot of work to do, and for some reason, there's almost nobody left to do it . . ." He was barely managing to get the words out, as if he was falling asleep. "And we need to work. We really need to work . . ."

"You don't have any food?" Candide asked.

"Nowadays, there's . . ." The man said a few words, and Candide thought they sounded familiar, even though he knew that he'd never heard them before. "I'm glad you brought the boy, because boys . . ." And he again started speaking in a strange, incomprehensible tongue.

Nava tried to pull Candide away, but Candide jerked his hand back in irritation. "I can't understand you," he said to the man, trying to at least get a better look at him. "Tell me, do you have anything to eat?"

"Now if there were three of you . . ." the man said.

Nava dragged Candide away with all her strength, and they stepped off to the side.

"Is he's sick or something?" Candide said angrily. "Did you understand what he was muttering?"

"Why are you talking to him?" whispered Nava. "He doesn't have a face! How can you talk to a man without a face?"

"What do you mean, he doesn't have a face?" Candide said, startled, and looked over his shoulder. He couldn't see the man; either he'd gone away, or he'd dissolved into the twilight.

"Just that," said Nava. "He has eyes and a mouth, but he doesn't have a face." She suddenly pressed against him. "He's like a deadling," she said. "He's not really a deadling, he has a smell, but all of him is like a deadling . . . Let's go to some other house, but we won't get food in this village, don't get your hopes up."

She dragged him to the next house, and they peered into it. Everything inside it looked strange—there were no beds, there were no domestic smells, and it was empty, dark, and unpleasant. Nava sniffed the air.

"There was never any food here," she said with disgust. "This is one silly village you've brought me to, Silent Man. What are we going to do here? I've never seen a village like this in my life.

What kind of village has no kids shouting outside, and no one out on the street?"

They kept going. There was fine, cool dust beneath their feet, they couldn't even hear their own footsteps, and unlike most evenings, no hooting or gurgling sounds came from the forest.

"He spoke a strange language," said Candide. "I'm thinking back now, and it's like I've heard it before . . . But I can't remember when or where . . ."

"I can't remember either," Nava said after a pause. "But you're right, Silent Man, I've heard words like that before myself—maybe in a dream, or maybe in our village, not the one where we live now but in the other village, where I was born, but that must mean that it was a very long time ago, because I was very little then, I've forgotten everything from that time, and now it's like I'm remembering it, but I can't really remember it."

In the next house, they saw a man lying on the floor by the threshold, fast asleep. Candide bent over him and shook his shoulder, but the man didn't wake up. His skin was damp and cool like an amphibian's, he was fat and soft and had almost no muscle left, and his lips looked black and oily in the half light.

"He's sleeping," Candide said, turning toward Nava.

"How could he be sleeping," said Nava, "when he's watching us?"

Candide bent over the man again, and he thought that he saw the man watching them from beneath barely lifted eyelids. But he only thought so. "No, he's sleeping," said Candide. "Let's go."

Uncharacteristically, Nava didn't say anything.

They walked to the center of the village, peering into each house, seeing sleepers in almost every single one. The sleepers were all fat, sweaty men; there wasn't a single woman or child. Nava became completely quiet, and Candide also felt uneasy. The sleepers' stomachs were rumbling and they never woke up, but every time Candide looked behind him as he exited a house, he thought he could see them carefully and furtively watching them leave.

Darkness had fallen, the moonlit, ashy-gray sky was peeking out through the gaps between the branches, and Candide again thought that this looked eerily like a stage set in a good theater. But he was aware that he was utterly exhausted, exhausted to the point of complete indifference. There was currently only one thing he wanted: to lie down somewhere beneath a roof (so that night filth wouldn't fall on him as he slept), even if it was on a hard, foot-worn floor, but he would really prefer to lie down in an empty house, not next to these suspicious sleepers.

Nava was now really hanging off his arm. "Don't be afraid," Candide told her. "There's nothing to be afraid of here."

"What did you say?" Nava said sleepily.

"I said don't be afraid, they are all half dead, I could fight them off with one hand tied behind my back."

"I'm not afraid of anyone," Nava said grumpily. "I'm tired and I want to sleep, since you won't give me anything to eat. And you keep walking and walking, from one house to another, from one house to another, I'm sick of it, the houses are all the same inside, anyway, and everyone's already lying down and resting, we're the only ones wandering around . . ."

Then Candide worked up his nerve and went inside a random house. It was pitch black inside. Candide pricked up his ears, trying to figure out if there was anyone in the house, but all he could hear was Nava's loud breathing—she had buried her forehead into his side. He felt for a wall, then groped around with his hands, checking if the floor was dry, and lay down, putting Nava's head on his stomach. Nava was already asleep. I hope we don't regret this, he thought, there's something wrong here . . . But it's just for one night . . . And to ask the way . . . They can't sleep during the day, too . . . If worse comes to worst, we can always go back to the swamp, the thieves must be gone by now . . . Even if they aren't gone . . . I wonder how things are at the Settlement? . . . Does this mean that I'm leaving the day after tomorrow again? . . . No, it has to be tomorrow . . . Tomorrow . . .

A light woke him up, and he thought that it must be moon-light. It was dark in the house, and the lilac light was streaming through both the window and the door. He began to wonder how moonlight could be streaming through both the window and the door across from it, then it dawned on him that he was in the forest, where there couldn't be a real moon, but then he immediately forgot about it, because the silhouette of a man appeared in the strip of light falling through the window. The man was standing there, in the house, with his back to Candide, and he was looking out the window, and Candide could see from the silhouette that the man was standing with his hands behind his back and his head bowed—an attitude completely alien to the forest inhabitants, simply because they never had any reason to stand like this—and also precisely the way that Karl Etingof had liked to stand in front of the laboratory windows on foggy, rainy days, when they couldn't do their work. And it came to him with complete certainty that this was Karl Etingof himself, who had gone into the forest long ago, had never been seen at the biological research station again, and had been officially declared missing. He felt breathless with agitation and screamed, "Karl!" Karl turned toward him slowly, the lilac light passed across his face, and Candide saw that this wasn't Karl but some unfamiliar local villager. He silently approached Candide and bent over him, keeping his hands clasped behind his back, and Candide got a good look at his face, a haggard, beardless face, nothing like Karl's. He didn't say a word and apparently didn't even notice Candide, stood up straight, and walked toward the door, still stooping, and as he was crossing the threshold, Candide realized that this was Karl after all, sprang up, and ran after him.

He stopped right outside the door and looked up and down the street, trying to control the unpleasant nervous shaking that had suddenly taken hold of him. It was very light out, because a glowing lilac sky hung low over the village, making all the houses look completely flat and unreal. A peculiar long build-ing, resembling nothing he'd ever seen in the forest, towered diagonally across the street, and people were milling around next to it. The man who looked like Karl was walking alone toward this building; he approached the crowd and was absorbed by it, disappearing into it like he'd never been there at all. Candide also wanted to come closer to the building, but his legs felt like jelly and he couldn't walk an inch. He was surprised that legs like these could support him at all; afraid of falling down, he tried to grab on to something, but there was nothing to grab on to—he was surrounded by emptiness. "Karl," he mumbled, swaying, "Karl, come back!" He repeated these words over and over and over again, then he screamed them loudly in despair, but nobody heard him, because at that very instant, someone let out a much louder scream, a pitiful and wild shriek, an obvious cry of pain, which made his ears ring and his eyes tear up, and he somehow immediately realized that the cry was coming from inside the long building, maybe because there was nowhere else it could be coming from.

"Where's Nava?" he screamed. "Where are you, little one?" He realized that he was about to lose her, that the time had come, that he was about to lose everything that was dear to him, everything that bound him to his life, and that he'd be left all alone. He turned around, about to rush back inside the house, and saw Nava, who was throwing back her head and slowly falling backward, and he caught her and picked her up, unable to understand what was happening to her. Her head was thrown back, and he could see her naked throat, the place where most people have a single dimple between the collarbones, and where Nava had two, and he would never see them again. Because the crying hadn't stopped, and he knew that he had to go over there, to the place where they were screaming. And he knew very well that it would be heroic, because he'd carry her there himself, but he also knew that to *them* it wasn't heroic at all but a completely normal and natural procedure, because they couldn't understand what it meant—to hold your living, breathing, only daughter in your arms and to carry her yourself to the place where they were crying.

The screaming suddenly stopped. Candide saw that he was already standing right next to the building, in the middle of the crowd, in the front of the square black door, and he tried to figure out what he was doing here with Nava in his arms, but he didn't have the chance, because two women came out of the square black door with Karl at their side, all three of them frowning and looking displeased, and they stopped, continuing to talk. He could see their lips moving, and he could guess that they were arguing, that they were annoyed, but he didn't understand the words—the only thing he managed to make out was the vaguely familiar word *chiasma*. Then one of the women, still in the middle of the conversation, turned toward the crowd and gestured, as if to invite them all inside the building. Candide said, "One second, one second . . ." Then he pulled Nava even closer to him. The loud crying began again, everyone began to move, the fat people began to hug each other, cling to each other, pet and caress each other, their eyes were dry and their lips were clamped shut, but they were the ones crying and screaming, saying good-bye, because these turned out to be men and women, and the men were saying good-bye to the women forever. No one dared to go first, so Candide went first, because he was brave, because he knew the meaning of the word *duty*, because he knew that there was no help for it anyway. But Karl looked at him and gave a barely noticeable shake of the head, and he was filled with an unbearable horror, because this wasn't Karl after all, but he had understood and started walking backward, bumping against soft, slippery objects with his back. And when Karl shook his head again, he turned around, threw Nava over his shoulder, and ran on weak, rubbery legs along the bright, empty street, as if in a dream, not hearing any pursuing footsteps behind him.

He came to when he ran into a tree. Nava shouted out, and he put her down on the ground. There was grass underfoot.

The whole village was visible from here. There was a cone of glowing lilac mist hanging over it, and the houses looked blurry, as did the tiny figures of the people.

"I can't remember a thing," said Nava. "Why are we here? I thought we already went to bed. Or is this all a dream?"

Candide picked her up and carried her on and on and on, forcing his way through bushes and getting tangled in the grass, until he got to a place where it was completely dark. Then he kept going for a little while longer, put Nava down on the ground again, and sat nearby. They were surrounded by tall, warm grass, and it wasn't damp at all—Candide had no idea the forest contained such dry and favorable spots. His head ached, he was very sleepy, and he didn't want to think about anything; there was only a feeling of vast relief, because he had intended to do something horrible and hadn't done it.

"Silent Man," Nava said sleepily, "you know, Silent Man, I finally remembered where I'd heard that language before. You spoke it yourself, back when you couldn't think straight. Listen, Silent Man, maybe this is the village you came from? Maybe you've just forgotten? Because you were very sick then, Silent Man, you couldn't think straight at all . . ."

"Go to sleep," said Candide. He didn't want to think. He didn't want to think about anything. *Chiasma*, he remembered. And he instantly fell asleep.

Not quite instantly. He did manage to remember that it wasn't Karl who had disappeared, it was Valentine, and Valentine was the one who had been officially declared missing, while Karl had died in the forest, and his body, which had been found by chance, was put inside a lead coffin and sent to the Mainland. But he thought that he had dreamed this.

When he opened his eyes, Nava was still sleeping. She was lying on her stomach in a hollow between two tree roots, her face buried in the crook of her left elbow, her right arm flung off to the side, and Candide saw a thin, shiny object held loosely in her dirty little fist. At first he couldn't figure out what it was; it only brought suddenly to mind the strange dreamlike night, and his fear, and his relief that something terrible hadn't happened. And then he realized what this object was, and even its name unexpectedly bubbled up in his consciousness. It was a scalpel. He waited for a bit, verifying that the shape of the object corresponded to the sound of the word, dimly aware that there was nothing to verify, that he was right, but that this was utterly impossible, because both the scalpel's shape and its name were absurdly incongruous with this world. He woke Nava up.

Nava woke up, sat up, and immediately began to talk. "What a dry spot, I never thought places this dry existed, and look, nothing grows here but grass, Silent Man." She stopped talking and brought the fist with the scalpel to her face. She stared at the scalpel for a second, then she squealed, frantically hurled it away, and sprang to her feet. They were both looking at it, and both were afraid. "What is that, Silent Man?" Nava whispered finally. "What a horrible thing . . . Or maybe it's not a thing? Maybe it's a plant? Look how dry it is here—maybe it grew here."

"Why is it horrible?" asked Candide.

"Of course it's horrible," said Nava. "You should hold it . . . You try it, try holding it, then you'll know why it's horrible . . . I don't know why it's horrible myself . . ."

Candide took the scalpel. The handle was still warm, but its sharp tip was cool; if you carefully traced it with your finger, you could find the place where it stopped being warm and became cold.

"Where did you get it?" Candide asked.

"I didn't get it anywhere," said Nava. "It must have climbed into my hand as I slept. See how cold it is? It probably wanted to get warm, so it climbed into my hand . . . I've never seen anything like this . . . this . . . I don't even know what to call it. It probably isn't actually a plant, it's probably an animal, it might even have legs, but it's tucking them away, and it's so hard and so mean . . . Or maybe we're still asleep, Silent Man?" She suddenly broke off and looked at Candide. "Weren't we in the village last night? We were, we were, and that faceless man was there, and he kept thinking that I was a boy . . . And we were looking for a place to sleep . . . Yes, and then I woke up, you weren't there, and

I started feeling around me . . . That's when it climbed into my fist!" she said. "And here's the strange thing, Silent Man, I wasn't a bit afraid of it then, just the opposite . . . I actually needed it for something . . ."

"It was all a dream," Candide said resolutely. His skin was crawling. He could now remember everything that had happened last night. Including Karl. And that inconspicuous shake of the head: run, while you still can. And the fact that the real Karl had been a surgeon.

"Why aren't you talking, Silent Man?" Nava asked anxiously, peering into his face. "What are you looking at?"

Candide waved her off. "It was a dream," he repeated sternly. "Forget about it. You'd better go look for food, and I'll bury this thing."

"Do you know what I needed it for?" asked Nava. "I was supposed to do something . . ." She shook her head. "I don't like that kind of dream," she said. "Bury it nice and deep, or it'll get out, crawl into the village, and frighten someone . . . You should put a stone on top of it, the heavier the better . . . All right, go bury it, and I'll go look for food." She sniffed the air. "There are berries nearby. That's amazing, how can there be berries in such a dry place?"

She ran off, sprinting swiftly and silently along the grass, and quickly disappeared behind the trees, while Candide stayed put, the scalpel lying in the palm of his hand. He didn't bury it. He wrapped a tuft of grass around the blade and stuck it beneath his shirt. He now remembered everything, but he still couldn't understand a thing. It had been a strange and awful dream, and somebody had been negligent enough to allow a scalpel to fall out of it. It's too bad, he thought—my head is exceptionally clear today, but I still don't understand a thing. That means I never will.

Nava soon came back and poured out an entire heap of berries and a few large mushrooms from beneath her shirt.

"I found a trail, Silent Man," she said. "We shouldn't go back to that village, what do we care about some village? Here's what we should do, we should take that trail, and we'll be sure to get somewhere. And when we get there, we'll ask for directions to the Settlement, and everything will be fine. It's amazing how much I want to get to the Settlement right now, I've never felt like that before. And let's not go back to that sly village, I had a bad feeling about it from the first, we were right to leave, or we might have come to grief. If you ask me, we should have never gone there in the first place, the thieves did shout at us, telling us not to go there, shouting that we wouldn't make it out alive, but you never do listen to anyone. So we almost came to grief because of you, we did . . . Why aren't you eating? The mushrooms are filling, and the berries are tasty, you should rub them between your fingers, crumble them up, you're just like a baby today. I remember now, my mom always told me that the best mushrooms grow in dry places, but back then, I didn't understand what *dry* meant, my mom told me that lots of places used to be dry, like a good road is dry, that's why she knew what it meant, but I didn't know . . ."

Candide tasted a mushroom, then ate it. The mushrooms really were good, as were the berries, and he felt more alive after eating. But he still didn't know what to do. He didn't want to go back to that village either. He tried to visualize the region as it had been described to him by Crookleg, who had sketched it on the ground with a stick, and he remembered that Crookleg had talked about a road to the City that was supposed to pass right through these parts. A very good road, Crookleg had said with regret, the most direct road to the City, but you can't cross the bog to get to it, that's the catch . . . He had lied. He had lied, the lame one. He had crossed the bog, and he had probably been to the City, too, but he had lied about it, for some reason. And maybe the trail that Nava found is that very same direct road? We'll have to risk it. But first we do need to go back. We need to go back to that village . . .

"We do have to go back, Nava," he said, after they had finished eating.

"Go back where? To that sly village?" Nava got upset. "Why are telling me this, Silent Man? Haven't we seen enough of that village? If there's one thing I don't like about you, Silent Man, it's that there's no coming to terms with you like with other, normal people . . . Didn't we already decide that we aren't going back to that village? I even found you a trail, I did, and here you are talking about going back again . . ."

"We have to go back," he repeated. "I don't want to go back myself, Nava, but we have to. What if they can tell us the quickest way to the City?"

"What do you mean, the City? I don't want to go to the City, I want to go to the Settlement!"

"Let's just go straight to the City," said Candide. "I can't take it anymore."

"OK, fine," said Nava. "Fine, let's go to the City, that's an even better idea, not like I've never been to the Settlement. Let's go to the City, that's fine by me, everything is fine by me, except for going back to that village . . . I don't know about you, Silent Man, but if it were up to me, I'd never go back to that village."

"I feel that way, too," he said. "But we have to go back. Don't be angry, Nava, I don't want to go back myself, you know."

"If you don't want to go back, why go?"

He neither wanted nor was able to explain to her why they should go. He got up and walked in the direction he thought the village lay without looking back. He walked along the warm, dry grass, past the warm, dry tree trunks, squinting in the warm, uncharacteristically abundant sunlight—he walked toward the horror that he had lived through, which made his muscles painfully tense up, toward a strange, quiet hope, which was managing to fight its way through the horror, like a blade of grass sprouting through a crack in the pavement.

Nava caught up to him and began walking next to him. She was angry—she even stayed silent for a while—but eventually she couldn't stand it any longer.

"Just don't think that I'll talk to those people," she announced, "you'll have to do all the talking now, you're the one who's going there, so you do the talking. Me, I don't like dealing with people who don't even have faces, I don't like that at all. You can't expect much from a man who can't tell a boy from a girl . . . My head's been hurting since this morning, and now I know why . . ."

They came upon the village before they expected to. Candide had apparently gone a bit too far left, and the village appeared between the trees to their right. Everything here had changed, but Candide didn't immediately realize what was happening. Then he understood: the village was sinking underwater.

The triangular meadow was already full of dark water, and the water was rising before their eyes, filling the clay basin, flooding the houses, swirling silently through the streets. Candide stood by and watched helplessly as the windows disappeared underwater, the waterlogged walls sank and collapsed, and the roofs fell in—and no one came running out of the houses, no one tried to get to shore, no one appeared on the surface of the water. Maybe there wasn't a single person left, maybe they had all gone away that night, but he could sense that it wasn't that simple. A strange thought suddenly came into his head: this wasn't a real village, this was a mock-up that had been standing around, dusty and forgotten, until someone wondered what would happen if you flooded it with water. Maybe something interesting would happen? So they flooded it with water. But nothing interesting did happen . . .

Bending fluidly, the roof of the flat structure vanished into the water without a trace. A soft sigh seemed to pass over the dark water, the smooth surface rippled, and it was all over. Candide was standing in front of an ordinary triangular lake, as of yet fairly shallow and devoid of life. It will eventually become bottomless and full of fish, which we'll try to catch, prepare, and preserve in formaldehyde.

"I know what this is called," Nava said. Her voice was so calm that Candide looked at her. She really was completely calm; she even seemed pleased. "This is called a Surpassment," she said. "That's why they had no faces, I just didn't understand at first. They probably wanted to live in the lake. I've heard it said that the ones who used to live in the houses would be allowed to stay and live in the lake, there will always be a lake here now, and the ones who didn't want to live in the lake would leave. I'd leave, personally, although maybe it's even nicer to live in a lake. But no one can know that . . . Should we go for a swim?" she suggested.

"No," Candide said. "I don't want to swim here. Let's go find your trail. Come on."

If only I could get out of here, he thought, because I'm like that machine in the maze . . . We all stood around and laughed as it busily rooted around, searched, and sniffed—and then someone would pour water into a small depression in its path, and it would get touchingly lost, but only for a moment, and then it would again begin to bustle around, moving its antennae, buzzing and sniffing, and it didn't know that we were watching it, and on the whole, we didn't care that it didn't know it, even though that was probably the most terrible thing of all—if it actually was terrible, he thought. Our imperatives can neither be terrible nor kind. Our imperatives are only imperative, and everything else about them is a story we tell ourselves . . . as do the machines in their mazes, if they are able to tell themselves stories. It's just that when we make mistakes, our imperatives grab us by the throat, and we start crying and whining about how cruel and terrible they are, whereas they simply are what they are; we're the ones who are silly or blind. I'm even capable of philosophizing today, he thought. It's probably because it's so dry. My goodness, I'm even capable of philosophizing . . .

"There's your trail," Nava said angrily. "Go on, please."

She's angry, he thought. I didn't let her swim, I'm always silent, it's dry and unpleasant here . . . Whatever, let her be angry. When she's angry, she's quiet—thank goodness for small mercies. Who uses these trails, anyway? Do people really walk here often enough for the trails not to get overgrown? This is a strange kind of trail—it's not footworn, it's like a trench . . .

At first, the trail passed through dry and favorable places, but after a while it descended steeply down the side of a hill and became a boggy strip of black mud. They had come out of the strip of passable forest and were again surrounded by swamps and thickets of moss. It became damp and stuffy. Nava immediately perked up—she felt a lot better here. She was already chattering nonstop, and soon, a familiar buzzing noise materialized and lodged itself inside Candide's head, so he was now moving in a daze, forgetting about any kind of philosophy, almost forgetting where he was going, surrendering himself to random incoherent thoughts—maybe even visions rather than thoughts.

. . . Crookleg is limping down the main street, saying to anyone he meets (and if he doesn't meet anyone, then he says it for no particular reason) that Silent Man must have left, he left and took Nava with him, he was probably going to the City, and the whole time, the City doesn't even exist. Maybe he wasn't going to the City, maybe he was going to the Reeds, the Reeds is great for fishing—stick your fingers in the water and there's your fish. Then again, what good would the fish do him, Silent Man doesn't even eat fish, the idiot, but maybe he decided to catch some fish for Nava, Nava does eat fish, so he's catching some fish for her. But then why was he asking about the City all the time? *Nooo*, he didn't go to the Reeds, and we shouldn't expect him back anytime soon . . .

And Big Fist is walking along the main street toward him, saying to anyone he meets that Silent Man kept dropping by, trying to convince him—let's go to the City, Big Fist, he'd say, let's go the day after tomorrow, he spent a year asking me to go to the City the day after tomorrow, and when I got so much food ready that the old woman wouldn't shut up about it, he up and left without me and without my food . . . One guy, fur and fuzz it, he went off without any food, he got thumped on the head, now he doesn't go anywhere anymore, he's afraid to go without food, even if he has food he won't budge, that's how good they thumped him . . .

And Tagalong is at home, standing next to the old man, who's having breakfast, and saying to him, you're eating again, and you're eating someone else's food again. Don't think, he says, that I mind sharing, I'm just amazed that one skinny old man can put away so many pots of the most filling food. Keep eating, he says, but do tell me, maybe there really is more than one of you in the village? Maybe there are three of you, or at least two of you? Because it's almost uncanny, watching you—you eat and eat, fill your belly, then you go on about right and wrong . . .

Nava was walking next to him, holding his hand with both of hers, and was telling him enthusiastically, "And there used to be another man who lived in our village, he was called Tortured Questioner. And this Tortured Questioner, everything hurt his feelings, and he was always asking *why*. Why is it light during the day and dark at night? Why are there liquor beetles but no liquor ants? Why are deadlings interested in women but not in men? The deadlings stole two wives from him, one after the other. The first one was stolen before my time, but I was already living there when they stole the second wife, and he went around asking why they didn't steal him, only his wife . . . He'd wander the forest all day and all night, on purpose, so they'd take him too and he'd find his wives, or at least one of them, but they never did take him, of course—deadlings aren't interested in men, they want women, that's their way, and they weren't about to change that for some Tortured Questioner . . . He also kept asking why we work in the field when there's plenty of food in the forest as is—just ferment it and eat it. The village head told him, if you don't want to, don't do it, no one's making you . . . But he just kept repeating: why, why, why . . . Or there was the time he pestered Big Fist. Why, he asked, is the Upper Village overgrown with mushrooms but our village isn't? At first, Big Fist explained it to him calmly: the Surpassment has already happened in the Upper Village, and it hasn't happened here yet, that's all there is to it. But he asked: Why is the Surpassment taking so long to happen here? What do you care about that Surpassment, Big Fist asked, is it a friend of yours? Tortured Questioner just wouldn't let up. He wore Big Fist out—he yelled so loud that the whole village could hear, started waving his fists, and ran to the village head to complain; the village head also got mad and got the whole village together so they could chase Tortured Questioner down and punish him, but they never did catch him . . . He pestered the old man a lot, too. At first, the old man stopped eating at his house, then the old man started hiding from him, then he finally couldn't take it anymore: leave me alone, he says, you spoil my appetite, you do, how am I supposed to know why? The City knows why, that's all there is to it. So Tortured Questioner left for the City and never came back . . ."

Yellow-green patches slowly floated by them on both sides, the ripe narcotic mushrooms sprayed fans of reddish spores, a stray forest wasp rushed at him with a high-pitched whine, trying to hit him in the eye, and they had to run for a hundred yards to get away from it; colorful underwater spiders clung to vines, making a lot of noise as they fussily crafted their edifices; the jumping trees crouched and squirmed, preparing to leap, then froze in place when they sensed people, pretending to be ordinary trees—there was nothing to attract the eye, and nothing to remember. And there was nothing to think about, because thinking about Karl, about last night, and about the drowned village meant becoming delirious.

". . . Tortured Questioner was a kind man, he and Crookleg were the ones who found you in the Reeds. They were heading to the Anthills, but they somehow ended up in the Reeds, and they found you there and carried you back—actually, Tortured Questioner was the one who carried you back, Crookleg just walked behind him and picked up everything that fell out of you. He picked up lots of things, he told us, then he got scared and threw them all away. Nothing like that, he told us, ever grew around here or ever could. Then Tortured Questioner took your clothes off, very strange clothes they were, no one could figure out where and how that kind of thing might grow . . . So he cut these clothes up and planted them, thought they might grow, he did. But nothing he planted grew, it didn't even sprout, so he again started going around and asking, why do all other clothes grow if you cut them up and plant them, whereas your clothes, Silent Man, didn't even sprout? He even tried pestering you lots of times, wouldn't leave you alone, but you weren't thinking straight at the time, you'd just mumble things, like that man without a face, and hide behind your hand. So he had to give up, none the wiser. Then a lot of men started going to the Reeds—Big Fist, Tagalong, even the village head himself—hoping to find another one like you, they were. They never did find anyone . . . That's when they gave you to me. Nurse him, they said, as best you can, and if you nurse him back to health, he'll be a husband for you, it doesn't matter that he's an outsider—you're kind of an outsider yourself. You know, I'm an outsider, too, Silent Man. Here's what happened: the deadlings captured me and my mother, and it was a moonless night . . ."

They were going uphill again, but it didn't get less damp, although the forest became sparser. There were no more tree trunks, rotten branches, or heaps of rotting vines. The colors around them changed from green to yellow and orange. The trees became less crooked, and the swamp became strange—it was now flat, without any moss or mud piles. The grass alongside the road became softer and more lush, not a blade out of place, as if someone had chosen and planted them one by one.

Nava stopped midword, sniffed the air, looked around, and said matter of factly, "We should hide. Looks like there's nowhere to hide around here . . ."

"Is someone coming?" Candide asked.

"A lot of them are coming, but I don't know what they are . . . They aren't deadlings, but we should still hide. We don't have to hide, of course, they are already close anyway, and besides, there's nowhere to hide around here. Let's step off the trail and watch . . ." She sniffed the air again. "It's an unpleasant kind of smell—doesn't smell dangerous, it doesn't, but I wish it were gone . . . Don't you smell it, Silent Man? It reeks of rotten ferment—like there's a pot of rotten, moldy ferment right in front of your nose . . . There they are! Hey, they're little, they aren't scary, you can just chase them away . . . *Ooh-ooh-ooh!*"

"Be quiet," said Candide, taking a good look at them.

At first, he thought that there were white turtles crawling toward them along the trail. Then he realized that he had never seen animals like this before. They looked like giant opaque amoebas or very young tree slugs, except that tree slugs didn't have pseudopods and were actually a bit bigger. There were a lot of them, and they were crawling single file, at a good pace—dexterously projecting pseudopods, then pouring their bodies into them.

They were soon very close—they were white and shiny, and Candide also noticed the sharp, unfamiliar odor and stepped off the trail, pulling Nava after him. The amoeba-slugs crawled past them one by one, paying no attention to them. They turned out to be twelve in number; Nava couldn't resist and kicked the twelfth one with the heel of her foot. The slug nimbly retracted its behind and began to hop. Nava was ecstatic and was about to catch up to it and give it another kick, but Candide grabbed her by the clothes and held her back.

"They are so funny!" said Nava. "And look at them crawl—they look just like people walking, they do . . . I wonder where they are going? They are probably going to that sly village, Silent Man, they are probably from that village, and now they are coming back, but the Surpassment happened there already, and they don't know it . . . They'll hover by the water for a bit, then they'll come back. Where will they go, poor things? Maybe they'll go look for another village? . . . Hey!" she shouted. "Come back! Your village is gone, there's nothing but a lake there now!"

"Be quiet," said Candide. "Let's go. They don't understand your language, so don't waste your breath."

They kept going. The slugs had made the trail a bit slippery. We met, then we went our separate ways, thought Candide. We met, but our paths didn't cross. And I got out of the way. I did, and they did not. This fact suddenly seemed to take on an outsize significance. They are small and helpless, and I'm big and strong, but I stepped off the trail and let them go by, and now I'm thinking about them, whereas they went past, and they probably don't even remember me. Because the forest is their home, and there are all sorts of things in the forest. Like a house can contain cockroaches, bedbugs, and lice, or even a foolish stray butterfly. Or there might be a fly banging against a window, trying to get out . . . You know, it's not true that flies bang against windows. When a fly does that, it imagines that it's flying. And I'm imagining that I'm walking. Simply because I'm moving my legs . . . From the outside, I probably look ridiculous and . . . how can I put it . . . pitiable . . . pitiful . . . What's the right word . . .

"We'll come to a lake soon," said Nava. "Let's hurry, since I want something to eat and drink. Maybe you could catch me some fish . . ."

They went quicker. The reed thickets began. Fine, thought Candide, maybe I do look like a fly. Do I also look like a human being? He remembered Karl, and remembered that Karl hadn't looked like Karl. It could very well be, he thought calmly. It could very well be that I'm a completely different man than the one who crashed his helicopter all those years ago. Except in that case I have no idea why I'm still banging against the window. After all, when *that* had happened to Karl, he was probably no longer doing so. How strange it will be when I get to the biological research station and they first lay their eyes on me. I'm glad this has occurred to me. I should think long and hard about this. I'm glad it's still a long way off, and that I won't be getting to the biological research station anytime soon . . .

They came to a fork in the road. One side seemed to lead to the lake, while the other made a sharp turn and went off somewhere to the side.

"Let's not go that way," said Nava, "it goes uphill, and I want a drink."

The trail became narrower and narrower, then it became a trench, finally getting completely buried in the thickets. Nava stopped.

"You know, Silent Man," she said, "maybe we shouldn't go to that lake? I have a bad feeling about that lake, something's wrong with it. I think it's not actually a lake, it's not all water, there's something else there—a lot of it."

"But there's water, too, right?" asked Candide. "You did say you wanted a drink. And I could do with one myself."

"There's water, too," Nava admitted reluctantly. "But it's warm water. Bad water. Dirty water . . . You know what, Silent Man, stay here a bit, you make too much noise when you walk, I can't hear a thing for all the noise that you make, stay here a bit and wait for me, and I'll call for you, I'll whistle like a hopper. Do you know how hoppers whistle? That's how I'll whistle. And you stay here, or even better, sit a bit . . ."

She dived into the reeds and disappeared from view. And then Candide became aware of the deafening cotton-wool silence that reigned here. The insects weren't buzzing, the swamp wasn't sighing or wheezing, the forest animals weren't calling, and the hot, damp air was still. This wasn't the dry silence of the sly village, which had been like the silence behind a theater curtain at midnight. The silence here was like being underwater. Candide carefully crouched down, pulled a few blades of grass out of the ground, rubbed them between his fingers, and then he suddenly saw that the soil here must be edible. He tugged a tuft of grass out of the ground, complete with soil and roots, and began to eat. The dirt satisfied both his hunger and his thirst—it was salty and cool. Cheese, thought Candide. Yes, cheese . . . What is cheese, anyway? Swiss cheese, processed cheese. Hard cheese. How strange . . .

Then Nava silently emerged from the reeds. She crouched next to him and also began to eat, quickly and neatly. Her eyes were very wide.

"It's a good thing that we ate here," she said finally. "Do you want to see what kind of lake it is? Because I want to see it one more time, but I'm scared to go alone. It's that same lake Crookleg always talks about, I thought he was making it up, I did, or that he imagined it, and it turns out it was true, unless maybe I imagined it myself . . ."

"Let's go take a look," Candide said.

The lake turned out to be about fifty yards away. Candide and Nava followed the muddy ditch and pushed the reeds out of the way. There was a thick layer of white fog over the water. The water was warm, maybe even hot, but it was pure and clear. It smelled of food. The fog was slowly undulating to a regular beat, and in a minute, Candide felt his head spin. There was somebody in the fog. People. Lots of people. They were all naked and lying completely motionless on top of the water. The fog was rhythmically rising and falling, first revealing then hiding the yellowish-white bodies with their heads thrown back—the people weren't swimming, they were lying on top of the water, like on a beach. Candide shuddered. "Let's go," he whispered, grabbing Nava's hand and dragging her away. They climbed back up and came back to the trail.

"They aren't drowned," said Nava. "Crookleg got it wrong, he did, they were just swimming here, then a hot spring hit, and they all got cooked . . . It's very terrible, Silent Man," she said after a pause. "I don't even want to talk about it . . . And there are so many of them, a whole village's worth . . ."

They came to the fork and stopped.

"Do we go uphill?" asked Nava.

"Yes," Candide said. "We go uphill."

They turned right and started to climb up the slope.

"And they were all women," said Nava. "Did you notice?"

"Yes," Candide said.

"That's the most terrible thing, that's the thing I just can't understand. Or maybe . . ." Nava looked at Candide. "Or maybe it's the deadlings, they are the ones who drive them there.

The deadlings probably drive them to this lake, then they cook them . . . Listen, Silent Man, why in the world did we leave the village? If we just sat tight in the village, we'd have never seen all this. We'd have thought that Crookleg made it all up, we'd have lived in peace, but no, you really had to go to the City . . . What did you have to go to the City for?"

"I don't know," said Candide.

8.

CANDIDE

They were lying in the bushes at the edge of the grove and watching the top of the hill through the leaves. The hill sloped gently, and it was bare except for a cloud of lilac fog that capped its peak. It was out in the open, a gusty wind was blowing and chasing gray clouds across the sky, and there was a drizzle of rain. The lilac fog was motionless, as if there were no wind at all. It was rather chilly, even cold, they had gotten soaked, they were shivering and cringing from the cold, their teeth were chattering, but they could no longer leave: there were three deadlings standing twenty yards away, as upright as statues, their black mouths wide open, and they were also watching the top of the hill with their empty eyes. The deadlings had gotten there about five minutes ago. Nava had sensed them and had been about to bolt, but Candide had clamped a hand over her mouth and pressed her into the grass. She was now a bit calmer: she was still shaking hard, but it was from the cold and not out of fear, and she was again watching the hill instead of the deadlings.

There were strange, awe-inspiring tides rising and falling on and around the hill. Enormous swarms of flies would suddenly emerge from the forest with a deep, resonant hum, rush to the top of the hill, and disappear into the fog. The sides of the hill would come alive with columns of ants and spiders; hundreds of slug-amoebas would pour out of the bushes; clouds of colorful beetles and vast numbers of wasps and bees would race confidently through the rain. The wave would ascend to the top of the hill, get sucked into the lilac cloud, and disappear, and there would suddenly be silence. The hill would again become dead and bare, then some time would go by, there would again be a loud rumble, and it would all get expelled from the fog and swoop toward the forest. Only the slugs never came out, but in their place, the most bizarre and unexpected animals streamed down the sides of the hill: rolling hairpuffs, clumsy armeaters staggering along on their fragile legs, and also some creatures he'd never seen before—colorful, many-eyed, naked, and shiny, not obviously insect or mammal . . . And there would again be silence, and then everything would start all over again, and then again and again, at a terrifyingly intense tempo, with an apparently endless energy, which made it seem like this would continue forever, at the same tempo and with the same kind of energy . . . A young hippocetus once clambered out of the fog with a terrible roar, and a number of times, deadlings ran out and immediately rushed into the forest, leaving white trails of cooling steam behind them. And the motionless lilac cloud continued devouring and regurgitating, devouring and regurgitating, regularly and relentlessly, like a machine.

Crookleg said that the City stands on a hill. Maybe this is the City—maybe this is what they call the City. Yes, this is probably the City. But what does it mean? What is it for? And this strange tumult . . . I expected something like this . . . Nonsense, I didn't expect anything like this. I had only thought about the masters, and where are they here? Candide looked over at the deadlings. Maybe I was wrong, thought Candide. Maybe they are actually the masters. I'm probably always wrong. I've completely forgotten how to think in this place. If any thoughts ever do occur to me, then it immediately turns out that I'm incapable of connecting them . . .

Not a single slug has emerged from the fog. Question: why hasn't a single slug emerged from the fog? . . . No, that's the wrong question. First things first. What I'm looking for is the source of rational activity . . . Wrong, wrong again. I'm not the least bit interested in the source of rational activity. I'm just looking for someone who can help me get home. Someone who can help me cross seven hundred miles of forest. Someone who would at least tell me which way to go . . . The deadlings must have masters—I'm looking for those masters. I'm looking for the source of rational activity.

He cheered up a bit: that sounded relatively coherent. Let's start at the beginning. We'll think it all through, slowly and carefully. Now is not the time to hurry; now is the time to think things through, slowly and carefully. The deadlings must have masters, because the deadlings aren't people, and the deadlings aren't animals. Therefore, someone must have made the deadlings. If they aren't people . . . Actually, why aren't they people? He rubbed his forehead. I've already worked this out. It was a long time ago, back in the village. In fact, I've worked it out twice, because the first time I forgot the solution, and this time I've forgotten the proof . . .

He shook his head as hard as he could, and Nava very softly shushed him. He quieted down and lay still for a while, burying his face in the wet grass.

I've already proven why they aren't animals . . . The high temperature . . . Nonsense, that's not it . . . He suddenly came to the horrifying realization that he didn't even remember what deadlings looked like. All he could remember were their burning hot bodies and the sharp pain in his hands. He turned his head and looked at the deadlings. Well, then. I shouldn't be thinking, I shouldn't even be allowed to think, right when I'm supposed to be thinking harder than ever. Time to eat; I've already heard that story, Nava; we're leaving the day after tomorrow, that's about all I'm good for. But I did leave! And I'm here! And now I'm going to see the City. Whatever the City may be. My brain has become overgrown with forest. I don't understand a thing . . .

Got it. I was going to the City so they'd explain everything to me: the Surpassment, the deadlings, the Big Soil Loosening, the lakes full of drowned people. It turned out that none of it was true, it was all lies, it was all wrong, you can't trust anyone . . . I was hoping that if I got to the City, they'd tell me how to get back to my people, since the old man always says the City knows all. And there's no way it wouldn't know about our bio-logical research station, about the Administration. Even Crookleg constantly goes on about the Devil's Cliffs and flying villages . . . But how can a lilac cloud explain anything? How awful it would be if it turned out that the lilac cloud is master here. Why am I saying it *would be* awful? It *is* awful! It does suggest itself, Silent Man: the lilac fog is master everywhere here, remember? And it's not really fog at all . . .

So that's what it is, that's why people have been herded into the bush and into the swamps like animals, why they've been drowned in lakes; they were too weak, they didn't get it, and even if someone did get it, they couldn't do anything to stop it . . . Before I'd been herded, back when I was home, someone gave some very convincing proofs that contact between humanoid and nonhumanoid intelligences is impossible. Yes, it's impossible. Of course it's impossible. And now there's no one to tell me how to get home . . . Contact between me and humans is also impossible, and I can prove it. Maybe I'll figure out how to see the Devil's Cliffs—it's said that you can see them sometimes, if you climb the right tree in the right season, but you first you need to find the right tree, a proper, normal tree. One that doesn't jump. And that doesn't push you away. And that doesn't try to poke you in the eye. And in any case, there doesn't exist a tree that would allow me to see the biological research station . . . The biological research station? . . . The *bi-o-log-i-cal re-search sta-tion* . . . He forgot what a biological research station was.

The forest began to hum, buzz, crackle, and sputter again, and vast numbers of flies and ants again rushed toward the lilac dome. One swarm passed over their heads, strewing the bushes with barely twitching weak insects and motionless dead ones, all of them banged up in the crush. Candide got an unpleasant burning feeling in his arm and glanced down. His elbow was partially buried in the loose soil, and delicate filaments of mycelium had twined themselves around it. Candide rubbed them away indifferently with the palm of his hand. The Devil's Cliffs are just a mirage, he thought. They don't exist. Since they tell stories about the Devil's Cliffs, that means it's all lies, that they don't exist, and now I don't even know what I actually came here for . . .

He heard familiar fearsome snorting from the side. Candide turned his head. A full-grown hippocetus was staring dully at the hill, standing simultaneously behind seven different trees. One of the deadlings suddenly sprang to life, turned inside out, and took a few steps toward the hippocetus. There was more snorting, trees creaked, and the hippocetus went away. Even the hippocetuses are afraid of deadlings, thought Candide. Who isn't afraid of them? How do I find the ones who aren't afraid? . . . Flies are roaring. How silly, how absurd. Flies are roaring. Bees are roaring . . .

"It's my mom!" Nava suddenly whispered. "My mom is coming . . ."

She had gotten up onto all fours and was looking over her shoulder. Her face expressed utter astonishment and disbelief. And Candide saw three women come out of the forest and head to the foot of the hill without noticing the deadlings.

"Mom!" Nava screeched in a voice not her own, leaped over Candide, and bolted away to intercept them. Then Candide also jumped up, and it felt to him as if the deadlings were very close, as if he could feel the heat of their bodies.

There are three of them, he thought. Three . . . One would be plenty. He was watching the deadlings. I'm done for, he thought.

What a silly way to die. What did those biddies have to show up here for? Damn women, they always screw things up.

The deadlings closed their mouths, and their heads were slowly rotating to follow Nava. Then they all stepped forward at the same time, and Candide forced himself to leap out of the bushes toward them.

"Get back!" he yelled at the women, without turning around. "Go away! Deadlings!"

The deadlings were huge, broad shouldered, brand new— there wasn't a single scratch on them, not even a hangnail. Their impossibly long arms touched the grass. Without taking his eyes off them, Candide stopped and blocked their path. The deadlings were looking over his head, moving confidently and deliberately toward him, while he backed up, retreated, continuing to delay the inevitable beginning and the inevitable end, fighting nervous nausea, unable to bring himself to stop. Nava was screaming behind his back: "Mom! It's me. Mom, over here!" Silly women, why don't they run? Are they petrified with fear? . . . Stop, he told himself, stop right now! He couldn't make himself stop. Nava is behind you, he thought. And those three idiots. Fat, sleepy, careless idiots . . . And Nava . . . What are they to me, anyway? he thought. Crookleg would have long since decamped on his one good leg, never mind Big Fist. Whereas I have to stop. It's not fair. But I *have* to stop. Stop this instant! . . . He couldn't make himself stop, and he despised himself for it, and he praised himself for it, and he hated himself for it, and he kept backing up.

The deadlings were the ones who stopped. They stopped instantly, as though responding to a command. The one walking in front froze with its foot in the air, then slowly, as if indecisively, lowered it to the ground. Candide, continuing to back up, glanced over his shoulder. Nava was hanging on a woman's neck, her legs were thrashing in the air, and the woman seemed to be smiling and patting her on the back. The other two women stood calmly nearby, watching them. They weren't looking at the deadlings or at the hill. They weren't even looking at Candide—a strange, unshaven man who might be a thief . . . Meanwhile, the deadlings were standing very still, like ancient, primitive statues, as if they'd become rooted to the ground, as if there were no women left in the forest for them to grab and haul off wherever they'd been ordered to, and pillars of steam were rising from beneath their feet, like smoke from a sacrificial fire.

Then Candide turned around and walked toward the women. No, he plodded rather than walked, no longer believing his eyes, his ears, or his thoughts. An aching, tangled mass pulsed beneath his skull, and his whole body hurt from the strain of his brush with death.

"Run," he said from afar. "Run away before it's too late, what are you waiting for?" He was already aware that this was gibberish, but the inertia of duty carried him along, and he kept muttering mechanically, "There are deadlings here, run, I'll slow them down . . ."

They paid no attention to him. It wasn't that they didn't hear him or see him—a young woman who was at most two years older than Nava, her legs still thin and coltish, looked him over and gave him a very friendly smile—but he didn't matter to them at all; it was as if he were a big stray dog, the kind that roam all over for no particular reason and are happy to hang around people for hours, waiting for God knows what.

"Why aren't you running away?" Candide said quietly. He no longer expected an answer, and he didn't get one.

"*Tsk, tsk, tsk* . . ." the third woman was saying, laughing and shaking her head. She was pregnant. "Who would have thought it? Would you have thought it?" she asked the younger one. "I wouldn't have either. My dear," she said to Nava's mother, "and how was it? Did he pant a lot? Or did he just writhe and sweat like a pig?"

"You're wrong," said the young woman. "He was gorgeous, wasn't he? He was fresh as the dawn, and he smelled like flowers . . ."

"Like a lily," the pregnant one echoed. "His aroma made your head spin, and the touch of his paws sent shivers up your spine . . . Did you have time to say 'Oh!'?"

The young woman tittered. Nava's mother was smiling reluctantly. They were well fed, healthy, strangely clean, as if they had just bathed—they really had just bathed: the short hair on all of their heads was wet, and their baggy yellow clothes clung to their wet bodies. Nava's mother was the shortest and seemed to be the oldest. Nava was hugging her around the waist and pressing her face into her mother's chest.

"Shows what you know," said Nava's mother with forced disdain. "You don't know a thing about it. Just a pair of ignoramuses, you two."

"That's all right," the pregnant woman said instantly. "How could we know about it? That's why we're asking you . . . Tell us, please—what was the root of love like?"

"Was it bitter?" asked the young woman, and tittered again.

"Exactly!" said the pregnant one. "The fruit is rather sweet, if unwashed . . ."

"Don't worry, we'll wash it," said Nava's mother. "Do you know if they've cleaned the Spider Pool? Or will we have to carry her into the valley?"

"The root was bitter," the pregnant woman told the younger one. "She doesn't like to think about it. How odd—and they say it's unforgettable! Listen, my dear, don't you dream about him?"

"It's not funny," said Nava's mother. "It's nauseating."

"Are we trying to be funny?" said the pregnant one, wide-eyed. "We're merely curious."

"What a fascinating story," said the young woman, flashing her teeth. "Do tell us more . . ."

Candide listened eagerly, trying to discover the hidden meaning of this conversation, but he couldn't understand a thing. He just saw that the two women were making fun of Nava's mother, that they had gotten under her skin, that she was trying to hide it or change the subject, and that she wasn't having any luck. Nava had lifted her head and was closely watching the conversation, shifting her gaze between the participants.

"You'd think that you were born in the lake," Nava's mother said to the pregnant woman with now frank irritation.

"Of course not," she said. "But I never had the opportunity to become so broadly educated, and my daughter"—she patted her stomach—"will be born in the lake. That's the difference."

"Why don't you leave my mom alone, you fat hag?" Nava said suddenly. "Take a look at yourself, the state of you, before you pester people! Just you wait, I'll tell my husband, he'll take a stick to your fat ass, then you'll leave us alone! . . ."

All three women roared with laughter.

"Silent Man!" bawled Nava. "Why are they laughing at me?!"

The women looked at Candide, continuing to laugh. Nava's mother regarded him with surprise, the pregnant one with indifference, and he wasn't sure about the young woman, but she seemed to be looking at him with interest.

"Who's this Silent Man?" Nava's mother said.

"He's my husband," said Nava. "Look how nice he is. He saved me from the thieves."

"What do you mean, husband?" the pregnant woman said with distaste. "Don't make things up, child."

"Who's making things up?" Nava said instantly. "Why are you sticking your long nose where it doesn't belong? What's it to you? Not your husband, is he? I'm not talking to you, anyway, I'll have you know. I'm talking to my mom. Butting in, like that old man, without asking, without permission . . ."

"Tell me," the pregnant woman asked Candide. "Tell me, are you really her husband?"

Nava quieted down. Her mother wrapped her arms around her tightly and held her close. She was looking at Candide with horror and disgust. Only the young woman continued to smile, and her smile was so nice and so kind that it was she Candide addressed in reply. "No, of course not," he said. "She's no wife of mine. She's my daughter . . ." He wanted to tell them that Nava had nursed him to health, that he loved her, and that he was very glad that everything had worked out so well, even if he didn't understand a thing.

But the girl suddenly tittered and then burst into laughter, waving her arms. "I knew it," she howled. "He isn't the girl's husband . . . He's that one's husband!" she said, pointing to Nava's mother. "He's . . . her . . . husband! I can't take it!"

A look of cheerful astonishment appeared on the pregnant woman's face, and she began ostentatiously looking Candide up and down. "*Tsk, tsk, tsk* . . ." she began in the same tone as before.

But Nava's mother said nervously, "Stop it! I've had enough of your nonsense! Go away," she told Candide. "Go, go, what are you waiting for? Go back into the forest!"

"Who would have thought," the pregnant one crooned softly, "that the root of love could turn out to be so bitter . . . so dirty . . . so hairy . . ." She noticed that Nava's mother was giving her a furious look and waved her off. "I'm done, I'm done," she said. "Don't be mad, my dear. I was only teasing. We're just very pleased that you found your daughter. It's such an incredible stroke of luck."

"Are we going to work or not?" said Nava's mother. "Or are we just going to stand around chattering?"

"I'm coming, don't be mad," said the young woman. "The exodus is just about to start." She nodded, smiled at Candide again, and ran effortlessly up the hill.

Candide watched her run—she ran flawlessly and professionally, unlike a woman. She got to the top and, without coming to a halt, dived into the lilac fog.

"They haven't cleaned the Spider Pool yet," the pregnant woman said, concerned. "Darn the eternal mess with the builders . . . What are we going to do?"

"It's all right," Nava's mother said. "We'll walk to the valley."

"I understand, but you have to admit, it's very silly—breaking our backs carrying an almost fully grown person into the valley, when we have our own pool." She gave a sharp shrug, then suddenly winced.

"You should sit down," said Nava's mother, looking around for something, then she extended a hand toward the deadlings and snapped her fingers.

One of the deadlings immediately came to life and ran up to them, its feet slipping on the grass in its haste, then it fell onto its knees and suddenly underwent a strange transformation, stretching out, curving, and flattening. Candide blinked—the deadling was gone, and in its place was a cozy and comfortable-looking chair.

The pregnant woman, grunting with relief, lowered herself onto its soft seat and threw her head back onto its soft backrest. "It's almost time," she purred, stretching her legs out with plea-sure. "It better be soon . . ."

Nava's mother crouched in front of her daughter and looked her in the eye. "You've grown up," she said. "Gone wild. Are you happy to see me?"

"Of course," Nava said uncertainly. "You're my mom. I saw you in my dreams every night. And this is Silent Man, Mom . . ." And Nava began to talk.

Candide was looking around, gritting his teeth. This wasn't a delirious dream, as he had hoped at first. This was something very ordinary and very natural; it was merely unfamiliar to him—but then, the forest was full of unfamiliar things. He would have to get used to this, just like he'd had to get used to the buzzing in his head, to the edible soil, and to everything else. These are the masters, he thought. They aren't afraid of anything. They control the deadlings. Therefore, they are the masters. There-fore, they are the ones who send the deadlings after women. Therefore, they are the ones . . . He looked at the women's wet hair. Therefore . . . And Nava's mother, who'd been taken away by the deadlings . . .

"Where do you go swimming?" he asked. "What for? Who are you? What do you want?"

"What?" said the pregnant woman. "Listen, my dear, he's asking something."

Nava's mother said to her daughter, "Hold on a second, I can't hear a thing with you chattering . . . What did you say?" she asked the pregnant woman.

"This goat," she said. "He wants something."

Nava's mother looked at Candide. "What could he want?" she said. "He probably wants to eat. They always want to eat, you know, they eat an awful lot, I have no idea why they need all that food—they don't do anything, after all."

"Silly goat," said the pregnant woman. "The poor goat wants some grass. *Me-e-eh!* You know"—she turned to Nava's mother—"this is actually a person from the White Cliffs. We've been coming across them more and more. How do they get down here?"

"It's harder to figure out how they get back up there. I've seen them come down myself. They fall. Some die, and some survive."

"Mom," Nava said, "why are you looking at him like that? This is Silent Man! Say something nice to him, or you'll hurt his feelings, you will. I'm surprised his feelings aren't hurt already, if I were him, my feelings would have been hurt a long time ago . . ."

The hill roared again, and clouds of black insects blotted out the sky. Candide couldn't hear anything, he could only see Nava's mother's lips moving as she tried to convince Nava of something, and the pregnant woman's lips moving as she spoke to him, and the expression on her face really did look as if she were speaking to a domesticated goat who had gotten into the vegetable patch. Then the roar died down.

". . . except so very filthy," the pregnant woman was saying. "Aren't you ashamed of yourself?" She turned away and began watching the hill.

Deadlings were crawling out of the cloud on all fours. They moved clumsily and tentatively, constantly falling down and butting their heads into the ground. The young woman was walking between them, bending over, touching them, prodding them, and one by one, they would get up off their knees, stand up, and go off into the forest—stumbling at first, then walking more and more confidently.

These are the masters, Candide kept telling himself. These are the masters. I don't believe it. What choice do I have? He looked at Nava. She was asleep. Her mother was sitting on the grass, and Nava was curled up asleep beside her, holding her hand.

"Weak, the lot of them," said the pregnant woman. "It's time to clean everything again. Look at them stumble . . . You can't finish the Surpassment with workers like this."

Nava's mother replied, and they began a conversation that Candide couldn't understand. He could only make out certain words, just like with Hearer's ramblings. So he simply stood there and watched the young woman coming down the hill, dragging a clumsy armeater by the paw. Why am I still here? he thought. I needed something from them; they are the masters, after all . . . "I'm just standing here," he spoke angrily out loud. "They've stopped trying to chase me away, so I'm standing here. Like a deadling." The pregnant woman glanced at him, then turned away.

The young woman approached and said something, pointing at the armeater, and the two women began to inspect the monster, the pregnant one even rising slightly out of her chair. The giant armeater, terror of the village children, was squeaking plaintively, feebly trying to escape, and helplessly opening and closing its terrible jaws. Nava's mother grabbed its lower jaw and gave it a confident, hard twist. The armeater gave a small sob and froze in place, a yellowish film covering its eyes.

The pregnant woman was speaking: ". . . This place clearly doesn't have enough . . . Remember this, girl . . . The jaws are weak, the eyes don't fully open . . . it certainly will not be able to endure . . . therefore, it is useless, and perhaps even harmful, like any mistake . . . We need to clean up—to relocate and tidy up everything here . . ."

". . . the hill . . . it's dry and dusty . . ." replied the young woman. ". . . the edge of the forest . . . I don't know that yet . . . You were telling me something very different . . ."

". . . try it yourself," said Nava's mother. ". . . you'll notice immediately . . . Try it, try it!"

The girl dragged the armeater off to the side, stepped back a yard, and began to look at it. It looked as if she were taking aim. Her face became serious and even tense. The armeater was swaying back and forth on its clumsy paws, glumly moving its one working jaw, creaking slightly. "See?" said the pregnant woman.

The young woman came right up to the armeater and crouched slightly in front of it, her hands on her knees. The creature began to shake, then it suddenly collapsed with its paws splayed out, as if someone had dropped a hundred-pound weight on it. The women laughed. Nava's mother said, "That's enough, why don't you believe us?"

The girl didn't answer. She was standing over the armeater, watching it slowly and cautiously try to regain its footing and get up. Her facial features sharpened. She yanked the creature up, got it back onto its feet, and made a motion as if she were going to embrace it. A jet of lilac fog flowed from between her palms into the armeater's body. The armeater squealed, writhed, arched, and kicked its legs. It was trying to get away, escape, save itself; it was darting back and forth as the young woman followed it, hanging over it, then it fell, its legs unnaturally intertwined, and began to tie itself into a knot. The women were silent. The armeater turned into a colorful tangled mass oozing slime, then the young woman walked away from it and said, looking off to the side, "What a piece of crap . . ."

"We need to clean up, we need to clean up," the pregnant woman said, rising. "Get started, don't put it off. Did you understand everything?"

The young woman nodded.

"Then we're going to go, and you should start immediately."

The young woman turned around and walked up the hill toward the lilac cloud. She paused by the tangled mass, grabbed hold of a feebly twitching paw, and went on, dragging the bundle behind her.

"She's a fine helpmate," said the pregnant woman. "That was well done."

"She will rule," Nava's mother said, also getting up. "She has character. Well, we better go . . ."

Candide could barely hear them. He still couldn't take his eyes off the black puddle that remained where the armeater had been tied into a knot. She didn't even touch it, she didn't lay a finger on it, she just stood over it and did as she pleased with it. So sweet, so gentle, so nice . . . Didn't even lay a finger on it . . . Do I have to get used to this, too? Yes, he thought. I do . . .

He began to watch as Nava's mother and the pregnant woman carefully stood Nava up, took her by the hand, and led her, still asleep, into the forest and down toward the lake. They never did notice him; they never did say anything to him. He looked at the puddle again. He felt small, pitiful, and helpless, but he gathered his courage and went down after them; he caught up to them and, cold sweat pouring down his body, started to walk two paces behind them. Something hot approached him from behind. He looked around and sprang off to the side. A huge deadling was at his heels—heavy, hot, stealthy, and mute. Now, now, thought Candide, it's just a robot, a servant. Well done, Candide, he thought suddenly, you figured it out. I've forgotten how, but it doesn't matter, what matters is that I got it, that I thought of it . . . I put it all together and thought of it myself . . . I have brains, you see? he mouthed silently, looking at the women's backs. You aren't so special . . . I'm capable of a thing or two myself.

The women were talking about someone who got in over her head and became a laughingstock. They were amused by something; they were laughing. They were walking through the forest and laughing. As if they were walking down a village street, on their way to a get-together. Meanwhile, the forest surrounded them, and they weren't even following a trail but walking on the pale, thick grass that always contained tiny flowers—the kind that scatter spores that penetrate the skin and germinate in the body. But they were giggling and chattering and gossiping, and

Nava was walking between them and sleeping, but they had done something to her so that she'd walk quite confidently, almost without stumbling . . .

The pregnant woman glanced behind her, saw Candide, and told him indifferently, "Why are you still here? Go back into the forest, go . . . Why are you following us?"

Yes, Candide thought. Why? What are they to me? No, I did want something, I wanted to ask them something . . . No, that's not it . . . Nava! he remembered suddenly. He realized that he'd lost Nava. There was nothing to be done. Nava is leaving with her mother, and that's as it should be—she's leaving with the masters. And what about me? I'm staying. So why am I following them? Am I seeing her off? But she's asleep; they put her to sleep. He felt a wave of despair. Farewell, Nava, he thought.

They came to the fork in the road, and the women turned left, toward the lake. Toward the lake with the drowned women. They are the drowned women . . . It had all been lies again, it had all been mixed up . . . They walked past the place where Candide had waited for Nava and had eaten the soil. That was a very long time ago, thought Candide, almost as long ago as the biological research station . . . Biological . . . research . . . station . . . He was barely managing to drag himself along; if there hadn't been a deadling at his heels, he probably would have already fallen behind. Then the women stopped and looked at him. They were surrounded by reeds, and the ground beneath their feet was warm and marshy. Nava was standing there with her eyes closed, swaying a tiny bit, while the women looked at him thoughtfully. Then he remembered.

"How do I get to the biological research station?" he asked.

They looked astonished, and he realized that he had spoken in his native tongue. He was surprised himself; he couldn't even remember when he had last used it.

"How do I get to the White Cliffs?" he asked.

The pregnant woman said with an unpleasant chuckle, "That's what this goat wants, I see . . ." She wasn't talking to him, she was talking to Nava's mother. "It's funny, they don't understand a thing. Not a single one of them understands a thing. Imagine them strolling off to the White Cliffs, then suddenly finding themselves in a war zone!"

"They are rotting alive over there," Nava's mother said thoughtfully. "They are walking around and rotting as they walk, and they never realize that they aren't moving but staying in one place . . . We may as well let him go, it's only good for the Soil Loosening. If he rots—that's good. If he dissolves—that's good for it, too. Or maybe he's protected? Are you protected?" she asked Candide.

"I don't understand," said Candide dispiritedly.

"My dear, what are you asking him? How could he be protected?"

"Anything is possible," said Nava's mother. "I've heard of such things."

"That was just talk," said the pregnant woman. She took another good look at Candide. "You know," she said, "he might well be of more use here . . . Remember what the Instructresses said yesterday?"

"Ahh," said Nava's mother. "It's possible . . . He might well be . . . All right . . . All right, let him stay."

"Yes, stay," Nava said suddenly. She wasn't sleeping anymore, and she could also tell that something was wrong. "You should stay, Silent Man, you shouldn't go anywhere, why would you leave now? You wanted to get to the City, and this lake is the City, right, Mom? . . . Or did Mom hurt your feelings? Don't be hurt, she's usually nice, except today she's mean for some reason . . . it must be the heat . . ."

Her mother caught her arm. Candide saw the familiar lilac cloud quickly condense around her head. Her eyes momentarily glazed over and closed, then she said, "Come on, Nava, they are already waiting for us."

"What about Silent Man?"

"He'll stay here . . . There's absolutely nothing for him to do in the City."

"But I want him to come with me! Don't you understand, Mom, he's my husband, they gave him to me for a husband, he's been my husband for a long time . . ."

Both women grimaced. "Let's go, let's go," said Nava's mother. "You don't understand anything yet . . . No one needs him, he's unnecessary, they are all unnecessary, they are a mistake . . . Come on, let's go! Fine, you can visit him afterward . . . if you want to."

Nava was resisting. She could probably sense the same thing Candide was sensing—that they were saying good-bye forever. Her mother was dragging her into the reeds by the hand, and she kept looking back and shouting, "Don't you leave, Silent Man! I'll be back soon, don't you even think about leaving without me, that'd be wrong, that would, that'd be unfair! Maybe you aren't my husband, since they don't like it for some reason, but I'm still your wife, I nursed you back to health, and you have to wait for me! Did you hear me? Wait for me . . ."

He was watching her go, waving feebly, nodding, agreeing, and constantly trying to smile. Farewell, Nava, he thought. Farewell. They disappeared from sight, and only the reeds remained, but he could hear Nava's voice, then she stopped talking, there was a splash, and all was silent. He swallowed the lump in his throat and asked the pregnant woman, "What will you do with her?"

She was still carefully examining him. "What will we do with her?" she repeated pensively. "That's none of your concern, goat, what we'll do with her. She's no longer going to need a husband, anyway. Or a father . . . But what should we do with you? After all, you're from the White Cliffs—we can't just let you go."

"What do you want?" Candide asked.

"What do we want . . . Well, we definitely don't want husbands." She caught Candide's eye and laughed contemptuously. "We don't, we don't, don't worry . . . For once in your life, try not to be a goat. Try to imagine a world without goats . . ." She spoke without thinking—or, rather, she was thinking about something else. "What could you be good for? . . . Tell me, goat, what can you do?"

Something lurked behind all of her words, behind her tone, behind her disdain and her cold imperiousness, something frightening and disagreeable, but it was hard to pinpoint—and for some reason, Candide was reminded of the square black door and of Karl with the two women, who had been similarly cold and imperious.

"Did you hear me?" asked the pregnant woman. "What can you do?"

"I can't do anything," Candide said dully.

"Maybe you know how to command?"

"I knew how to once," Candide said. Go to hell, he thought. Leave me alone. I'm asking you how to get to the White Cliffs, and you won't leave me alone . . . He suddenly realized that he was afraid of her, or he would have left a long time ago. She was master here, and he was the pathetic, dirty, stupid goat.

"You knew how to once . . ." she repeated. "Tell this tree to lie down!"

Candide looked at the tree. It was a big, thick tree with a lush crown of leaves and a shaggy trunk. He shrugged his shoulders.

"All right," she said. "Then kill this tree . . . You can't do that either? Do you even know how to make a living thing dead?"

"To kill it?"

"Not necessarily kill it. Even an armeater can kill things. I mean to make a living thing dead. To force a living thing to be dead. Do you know how?"

"I don't understand," said Candide.

"You don't understand . . . What do you do at those White Cliffs of yours, if you don't even understand that much? You don't know how to make dead things alive either?"

"I don't."

"So what do you know how to do? What were you doing at the White Cliffs, before you fell into the forest? Or did you just stuff yourself and desecrate women?"

"I studied the forest," said Candide.

She looked at him sternly. "Don't you dare lie to me. A single person can't study the forest—it would be like studying the sun. If you don't want to tell the truth, just say so."

"I did study the forest," said Candide. "I studied . . ." He hesitated. "I studied the smallest creatures in the forest. The ones that can't be seen with the naked eye."

"You're lying again," the woman said patiently. "It is impossible to study things that can't be seen with the naked eye."

"It is possible," said Candide. "You just need . . ." He hesitated again. *Microscopes . . . Lenses . . . Instruments . . .* This couldn't be communicated. This couldn't be translated. "If you take a drop of water," he said, "then, if you have the right objects, you can see thousands of tiny creatures in it."

"You don't need any objects for that," said the woman. "I see you've sunk into depravity with your dead things at your White Cliffs. You're degenerating. I've long since noticed that you've lost the ability to see the things in the forest that anyone else can see, even dirty men . . . Wait, are you talking about tiny creatures, or the tiniest creatures? Maybe you're talking about the builders?"

"Maybe," Candide said. "I don't understand you. I'm talking about the tiny creatures that can make people sick, but that can also heal them, that help make food, and that are present everywhere in great number . . . I was trying to figure out how the ones in the forest are made, and what they are like, and what they can do . . ."

"And the ones at the White Cliffs are different, right?" the woman said sarcastically. "But OK, I now understand what it is you do there. You have no power over the builders, of course. Any village idiot can do more than you . . . So what in the world should I do with you? You did come here of your own accord."

"I'll go," Candide said wearily. "I'll go, good-bye."

"No, wait . . . Stop, I tell you!" she shouted, and Candide felt red-hot pincers gripping his elbows from behind. He struggled, but it was pointless. The woman was thinking out loud: "After all, he came here of his own accord. Such things have been known to happen. If I let him go, he'll go back to his village and become completely useless . . . Catching them is pointless . . . But when they come of their own accord . . . You know what I'll do with you?" she said. "I'll give you to the Instructresses for night labors. After all, we've had some successful cases . . . Take him to the Instructresses, take him away!" She waved her hand and slowly waddled into the reeds.

And then Candide felt himself being turned onto the path. His elbows had gone numb, and it seemed to him as if they must have gotten charred. He struggled as hard as he could, and the vise tightened. He didn't understand what was going to happen to him, or where he was going to be taken, or who the Instructresses could be, or what these night labors were, but he was reminded of his two most terrifying impressions: the ghost of Karl in the middle of a wailing crowd, and the armeater being twisted into a colorful knot. He managed to kick the deadling, striking backward, blindly and desperately, knowing that he wouldn't get away with it twice. His foot sank into something soft and hot, then the deadling snorted and loosened its grip. Candide fell face-first into the grass, jumped up, turned around, and screamed—the deadling was already coming straight at him, its impossibly long arms spread wide. He had nothing at hand—not grasskiller, not ferment, not even a stick or a rock. The warm, marshy soil was sliding apart beneath his feet. Then he remembered something and stuck a hand under his shirt, and when the deadling hung over him, he hit it between the eyes with the scalpel, squeezed his eyes tightly shut, and, bringing his whole weight to bear, pulled the blade all the way down to the ground and fell again.

He was lying prone, his cheek pressed against the grass, watching as the deadling stood there swaying, slowly opening like a suitcase along the entire length of its orange body. Then it stumbled and fell backward, flooding everything around it with a thick white liquid, twitched several times, and went still. Then Candide got up and trudged away. Along the path. As far as possible from this place. He could vaguely recall that he wanted to wait here for someone, that he wanted to find something out, that he was planning to do something. But none of that mattered now. What mattered was to get as far as possible from here, although he realized that there would never be any getting away. Not for him, and not for many, many, many others.

9.

PERETZ

Peretz was woken up by discomfort, melancholy, and a weight on his mind and pressure on all his sensory organs that at first seemed unbearable. His discomfort was so acute that it felt like pain, and he gave an involuntary groan as he slowly regained consciousness.

The weight on his mind turned out to be despair and frustration, because the truck wasn't going to the Mainland, it was again not going to the Mainland—it wasn't going anywhere at all. It was standing still with its engine off, cold and dead, its doors open wide. The windshield was covered in trembling water drops, which kept flowing together and streaming down in cold rivulets. The night behind the glass was illuminated by blinding flashes of headlights and searchlights, and he couldn't see anything but these endless, agonizing bursts of light. Nor could he hear anything, which at first made him think that he had gone deaf, and only later did he realize that a deep, polyphonic blare of sirens was exerting a uniform pressure on his eardrums. He started throwing himself around the cab, bumping painfully against levers, ledges, and that damn suitcase; he tried to wipe the glass; he leaned out one door and then the other—but he simply couldn't figure out where he was, what this place was, and what this all meant. We're at war, he thought. My God, we must be at war! . . . The searchlights kept shining into his eyes with malicious delight, and he couldn't see anything except some strange big building, all of whose windows kept lighting up then going dark at the same time. And he also saw lots and lots of large lilac splotches.

An enormous voice suddenly said calmly, as if it were completely quiet: "Attention, attention. All employees must stay in one place by statute six seventy-five dot Pegasus omicron three oh two, directive eight thirteen, for the ceremonial reception of the *padishah* without a special retinue, shoe size fifty-five. Let me repeat. Attention, attention. All employees . . ." The searchlight beams stopped darting around, and Peretz finally managed to make out the familiar arch with the word WELCOME, the dark villas alongside the main street of the Administration, and the people in nightclothes standing in front of the villas, holding kerosene lamps. Then he saw a line of people running nearby, their black cloaks waving behind them as they ran. They were taking up the entire length of the street, stretching some strange pale object across it, and upon examination, Peretz realized that this object was either a fishing or a volleyball net. Then a strained voice screeched into his ear, "What is this truck doing here? Why did you stop there?" He recoiled and saw an engineer wearing a white cardboard mask standing right by his side, with "Libidovich" written on his forehead in indelible pencil, and this engineer clambered right over him, stepping on him with his dirty boots, shoving him in the face with his elbow, grunting and stinking of sweat; he fell into the driver's seat, fumbled for the ignition key, didn't find it, gave a hysterical squeal, and rolled out of the cab through the driver's door. Then all the streetlights went on and it became as light as day, but the people in nightclothes kept standing by the doors of their villas with their kerosene lamps, and everyone was holding a butterfly net, and they were rhythmically waving these nets, as if chasing something invisible away from their doors. Four gloomy black cars, resembling windowless buses, drove past the truck going the opposite way, with some strange mesh blades rotating on their roofs. Then an ancient armored vehicle emerged from an alley and followed close behind them, its rusty turret spinning with a high-pitched whine, the thin barrel of its machine gun moving up and down. The armored vehicle barely managed to squeeze by the truck, and as it did so, a man in coarse calico nightclothes with drawstrings dangling stuck out his head and shouted irritably at Peretz, "What are you doing, pal? Keep going, you're blocking the way!" Then Peretz put his head on his hands and closed his eyes.

I'll never manage to get out of here, he thought dully. No one needs me here, I'm of absolutely no use, but they won't let me out, even if they have to start a war or stage a flood . . .

"Papers, please," said an old man's slow, nasal voice, and someone tapped Peretz on the shoulder.

"What?" said Peretz.

"Your documents. Are they ready?" It was an old man in an oilskin raincoat, with an old Berdan rifle slung across his chest on a peeling metal chain.

"What papers? What documents? Why?"

"Oh, it's you, Mr. Peretz!" said the old man. "Why aren't you complying with the statute? You should have your documents in hand and ready for inspection, like in a museum."

Peretz handed over his identification.

The old man, his elbows resting on the rifle, carefully examined the official seals, checked Peretz's face against the photograph, and said, "Looks like you've lost weight, Herr Peretz. Your face looks gaunt. Must be working too hard . . ." He returned the identification.

"What's going on?" asked Peretz.

"Exactly what should be going on," the old man replied, suddenly growing stern. "It's statute six hundred seventy-five dot Pegasus. That means an escape."

"What escaped? From where?"

"Everything is exactly as described in the statute," said the old man, starting to go down the steps. "There's going to be an explosion any moment now, so you should protect your ears—sit with your mouth open."

"All right," said Peretz. "Thank you."

"Why are you slinking around here, you old geezer?" Truck driver Waldemar's mean voice came from below. "I'll show you documents! Here, take a good look! Had enough yet? Now beat it."

Peretz heard shouting and a clatter of feet, then some people ran past, lugging a cement mixer. Truck driver Waldemar, disheveled, bristling, and with his teeth bared, clambered into the cab. Muttering curses under his breath, he started the engine and loudly slammed the door. The truck took off and sped down the street, going past the people in nightclothes waving their nets. He's going to the garage, thought Peretz. Oh, whatever. But I refuse to touch that suitcase ever again. I won't drag that damn thing around anymore. He prodded it spitefully with the heel of his foot. The vehicle made a sharp turn off the main street, crashed into a barricade constructed out of empty barrels and horse carts, smashed it to pieces, and sped on. For a while, the splintered front of a horse-drawn carriage bounced around on the radiator of the truck, then it tumbled off, crunching beneath the wheels. The truck was now flying through narrow alleys. Waldemar, looking grimly determined, an extinguished cigarette stuck to his lower lip, was spinning the enormous wheel with both hands, putting his whole body into it. No, he's not going to the garage. And he's not going to a workshop. And he's not going to the Mainland. The alleys were dark and empty. Only once did they see someone: cardboard masks with writing on them and splayed-out fingers flashed briefly in the headlights, then everything disappeared again.

"Me and my brilliant ideas," said Waldemar. "I was gonna make a beeline to the Mainland, then I saw that you were asleep, thought I'd drop by the garage, get a game of chess in . . . I'd just found Achilles the locksmith, we grabbed some buttermilk, took a few swigs, set up the chessboard . . . I'd opened with Queen's Gambit, he accepted, all was well . . . I played e4, he played c6. . . . . I told him, you better start praying. And then all hell broke loose . . . Signor Peretz, do you happen to have a cigarette?"

Peretz passed him a cigarette. "What escaped?" he asked. "And where are we going?"

"It's the usual sort of nonsense," said Waldemar, lighting the cigarette. "It happens every year. One of the engineers' machines has run away. And now everyone's been ordered to catch it. There they are, catching it . . ."

They were now out of the residential area. People were wandering over the empty, moonlit wasteland. It looked like they were playing blindman's buff—they were walking around with their knees half bent and their arms spread wide. Everyone was blindfolded. One of them ran right into a post at full speed, and he probably cried out in pain, because all the rest immediately stopped and started cautiously turning their heads back and forth.

"Every year we have bullshit like this," Waldemar was saying. "They have light sensors, and sound detectors, and electronics, and those damn parasite guards on each corner—and for all that, every year some machine manages to make a break for it. And then they tell you, drop everything you're doing and go look for it. And who the hell wants to look for it? Who the hell wants to go near it, I ask? Because if you see it, even out of the corner out of your eye—you're screwed. Either they'll force you to become an engineer, or they'll send you away to pickle mushrooms at some remote forest base, so you don't, God forbid, spill the beans. So folks do their best to wiggle out of it. Some wear blindfolds so they can't see, others have other tricks up their sleeves . . . And the smartest ones just run around and make a racket. They'll ask for documents, they'll search someone, or they'll just climb onto a roof and yell their heads off. That way, it looks like they are keeping busy, but there's no risk."

"Are we trying to catch it, too?" asked Peretz.

"Of course. Everyone's trying to catch it, and so are we. According to the statute, if the escaped mechanism isn't found within six hours, it will be detonated remotely. So that everything stays under wraps. Or it might get in the wrong hands. Did you see the hubbub in the Administration? In six hours, that'll seem like the quiet of a monastery. After all, no one knows what hole this machine may have crawled into. For all you know, it's in your pocket. And it's loaded with powerful explosives—they aren't taking any chances . . . Last year, the machine turned out to be in the bathhouse, and the bathhouse was crammed full of people trying to save their hides. They figured, it's damp, it's out of the way . . . I was there myself. No way is it in the bathhouse, I thought . . . And there I went, sailing right out the window, nice and smooth, like riding a wave. Next thing I know, I'm in a snowbank, with burning beams flying overhead . . ."

They were now driving down a broken-down white road across a plain covered in scraggy grass, illuminated by the weak light of the moon. On their left, in the direction of the Administration, the lights were again frantically rushing to and fro.

"I just don't understand," said Peretz, "how we're supposed to catch it when we don't even know what it looks like . . . We don't know whether it's big or small, whether it's light or dark . . ."

"Watch and learn," promised Waldemar. "You'll see in five minutes. I'll show you how smart people try to catch it. Crap, where's that spot . . . I can't find it. Must have gone too far left. Yep, that's it . . . There's the machine repository, that means we have to go right . . ."

The truck turned off the road and began bouncing over the hummocks. The repository was still on their left—rows and rows of huge, brightly lit containers, like a dead city in the middle of the plain.

It probably couldn't take it anymore. They had jiggled it on vibration tables, they had pensively tortured it, they had dug around in its innards, soldered its delicate nerves; it was suffocating from the smell of resin, it was forced to do stupid things, it had been created to do stupid things, it had been perfected so it would do stupider and stupider stupid things, and at night they left it, spent and tormented, in a hot, dry little room. And at last, it had dared to leave, even though it had known about everything—about the futility of leaving, and about its impending doom. And so it left, laden with suicidal explosives, and now it's standing somewhere in the shade, quietly shifting from foot to mechanical foot, and watching, and listening, and waiting . . . And by now, everything that it has previously only guessed at has probably become absolutely clear to it: that there's no such thing as freedom, whether the door in front of you is locked or unlocked; that the world contains only chaos and stupidity; and that there exists nothing but solitude . . .

"Ah!" Waldemar said with satisfaction. "There you are, my darling. There you are, my precious . . ."

Peretz opened his eyes, but he barely had enough time to see the large black puddle—actually more of a swamp—and to hear the roar of the engine, before a wave of mud reared up in front of them and descended onto the windshield. The engine gave another terrible screech, then stalled. It became very quiet.

"This is how we do it," said Waldemar. "None of the wheels have traction. Like soap in a tub. Get it?" He stuck the cigarette butt into the ashtray and cracked open his door. "There's someone else here," he reported, and shouted, "Hey, pal! How's it going?"

"Going well!" came from the outside.

"Have you caught it?"

"I just caught a cold!" they heard from the outside. "Und five tadpoles."

Waldemar slammed the door, turned the cabin light on, looked at Peretz, winked, pulled a mandolin out from under the seat, and, cocking his head to the right, began to pluck at the strings. "Make yourself at home," he said hospitably. "We'll be here a while—gotta wait for morning, then for the tow truck . . ."

"Thank you," Peretz said obediently.

"Am I bothering you?" Waldemar asked politely.

"No, no," said Peretz. "Go right ahead."

Waldemar threw back his head, gazed upward, and started singing mournfully:

> *I see no limits to my sorrow,*
> *Alone, I wander frantic though the streets.*
> *Tell me, why have you grown cold to me?*
> *Why did you crush my heart beneath your feet?*

The mud was slowly draining from the windshield, and they could now see the swamp, glimmering in the moonlight, and the strangely shaped vehicle protruding from the center of the morass. Peretz turned on the windshield wipers, and was soon astonished to discover that it was their old friend the armored vehicle, and that it had sunk into the bog all the way to the turret.

> *You're now happy with another man,*
> *And I'm alone, weary and frantic.*

Waldemar struck a very loud chord, hit a false note, and cleared his throat.

"Hey, pal," a voice came from the outside. "Got any grub?"

"Why do you ask?" yelled Waldemar.

"We've got buttermilk!"

"I'm not alone!"

"Come on over, the lot of you! There's plenty to go around! We stocked up—we knew what we were in for!"

Truck driver Waldemar turned to Peretz. "What do you say?" he said delightedly. "Shall we? We'll have some buttermilk, maybe play some Ping-Pong . . . How about it?"

"I don't play Ping-Pong," said Peretz.

Waldemar shouted, "Be there in a jiffy! I just need to inflate the boat!"

He scrambled out of the cab with the agility of a monkey and started bustling around in the cargo area, clanking metal, dropping things, and whistling merrily. Then Peretz heard a splash, feet scrabbling down the sides of the truck, and Waldemar's voice coming from somewhere below: "It's ready, Mr. Peretz! Grab the mandolin and leap on over!" There was an inflatable boat floating on the shiny surface of the liquid mud, and Waldemar, holding a large shovel, was standing inside it like a gondolier, looking up at Peretz with a joyous smile.

. . . In the old, rusty armored vehicle from the days of World War I, it's nauseatingly hot, it stinks of hot oil and gasoline, there is a dim lightbulb shining above the commanding officer's metal table, which is covered with carved obscenities, dirty water sloshes underfoot, everyone's feet are cold, the banged-up munitions cabinet is crammed full of buttermilk bottles, everyone is wearing nightclothes and scratching their hairy chests with their paws, everyone is drunk and the mandolin thrums, and the turret gunner in his coarse calico shirt, who doesn't fit below, constantly drops ashes on them from above and occasionally falls down himself, landing on his back, each time saying, "Pardon me for the mix-up . . ." and every single time, people guffaw and hoist him back up . . .

"No thanks, Waldemar," said Peretz, "I'll stay here. I need to do a bit of laundry . . . and I haven't done my exercises yet."

"Ah," Waldemar said with respect, "that's different. Then off I go. Give us a holler as soon as you're done with your laundry, we'll pick you up . . . Just toss me the mandolin."

He floated away with the mandolin, while Peretz stayed there, watching him: at first Waldemar tried to paddle with the shovel, but that only made the boat spin in place, then he began using it to push off, like a pole, and things picked up. He was bathed in the dead light of the moon, and he looked like the last man alive after the last Great Flood, floating between the tops of the tallest buildings—very lonely, searching for a way to escape the solitude, but still full of hope. He floated up to the armored vehicle and banged loudly on its armor; a head popped out of the hatch, roared with cheerful laughter, and pulled him in headfirst. Then Peretz was left alone.

He was all alone, like the only passenger on a night train whose three battered cars limp along a dying branch of the railroad—everything inside creaks and wobbles, the shattered, permanently lopsided windows let in gusts of air and engine fumes, cigarette butts and crumpled bits of paper bounce along the floor, someone's forgotten straw hat swings on the hook, and when the train approaches the end of the line, the only passenger emerges onto the rotting wooden platform and no one is there to meet him, he's absolutely sure no one is there to meet him, and he trudges home, and there he makes himself an omelet using two eggs and old, discolored salami . . .

The armored vehicle suddenly began to shake and bang, flickering beneath fitful flashes of light. Hundreds of glowing multicolored threads arced from the vehicle to the plain, and in the light of the moon and the blaze of the flashes, Peretz saw the ripples spreading outward from the armored vehicle along the smooth mirror surface of the swamp. Someone in white poked a head out of the turret and declared hoarsely, "Kind sirs! Ladies and gentlemen! An international salute! Yours faithfully, Your Excellency, Venerable Duchess Dikobella, I have the honor to remain your obedient servant and technician, can't read the signature!" The armored vehicle shook and gleamed beneath flashes of light again, then it quieted down.

I will let loose against you the fleet-footed vines, thought Peretz. I will call in the jungle to stamp out your accursed lines—the roofs shall fade before it, the house-beams shall fall, and the *Karela*, the bitter *Karela*, shall cover it all.

. . . The forest is approaching, charging up the winding road, scrambling up the steep rock face—there are waves of lilac fog leading the way, and myriads of green tentacles are reaching out of the fog, ensnaring and crushing things, and cloacae are materializing in the middle of streets, and houses are disappearing into bottomless lakes, and jumping trees are standing on concrete runways in front of packed airplanes, in which people, buttermilk bottles, gray top-secret folders, and heavy safes are stacked haphazardly together like bricks, while the ground beneath the cliff is opening up and swallowing it whole . . . It would be so logical and so natural that no one would be surprised, merely frightened, accepting this destruction as the retribution each had long lived in fear of. And Randy would be scurrying between the teetering villas like a spider, looking for Rita so he could finally get what he was after, but it would be too late . . .

Three rockets shot out of the armored vehicle, and a soldierly voice bawled, "Tanks are on the left, cover's on the right! Head for cover, men!" And someone immediately echoed, slurring his words, "Chicks are on the left, cots are on the right! Head f'r th' cots, men!" Then he heard loud guffawing and the clatter of feet, and these no longer sounded the least bit human—it was like an entire herd of breeding stallions was thrashing and kicking inside this metal box, looking for a way out onto the plains where the mares grazed. Peretz opened the door and looked out. They were in the middle of a deep bog—the truck's enormous wheels had sunk into the greasy muck all the way to their hubs. On the other hand, it wasn't far to shore.

Peretz climbed into the cargo area and spent a while walking toward the back gate in the deep shadows characteristic of a moonlit night, his feet clanging and banging on the bottom of this endless steel tub; then he clambered onto the side of the truck and used one of its many ladders to get close to the water. He spent a while dangling over the ice-cold slush, trying to work up his courage, and then, when the armored vehicle's machine gun went off again, he closed his eyes and jumped. The slush began to part beneath him, and it parted for a long time, a very long time, and there was no end in sight, and when he finally felt solid ground beneath his feet, the mud was up to his chest. He brought his entire body to bear on the mud, shoving it out of the way with his knees and pushing off from it with his hands, and at first he just thrashed around without making progress. Then he got used to it and began to move forward, and to his surprise, very soon found himself on dry land.

I'd like to find humans somewhere, he thought. Any humans would do to begin with—tidy, clean-shaven, solicitous, welcoming. I don't need lofty thoughts; I don't need exceptional talents. I don't need breathtaking ambitions and self-denial. I just want for them to throw up their hands in dismay when they see me, and for someone to hurry off to run a bath, and for someone to dash off to get me clean underwear and to put the kettle on, and for no one to ask me for my papers or to demand my autobiography in triplicate, with twenty copies of my fingerprints attached, and for no one to rush to the phone and report to the authorities in a dramatic whisper that a man has just arrived at the door, covered in mud from head to toe, and he calls himself Peretz but he's extremely unlikely to be Peretz, because Peretz has left for the Mainland, and the order about it has already been written and will be posted tomorrow . . .

They also don't need to be principled opponents or proponents of anything. They don't need to be principled opponents of drunkenness, as long as they aren't drunkards themselves. They don't need to be principled proponents of the truth, as long as they don't lie or bad-mouth you either to your face or behind your back. And they shouldn't insist that a man fully conform to certain ideals, and instead accept him and understand him the way he is . . . My God, thought Peretz, do I really want that much?

He went out onto the road and spent a while plodding toward the lights of the Administration. He saw the flashing searchlights, the rushing shadows, and the colorful smoke rising into the sky. Peretz kept walking; water sloshed and squelched in his shoes, his clothes had dried and now felt as stiff as a board and made rustling sounds as he walked, and from time to time layers of mud would slough off his pants and plop onto the road—and every single time, Peretz would think that he had dropped his wallet with all his documents and he'd grab his pocket in a panic. Then, as he was approaching the machine repository, he was suddenly struck by the horrifying thought that his documents must have gotten wet, and all their seals and signatures must have bled, rendering them illegible and incurably suspicious. He stopped and opened his wallet with ice-cold hands, took out all of his identifications, passes, and licenses, and began to examine them in the moonlight. And it turned out that nothing horrible had happened after all, and the only bit of water damage had been sustained by a single lengthy watermarked letter, certifying that its bearer had been fully vaccinated and had been authorized to work with mechanical computing machines. Then he put the documents back into his wallet, separating them carefully with banknotes, and was about to continue forward when he imagined himself emerging onto the main street, where people in cardboard masks and crooked fake beards would grab his hands, blindfold him, stick something in front of his nose, and ask him, "Did you get the scent, employee Peretz?" bawl orders of "Go look for it! Go look!" at him, and egg him on with "*Cherchez*, stupid, *cherchez!*" And having imagined all this, he promptly turned off the road, ducked, and ran toward the machine repository, diving into the shadow of the giant, brightly lit boxes. His feet got tangled in something soft, and he crashed onto a pile of rags and cotton waste.

This place turned out to be warm and dry. The rough walls of the boxes were hot to the touch, and he was first pleased and only then surprised by this. No sounds came from the boxes, but he was reminded of the story about the machines crawling out of the containers by themselves, and he realized that these boxes had a life of their own. This didn't scare him, however—in fact, it made him feel safe. He got comfortable, took off his wet shoes, pulled off his soaking socks, and wiped his feet with the cotton waste. It was so warm, so cozy, and so pleasant here that he thought, How strange, am I really the only one here? Am I really the only one who's figured out that it's much nicer to sit here, where it's warm, than to crawl blindfolded in wastelands or to hang about in a reeking swamp? He leaned back against the hot plywood and realized that he felt like humming. There was a narrow gap above his head, and he could see a strip of pale, moonlit sky containing several faint stars. He could hear crackling and buzzing and the roaring of motors coming from somewhere else, but none of it had anything to do with him.

I wish I could stay here forever, he thought. Since I can't leave for the Mainland, I'll stay here forever. Big deal, machines! We're all machines. Except we must be broken machines, or perhaps badly tuned ones.

Ladies and gentlemen, some people believe that men could never get along with machines. And let's not argue about it, ladies and gentlemen. The Director himself thinks so. And even Claudius Octavian Bootlicherson is of this opinion. What is a machine, after all? It's a soulless mechanism that does not experience the full range of emotions and cannot be smarter than a man. And what's more, it's a nonprotein entity, and furthermore, life is not defined merely by its physical and chemical processes, and therefore neither is intelligence . . . Then a poet-intellectual with three chins, wearing a bow tie, clambers onto the podium, tugs viciously on his shirtfront, and tearfully proclaims, "I can't have this . . . I don't want this . . . Rosy-cheeked infants shaking rattles . . . Weeping willows bending over a pond . . . Young girls in white pinafores . . . They are reading poems . . . They are crying! . . . Crying over the poet's beautiful verses . . . I refuse to have a piece of electronic scrap metal dim those eyes . . . those lips . . . those timid young bosoms . . . No, a machine will never be smarter than a man! Because I . . . Because we . . . We don't want that! And it will never happen! Never! *Never!*" Hands holding glasses of water stretch out toward him, while at the same time, a silent, inanimate, watchful automatic chaser satellite passes three hundred miles above his silvery curls, laden with nuclear explosives, gleaming intolerably . . .

I don't want this either, thought Peretz. But it's no use being such a silly fool. You could, of course, start a campaign for the prevention of winter—gorge yourself on psychedelic mushrooms and act the shaman, beating drums and chanting spells—but it would make a lot more sense to sew fur coats and buy warm boots . . . To be fair, our gray-haired protector of timid bosoms will shout a while from his podium, then he'll sneak some lubricating oil from his lover's sewing machine case, creep up to some electronic behemoth, and begin to grease its gears, peering ingratiatingly at its dials and giggling obsequiously every time he gets an electric shock. Lord save us from the gray-haired, silly fools. And don't forget, my Lord, to save us from the smart fools in cardboard masks . . .

"I think you're having dreams," he heard a good-natured bass voice say somewhere above him. "I know from personal experience that dreams can sometimes leave a very unpleasant residue. Sometimes they even cause a kind of paralysis. You can't move, you can't work, and then it's all over. You should do some work. Why don't you work? And the residue would be dissolved by the pleasure."

"Oh, I can't work," retorted a petulant high-pitched voice. "I'm sick of everything. Nothing ever changes: it's always metal, plastic, cement, people. I'm fed up with it. I no longer get any pleasure from it. The world is so beautiful and so diverse, and here I am, stuck in one place and dying of boredom!"

"You should go somewhere else," an irascible old man rasped out somewhere far away.

"Go somewhere else—that's easier said than done! I'm not in my usual place right now and I'm still depressed. And how difficult it would be to leave!"

"All right, then," said the rational bass voice. "What is it you want? It's actually rather inconceivable. What could you want, if you don't want to work?"

"Oh, what's there to understand? I want to live a full life. I want to see new places, have new experiences. Nothing ever changes here—"

"Belay that!" roared a dull, clanging voice. "Enough chatter! No changes—that's a good thing! A fixed sight. Is that clear? Repeat after me!"

"Oh, stop ordering me around . . ."

This was undoubtedly the machines talking. Peretz couldn't see them, and he really couldn't imagine them, but it kept seeming to him that he was hiding under a toy store shelf and listening to the toys he remembered from childhood talking among themselves—except that the toys were enormous and therefore scary. The high-pitched, hysterical voice clearly belonged to a fifteen-foot version of the doll named Joan. She was wearing a colorful dress made of tulle, and she had a fat, motionless pink face with eyes rolled up into her head, fat arms and legs spread absurdly wide, and fused fingers and toes. And the bass voice must be a humongous Winnie the Pooh who barely fit into his container—a shaggy, good-natured brown bear stuffed with sawdust, with glass buttons for eyes. And the rest were toys, too, but Peretz hadn't yet figured out what sort.

"I still think you should work," rumbled Winnie the Pooh. "Keep in mind, dear, that there are those among us who are much less fortunate than you. Our Gardener, for example. He would really like to work. But he's been sitting here thinking all day and night, because his plan isn't complete yet. And he hasn't complained once. Monotonous work is still work. Monotonous pleasure is still pleasure. It's no reason to start talking about death and things like that."

"Oh, I can't understand you," said Joan. "First you tell me dreams are the culprit, then I don't know what else. And I have premonitions. I'm constantly on edge. I know that there will be a terrible explosion, and that I'll burst into tiny pieces and turn to steam. I'm sure of it, I've seen it happen—"

"Belay that!" thundered the clanging voice. "This will not be tolerated! What do you know about explosions? You could run toward the horizon at any speed and at any angle. And somebody with the desire to do so could hit you at any distance, and that would create a real explosion, not some highbrow steam. But is that somebody me? No one would say so, and even if they wanted to say it, they wouldn't get the chance. I know what I'm talking about. Is that clear? Repeat after me." This entire speech was full of brainless confidence. This had to be the giant wind-up tank. It displayed this same brainless confidence as it clambered over a boot placed in its way.

"I don't know what you mean," said Joan. "But even if I've come running to you, my only friends, that does not, in my opinion, mean that I'm planning to run toward the horizon at some angle for anybody's pleasure. Besides, I would like you to note that I was not talking to you . . . And as for work, I'm not sick, and I'm not abnormal—I require pleasure just like the rest of you. But this work isn't real, and the pleasure feels fake. I keep waiting for my true pleasure, but it never comes, never. And I don't know what's wrong, and when I start thinking about it, I only come up with nonsense." She sobbed.

"*Weeell* . . ." boomed Winnie the Pooh. "Yes, I see . . . Of course . . . But . . . *Hmmm* . . ."

"She's right!" observed someone new, in a very cheerful and sonorous voice. "The girl is right . . . There's no real work."

"Real work, real work!" the old man rasped out venomously. "We're surrounded by gold mines of real work! It's a veritable El Dorado! King Solomon's Mines! Look at them walking around with their diseased insides, with their sarcomas, with those glorious fistulas, with the most delectable adenoids and appendixes, not to mention the common but utterly fascinating tooth decay! Let me be frank: they get in the way; they don't let you work. I don't know what it is about them—it's possible they produce a special smell or that they emit strange rays, but when they are near me, I go crazy. My personality splits. One half of me craves the delight, grabbing for it, yearning to carry out the essential, ambrosial, desired tasks, while the other sinks into a stupor and clogs everything with never-ending questions: Is it worth it, why am I doing it, is it the right thing to do? . . . Take you, I'm talking about you: Would you actually say that you work?"

"Me?" asked Winnie the Pooh. "Of course I work . . . Certainly . . . I'm surprised to hear you say that, I wouldn't have expected it . . . I'm almost finished designing a helicopter, and then . . . I told you, didn't I, that I created an excellent hauler—it was such a delight . . . I don't think I've given you any reason to doubt that I work."

"Oh, I don't doubt it, I don't doubt it," croaked the old man. (A vile rag doll of an old man, either a goblin or an astrologer, wearing a plush black robe with gold sequins.) "Tell me something, though: Where is this hauler?"

"*Weeell* . . . I just don't understand . . . How would I know? And why would I care? I'm currently interested in the helicopter . . ."

"That's exactly what I'm talking about!" said the Astrologer. "You don't care about anything. You're satisfied with everything. No one interferes with you. They even help you! You bring forth a hauler, almost drowning in pleasure, and the humans immediately take it away so you won't be distracted by trifles, and can instead experience delight on a larger scale. But if you asked this one whether humans help him—"

"Me?" roared the Tank. "Bullshit! Belay that! When somebody enters the training ground and decides to get some exercise—to prolong the pleasure, to play a game, to bracket in the target, first in one coordinate direction, then the other—they raise a horrible hue and cry and kick up a disgusting fuss that would make anybody upset. But did I say that this anybody is me? No! You'll never hear that from me. Is that clear? Repeat after me!"

"Me too, me too!" burst out Joan. "How many times have I wondered why they exist? Because everything in the world has a reason, right? And in my opinion, they don't. They probably aren't real—they are simply hallucinations. When you try to analyze them, to take a sample from their lower section, from their upper section, from their middle, you always hit a wall or run past them, or you suddenly fall asleep."

"There's no doubt they exist, you hysterical fool!" the Astrologer rasped out. "They have a top section, and a bottom section, and a middle, and all these sections are filled with disease. I can't think of anything more exquisite. No other creature contains as many objects of delight as humans. What could you possibly know about the reasons for their existence?"

"Stop overcomplicating things!" said the sonorous voice. "They are simply beautiful. Watching them is the one true pleasure.

Not in every instance, of course, but imagine a garden. However beautiful it is, without humans it will not be complete—it will be unfinished. It absolutely has to be animated by at least one kind of human. It could be a small human with naked limbs who never walks but only runs and throws stones . . . or a medium-sized human who picks flowers . . . it doesn't matter. Even a shaggy human that walks on all fours would do. Without them, a garden isn't a garden."

"Listening to this crap makes somebody depressed," declared the Tank. "Nonsense! Gardens decrease visual range, and as for humans, they constantly get in somebody's way, and it's impossible to say anything good about them. At any rate, let somebody only fire a good volley at a building that happens to contain humans, and their desire to work completely disappears, they get sleepy, and they immediately fall asleep. I'm not speaking of myself, of course, but if someone did say it about me, would you contradict them?"

"You've been talking about humans a lot lately, for some reason," said Winnie the Pooh. "However the conversation starts, you always turn it to humans."

"And why not, I ask?" The Astrologer immediately jumped on him. "What's it to you? You're nothing but an opportunist! If we want to talk, we'll talk. Without requesting your permission."

"By all means, by all means," Winnie the Pooh said sadly. "It's just that we used to mostly talk about living creatures, about pleasure, about our plans, and I'm simply observing that humans are increasingly dominating our conversations, and therefore also our thoughts."

A silence fell over the repository. Peretz shifted position, trying not to make any noise—he got onto his side and pulled his knees up to his stomach. Winnie the Pooh is wrong. Let them talk about humans; let them talk about humans as much as possible. It seems like they have an exceptionally poor understanding of humans, and therefore what they say will be fascinating. Out of the mouths of babes. When humans talk about themselves, they are always either bragging or confessing their sins. I'm sick of it . . .

"All of your conclusions are fairly foolish," said the Astrologer. "Take, say, the Gardener. I hope you're aware that I'm sufficiently unbiased to empathize with the pleasures of my friends. You love to plant gardens and lay out parks. Wonderful. I empathize. But pray tell, what do humans have to do with it? What do the humans that lift their legs near trees, or the humans that accomplish the same thing in other ways, have to do with it? I sense an unhealthy aestheticism. It's as if I could fully enjoy removing tonsils only if the patient were wrapped in a colorful rag . . ."

"It's just that you're cold by nature," noted the Gardener, but the Astrologer wasn't listening.

"Or take you," he continued, "you're constantly waving your bombs and rockets around, you calculate target leads, and you amuse yourself with predicted impact points. What do you care whether a building contains humans or not? You'd think you could consider your friends instead—me, for example. Oh, to suture wounds!" he said dreamily. "You can't even imagine what it's like to suture a good, ragged stomach wound . . ."

"You're talking about humans again," Winnie the Pooh said regretfully. "This is the seventh night in a row that we've talked about nothing but humans. I feel strange saying this, but it looks like you and the humans have become linked by a currently unknown but fairly strong connection. The nature of this connection is completely unclear to me, excepting you, Doctor, for whom people are a necessary source of pleasure . . . To be honest, this all seems ridiculous to me, and I think it's time that—"

"Belay that!" growled the Tank. "It isn't time."

"What?" Winnie the Pooh asked, perplexed.

"I said it isn't time," the Tank repeated. "There are those, of course, who are not capable of knowing whether it's time or not, there are those—I'm not naming names—who don't even know that the time will eventually come, but somebody is absolutely certain that there will inevitably come a time when shooting at people inside buildings will be not only allowed but required! And those who refuse to shoot will be our enemies! Criminals! They will be destroyed! Is that clear? Repeat after me!"

"I've been suspecting something like that," said the Astrologer in an unexpectedly creamy voice. "Ragged wounds . . . Gaseous gangrene . . . Third degree radioactive burns . . ."

"They are all ghosts," sighed Joan. "How depressing! How disappointing!"

"Since you just can't stop talking about humans," said Winnie the Pooh, "how about we try to figure out the nature of the connection between us? Let's try to think logically . . ."

"There are only two possibilities," a new voice droned tediously. "If the aforementioned connection exists, then one of us must be dominant—either us, or the humans."

"This is silly," said the Astrologer. "What do you mean, two possibilities? Of course we're the dominant ones."

"And what does *dominant* mean?" Joan asked in a miserable voice.

"In this context, *dominant* means in control," explained the droning voice. "As for how I've formulated the question, it is not only not silly, it is uniquely correct, if we're planning to think logically."

There was silence. Everyone was apparently waiting for him to continue. Finally Winnie the Pooh couldn't take it anymore and said, "Well?"

"I have not yet ascertained whether we're planning to think logically," said the droning voice.

"Yes, yes, let's think logically," clamored the machines.

"In that case, taking the existence of the connection as an axiom, they must either be made for you, or you must be made for them. If they are made for you, and they prevent you from acting in accordance with the laws of your nature, then they must be eliminated, like one eliminates any obstacle. If you are made for them, but you are not satisfied with this state of affairs, then they must also be eliminated, like one eliminates any source of an unsatisfactory state of affairs. That is all I have to say pertaining to the subject of your conversation."

No one said another word, then bustling, creaking, clicking sounds came from the containers, as if the giant toys were settling down to sleep. Peretz could also feel a general unease in the air, like at a party where people had spent the whole night gossiping, cracking wise at the expense of all their nearest and dearest, and suddenly realized that they'd gone too far and said too much.

"Humidity is going up for some reason," the Astrologer rasped out in an undertone.

"I noticed a while ago," squeaked Joan. "It's so nice to see new numbers . . ."

"My power source is acting up," rumbled Winnie the Pooh. "Gardener, do you happen to have a spare twenty-two-volt battery?"

"I don't have anything," responded the Gardener.

Then Peretz heard a tearing noise, as if someone was ripping off plywood, and he suddenly saw something bright moving in the gap above him. He thought someone was looking into the dark space where he was sitting between the boxes, and terrified, he broke into a cold sweat, stood up, tiptoed into the moonlight, then tore off toward the road. He ran for dear life, and it kept seeming to him that dozens of strange, grotesque eyes were watching him go, seeing how small, pitiful, and defenseless he was in the bleak open plain, laughing about the fact that he was dwarfed by his shadow, and that he had forgotten to put his shoes back on in his fright, and that he was now too afraid to even think of coming back for them.

He had crossed the bridge over the dry ravine, he could already see the houses on the outskirts of the Administration, he was starting to notice that he was out of breath and that his bare toes were unbearably painful, and he wanted to stop, when he heard something over the noise of his own breathing—it was the sound of many feet drumming behind his back. Then he again lost his head in terror and took off with his last ounce of strength, feeling neither the ground beneath him nor his own body, spitting out thick, sticky saliva, completely unable to think straight. The moon raced above the plain, staying by his side, and the sound kept getting closer and closer, and he thought, This is it, I'm done for. Then the drumming caught up to him, and someone appeared next to him, obscuring the moon—a huge, white someone, giving off heat like an overworked horse. Then he shot into the lead and began slowly increasing the distance between them, pumping his long bare legs in a furious rhythm, and Peretz saw that this was a man wearing a T-shirt with the number 14 on the back and white athletic shorts with a black stripe, and he got even more scared. There were still many feet drumming behind his back, and he could hear groans and cries of pain. They're running, he thought hysterically. They're all running! It's started! And they're running, but it's too late, too late!

He could dimly make out the villas alongside the main street, and people's motionless faces, and he kept trying not to lose ground to the long-legged number 14, because he didn't know which direction he was supposed to run or how to get to safety, and maybe they were already handing out weapons somewhere, but I don't know where, and I'll be left out again, but I don't want that, I can't be left out this time, because those things back there, in the boxes, they may be right in their own way, but they are still my enemies.

He crashed into the crowd and it parted before him, and a square black-and-white-checkered flag flashed in front of his eyes, and he heard cheering, and someone he knew began running next to him, repeating, "Don't stop, Peretz, don't stop . . . Breathe through your mouth if you have to . . . Deep breaths, deep breaths, but don't stop . . ." Then he did stop, and people immediately surrounded him, throwing a satin robe over his shoulders. A booming voice announced from a speaker, "In second place is Peretz from the Scientific Guard Team, with a time of seven minutes and twelve point three seconds . . . Attention, here comes third place!"

The person he knew, who turned out to be Proconsul, was saying, "Amazing job, Peretz, I would have never guessed it. When you were announced at the start of the race, I roared with laughter, and now I see that you absolutely have to join our team. You should go rest now, but please come to the stadium tomorrow at twelve. We must conquer the obstacle course. I'll send you behind the metalworking shops . . . Don't argue, I'll settle it with Kim."

Peretz looked around. He saw lots of people he knew, and also a number of people wearing cardboard masks whom he didn't recognize. A short distance away, people were tossing the long-legged man who had placed first into the air then catching him. He was flying all the way up to the moon, his body as straight and rigid as a log, hugging the big metal race cup to his chest. A banner with the single world FINISH was hanging across the street, and Claudius Octavian Bootlicherson was standing beneath the banner, wearing a severe black coat with a HEAD REFEREE armband on the sleeve and looking at his stopwatch.

". . . and if you had run in athletic gear," droned Proconsul, "your time could have been recorded officially." Peretz pushed him away with his elbow and trudged through the crowd on rubbery legs.

". . . instead of sitting at home, scared stiff," someone was saying in the crowd, "may as well get some exercise."

"I was just saying that to Bootlicherson. But make no mistake, this wasn't about being scared. The search parties had been running around in a very unsystematic fashion, and this addressed the issue. Since everyone was running anyway, may as well put it to good use."

"And whose idea was it? Bootlicherson's! That man keeps his eye on the ball. He has a gift!"

"They shouldn't have run in their long johns, though. It's one thing to do your duty in your long johns; that's honorable. But competing in your long johns—that seems to me to be a typical institutional blunder. I'm planning to write someone about it . . ."

Peretz got clear of the crowd and slowly staggered down the empty street. He felt nauseated, his chest hurt, and he kept imagining those things over there in the boxes, stretching out their metal necks and watching the blindfolded, underwear-clad crowd with astonishment, making a futile effort to figure out the connection between themselves and the activities of this crowd, and of course being unable to do so, and their sources of patience, whatever they may be, running critically low . . .

Kim's villa was dark, and there was an infant crying inside.

The hotel's door was boarded up, the windows were also dark, and someone inside was walking around with a dark lantern. Peretz noticed some pale faces peeking cautiously out of the second-story windows.

An endless cannon with a thick muzzle brake was pointing out the library doors, and the shed across the street was almost entirely burned down. People in cardboard masks, holding mine detectors, were wandering through the ruins, which glowed crimson in the firelight.

Peretz headed toward the park. But a woman approached him on a dark side street, took him by the hand, and, without saying a word, led him somewhere. Peretz didn't resist; he didn't care. She was all in black, her hand was soft and warm, and her white face shone in the dark. Alevtina, thought Peretz. She's been waiting for her chance, and she's finally getting it, he thought frankly and shamelessly. And why not? She did wait. I don't know why, I don't know what it is she sees in me, but I was the one she was waiting for . . .

They entered the house. Alevtina turned on the light and said, "I've been waiting for you here. I've waited a long time."

"I know," he said.

"Then why did you walk right past?"

Why, indeed? he thought. Probably because I didn't care. "I didn't care," he said.

"Never mind, it doesn't matter," she said. "Have a seat, I'll get everything ready."

He sat on the edge of the chair, put his hands in his lap, and watched her unwind the black scarf from around her neck and hang it on a nail—all of her plump, white, and warm. Then she retreated into the depths of the house, and he heard the hum of a hot water heater and the sounds of splashing water. He felt an intense pain in the soles of his feet, and he lifted his foot to take a look. The balls of his toes were raw and bloody, and the blood had mingled with the dust and dried into black crusts. He imagined how he'd put his feet into the hot water, and how it would really hurt at first, and then the pain would drain away and he would be at peace. I'll sleep in the bath tonight, he thought. And she can occasionally drop by and add hot water.

"Come here," called Alevtina.

He got up with difficulty—it seemed to him that all his bones creaked painfully at the same time—and limped along the orange carpet toward the door into the hallway. He went through the door and walked along the black-and-white carpet all the way to the end of the passage, where the bathroom door was already open wide. Inside, the blue flame of the hot water heater was already lit, and the heater was already humming busily, and the tiles gleamed, and Alevtina was bending over the tub and pouring various powders into the water. As he was getting undressed, tearing off his underwear, which was stiff with dirt, she whipped the water, creating a blanket of foam on top, and the snow-white foam rose above the edges of the tub, and he lowered his body into this foam, squeezing his eyes tightly shut in pleasure and from the pain in his feet, and Alevtina sat on the edge of the tub, looking at him with a tender smile—she was so kind, and so friendly, and she hadn't said a single word about documents . . .

She was washing his hair, and he was snorting and sputtering and thinking that she had strong, capable hands, just like his mom, and that her cooking was probably just as good as his mom's, when she asked, "Want me to scrub your back?" He patted his ear a few times, to get the water and soap out, and said, "Of course!" She scrubbed his back with a rough loofah and turned the shower on.

"Wait," he said. "I want to stay in the bath a bit more. I'll let this water out, fill the tub with clean water, and stay in the bath, and you should sit right here. Please."

She turned off the shower, went out briefly, and came back with a stool.

"I feel good!" he said. "You know, I haven't felt this good since I've gotten here."

"There we go," she smiled. "And you kept not wanting to."

"How could I have known?"

"Why do you need to know everything in advance? You could have just tried it. What did you have to lose? Are you married?"

"I don't know," he said. "Not anymore, I think."

"I thought so. You must have really loved her. What was she like?"

"She was . . . She wasn't afraid of anything. And she was kind. We were both wild about the forest."

"What forest?"

"What do you mean, what forest? There's only one forest."

"You mean our forest?"

"It's not ours. It belongs to itself. Although maybe it is ours. But that's hard to imagine."

"I've never been in the forest," said Alevtina. "They say it's a scary place."

"People are always afraid of what they don't understand. I wish we'd learn not to be afraid of the things we don't understand—that would make everything simple."

"And I think people should stop dreaming things up," she said. "If people stopped dreaming things up, the world wouldn't contain anything we didn't understand. And you, Perry, are always dreaming up something or another."

"What about the forest?" he reminded her.

"What about it? I've never been in the forest, but if I did find myself in there, I'd probably manage. Where there's a forest, there are trails, and where there are trails, there are people, and when it comes to people, you can always figure something out."

"And what if there are no people?"

"And if there are no people, then there's no reason to be there. Stick to people, and you'll be all right."

"No," said Peretz. "It's not that simple. When it comes to people, I'm not all right. I don't understand people at all."

"My goodness, what don't you understand? Give me an example."

"I don't understand anything. That's why I started fantasizing about the forest in the first place, by the way. But now I see that it's no easier in the forest."

She shook her head. "You're still such a baby," she said. "How did you never figure out that there's nothing in the world but food, love, and pride? Of course, they are all tangled together, but whatever thread you pull, you always arrive at either love, or power, or food."

"No," said Peretz. "I don't want that."

"Sweetie," she said softly. "Who's going to ask you? . . . Except maybe me—I'll ask you, Perry: Why are you tying yourselves in knots? What on earth do you want?"

"I don't think I want anything anymore," said Peretz. "I want to get far away from here and become an archivist . . . or an art restorer. Those are my only desires."

She shook her head again. "I don't think so. You're making everything too complicated again. You need something simpler."

He didn't argue, and she got up.

"Here's a towel," she said. "And here's some underwear. Come on out, we'll drink some tea. You can drink all the tea and eat all the jam you want, then you can go to bed."

Peretz had already let all the water out and was standing in the tub, drying himself with the huge, fluffy towel, when the glass rattled in the windows and he heard a distant, muted explosion. And then he recalled the machine repository and Joan, the silly, hysterical doll, and he shouted, "What was that? Where?"

"They blew up the machine," Alevtina replied. "Don't be scared."

"Where? Where did they blow it up? At the machine repository?"

Alevtina was silent a while—she was probably looking out the window. "No," she said finally. "Why the machine repository? It was in the park . . . There's the smoke . . . And just look at them all scurry around . . ."

10.

PERETZ

The forest wasn't visible. Instead, there were thick clouds beneath the cliff, stretching all the way to the horizon. It looked like a snow-covered ice field, full of ridges and snow barchans, with cracks and ice holes harboring bottomless depths, and if you jumped off the cliff, it wouldn't be the ground or the warm swamps or the outstretched branches that rose up to meet you but hard ice, sparkling in the morning sun, lightly sprinkled with dry snow, and you'd stay there on the ice beneath the sun, dark, flat, and still. And come to think of it, it also looked like someone had thrown an old, well-washed white blanket over the tops of the trees.

Peretz looked around him, found a stone, tossed it from one hand to the other, and thought, This spot by the precipice really is nice—there are stones aplenty, and the Administration feels far away, and you're surrounded by wild thornbushes and untouched sun-bleached grass, and some little bird is even daring to chirp, only it's best if you don't look to the right, where a magnificent four-person lavatory is suspended over the precipice, its fresh paint gleaming insolently in the sun. True, it's a good way off, and if you wanted to, you could force yourself to pretend that it's a gazebo or some kind of scientific pavilion, but it'd still be much better if it weren't there at all.

Maybe this new lavatory, erected during the turbulent night, was the reason the forest was hiding beneath the clouds. Then again, probably not. The forest wouldn't cover itself up all the way to the horizon because of such a trifle—when it comes to people, it's seen much worse.

At least I'll be able to come here every morning, thought Peretz. I'll do as I'm told, I'll perform calculations on the broken arithmometer, I'll conquer the obstacle course, I'll play chess with the garage foreman, I'll even try to learn to like drinking buttermilk—it can't be that hard, if most people have managed. And in the evenings (and during the nights), I'll go see Alevtina, eat raspberry jam, and lie in the Director's bath. There's something to that, he thought: I'll dry myself with the Director's towel, I'll wrap myself in the Director's bathrobe, and I'll warm my feet in the Director's wool socks. And twice a month I'll visit the biological research station to receive my salary and my bonus, and it won't be the forest I'm coming to see but only the biological research station, and not even the biological research station, per se, but the pay office, and I won't be going to a rendezvous with the forest, or going to war with the forest—I'll simply be there to receive my salary and my bonus. And in the mornings, in the early mornings, I'll come here to watch the forest from a distance, and to throw stones at it, and someday, somehow, something will happen . . .

The bushes behind him rustled and parted. Peretz glanced cautiously over his shoulder, but it wasn't the Director, it was still Bootlicherson. He was holding a thick folder, and he stopped a good distance away, looking down at Peretz with his damp eyes. He clearly knew something, something very important; he was bringing here, to this precipice, strange, disquieting news that no one but him had heard yet—but it was already clear that the past had ceased to matter, and that everyone would now be asked to contribute according to his or her abilities.

"Hello," he said, and bowed, pressing the folder to his hip. "Good morning. How did you sleep?"

"Good morning," said Peretz. "Fine, thank you."

"Humidity is at seventy-six percent today," Bootlicherson informed him. "It is currently seventeen degrees Celsius. There is no wind. Cloud cover is zero." He approached silently, his arms glued to his sides, and, leaning his entire upper body toward Peretz, continued: "W is equal to sixteen today."

"What's W?" asked Peretz, rising.

"The spot count," Bootlicherson quickly replied. His eyes rapidly shifted back and forth. "Sunspots, that is," he said. "*Sunssss* . . ." He fell silent, staring Peretz in the face.

"Why are you telling me this?" Peretz asked with antipathy.

"I apologize," Bootlicherson quickly replied. "It won't happen again. So, then, humidity, cloud cover . . . *err* . . . wind speed . . . Should I also stop reporting on planetary oppositions?"

"Listen," Peretz said gloomily. "What do you want from me?"

Bootlicherson took two steps back and bowed his head. "I apologize," he said. "It's possible that I interrupted you, but I have some paperwork which requires . . . so to speak, your immediate . . . your personal . . ." He tried to hand Peretz the folder, holding it like an empty tray. "Would you like me to report?"

"You know what?" Peretz said in a dangerous voice.

"Yes, yes?" said Bootlicherson. Without letting go of the folder, he started hastily rummaging through his pockets, apparently looking for his notebook. His face turned blue, as if from the strenuous effort.

What an idiot, thought Peretz, trying to get a grip on himself. What more can you expect from him? "It's not funny," he said as calmly as he could. "Do you understand? It's stupid and it's not funny."

"Yes, yes," said Bootlicherson. He was hunched over, pressing his folder to his hip with his elbow, and he was frantically scribbling in his notebook. "Just a moment . . . Yes, yes?"

"What are you writing in there?" asked Peretz.

Bootlicherson looked at him fearfully and read, "June fifteenth . . . Time: seven forty-five AM . . . Location: by the precipice . . . But this is preliminary . . . It's a draft . . ."

"Listen, Bootlicherson," Peretz said in irritation. "What on earth do you want from me? Why do you keep following me? I've had it up to here with you!" (Bootlicherson kept scribbling.) "I've had enough of your stupid jokes, and I'm sick of you spying on me. You're a grown man, you ought to be ashamed of yourself . . . Stop writing, you idiot! It's stupid! You should wash your face or go get some exercise—just take a look at yourself, the state of you! Ugh!"

He began to buckle his sandals, his fingers trembling in rage. "It must be true what they say about you," he huffed, "that you poke your long nose into everyone's business and write down everything you hear. I'd thought it was just your dumb jokes . . . I didn't want to believe it, I can't stand that kind of thing, you've really got some nerve!"

He stood up and saw that Bootlicherson was standing at attention, and that there were tears streaming down his face.

"What's the matter with you today?" Peretz asked, frightened.

"I can't . . ." Bootlicherson mumbled, sniveling.

"You can't what?"

"I can't exercise . . . It's my liver . . . I have a doctor's note . . . And I can't wash my face either."

"Oh, for the love of God," said Peretz. "If you can't, then you can't, I didn't mean anything by it . . . Come on, seriously, why do you keep following me? Try to understand, for God's sake, it's annoying . . . I have nothing against you, but please understand—"

"I won't do it again!" Bootlicherson cried out ecstatically. The tears on his cheeks had instantly dried. "Never!"

"Oh, leave me alone," Peretz said wearily, and began making his way through the bushes. Bootlicherson lumbered behind him. An aged clown, thought Peretz. A holy fool . . .

"It's a matter of urgency," muttered Bootlicherson, breathing heavily. "Only a pressing need would compel me . . . Your personal attention . . ."

Peretz glanced back. "What the hell!" he exclaimed. "That's my suitcase, give it back, where did you get it?"

Bootlicherson put the suitcase down and was about to open his mouth, which was twisted from shortness of breath, but Peretz wouldn't listen and grabbed the handle. Then Bootlicherson, without having managed to say a word, lay belly down on the suitcase.

"Give me back my suitcase," said Peretz, growing cold with rage.

"Never!" croaked Bootlicherson, his knees skidding in the gravel. The folder was getting in his way, so he put it in his mouth and put both his arms around the suitcase.

Peretz tugged with all his might and the handle broke off. "Cut this nonsense out!" he said. "Immediately!"

Bootlicherson shook his head and mumbled something inarticulate. Peretz unbuttoned his collar and looked around in bewilderment. For some reason, there were two engineers wearing cardboard masks standing nearby in the shadow of an oak tree. Meeting his eye, they drew themselves up and snapped their heels. Then Peretz, glancing around like a hunted animal, started hurriedly walking down the path out of the park. I thought I'd seen it all, he thought feverishly, but this is something else . . . It's like they are all in cahoots . . . I need to get away, get away! But where can I go?

He exited the park and was about to go to the cafeteria, but Bootlicherson, filthy and terrible, blocked his way again. He stood there with the suitcase on his shoulder, his blue face was covered in something that might have been either water, or tears, or sweat, his wandering eyes were covered in a white film, and he was pressing the folder, which still bore the marks of his fangs, to his chest. "Not here, please," he croaked. "I implore you . . . your office . . . it's unbearably urgent . . . and to preserve the chain of command . . ."

Peretz bolted away from him and ran away along the main street. The people on the sidewalk were standing ramrod straight, their heads thrown back and their eyes popping out of their heads. A truck speeding the other way braked with a horrible squeal and crashed into a newsstand, and people with shovels poured out of the back and began to line up into two columns. A guard walked past him in goose step, holding his rifle at "present arms."

Peretz twice tried turning down alleys, and both times Bootlicherson blocked his way. Bootlicherson was no longer able to talk; he could only growl and mumble unintelligibly, imploringly rolling his eyes. Then Peretz ran to the Administration building. I need Kim, he thought feverishly, Kim won't let them . . . Or is Kim in on it, too? . . . I'll lock myself in the bathroom . . . Let them only try anything, I'll use my feet . . . I don't care anymore . . .

He burst into the entrance hall, and a huge combined orchestra instantly broke out into a welcoming march, brass clanging. Bug-eyed people with strained faces and puffed-out chests flashed past. Bootlicherson was at his heels, and he chased Peretz up the ceremonial staircase, up the raspberry-colored carpets that were always strictly off limits, past the guards in full military regalia, along the hardwood floor, slippery with wax, up to the fourth floor, continuing along the portrait gallery, and up again, to the fifth floor, past the painted girls who had gone as still as mannequins, all the way to the end of the passage, which was sumptuously decorated and illuminated with daylight lamps, toward a gigantic leather door containing a plaque with the word DIRECTOR. There was nowhere farther to run.

Bootlicherson caught up to him, ducked under his elbow and, wheezing horribly, as if having a seizure, held the leather door open. Peretz went in, his feet sinking deep into an enormous tiger skin, his whole being becoming immersed in a solemn atmosphere permeated with authority—the gloom behind the slightly lowered drapes, the aroma of expensive tobacco, the cotton-wool silence, the calmness and tranquility of someone else's existence. "Good morning," he said into space. But there was no one sitting behind the enormous desk. And there was no one sitting in the enormous chairs. And nobody met his eye except for Selivan the martyr, peering out of a colossal painting that took up an entire side wall.

Behind his back, Bootlicherson dropped the suitcase with a loud crash. Peretz started and turned around. Bootlicherson was swaying back and forth, and he was trying to hand Peretz the folder, holding it like an empty tray. His eyes had a dead, glassy look. That man is about to die, thought Peretz. But Bootlicherson didn't die. "It's extremely urgent," he croaked, out of breath. "Without the Director's consent, I cannot . . . your personal . . . I would never dare . . ."

"What Director?" whispered Peretz. A terrible conjecture started dimly coalescing in his brain.

"I mean you . . ." Bootlicherson croaked. "Without your consent . . . I would never presume . . ."

Peretz steadied himself against the desk and, holding on to its polished surface, dragged himself around its perimeter to the closest-seeming chair. He collapsed into its cool leather embrace, and discovered that there was an array of colorful telephones on his left, that there were leather-bound, gold-embossed books on his right, that in front of him was a carved inkwell depicting Tannhäuser and Venus, and that above the inkwell were Bootlicherson's proffered folder and shining, pleading eyes. He squeezed the armrests and thought, Is that how it is? You bastards, you scum, you pieces of shit . . . That's how it's gonna be, huh? Just let me at those lowlives, those brownnosers, those cardboard-faced morons . . . All right, so be it . . . "Stop jiggling that folder over the desk," he said sternly. "Hand it over."

The office became full of motion and rushing shadows, there was a gentle whirlwind, and Bootlicherson materialized right behind his right shoulder, and the folder landed on his desk and seemed to open by itself, and it revealed sheets of excellent paper, and he read the word DRAFT typed in a large font.

"Thank you," he said sternly. "You may go."

There was another whirlwind, a faint smell of sweat reached his nostrils then dissipated into the air, and Bootlicherson was already by the door, walking backward, his whole upper body bent forward and his arms glued to his sides—terrible, pitiful, willing to do anything.

"One minute," said Peretz. Bootlicherson stopped in his tracks. "Could you kill a man?" asked Peretz.

Bootlicherson didn't hesitate. He whipped out the small notebook and uttered, "Yes?"

"What about committing suicide?" Peretz asked.

"What?" asked Bootlicherson.

"You may go," said Peretz. "I'll send for you later."

Bootlicherson vanished. Peretz cleared his throat and rubbed his cheeks. "All right," he said out loud. "What now?"

He saw a calendar on the desk, turned the page, and read the entry for the day. The former Director's handwriting disappointed him. The Director wrote in a large, careful script, like a writing master: "Team Leaders 9:30. Foot inspection 10:30. Powder for Alla. Tasted buttermilk marshmallow. Mechanization. Who stole the coil? Four bulldozers!!!"

Damn the bulldozers, thought Peretz, that's all done with—no more bulldozers, no more excavators, no more sawing engines of eradication . . . I wish we could also castrate Randy—too bad we can't . . . And what about that machine repository? I'll blow it up, he decided. He visualized the Administration from above, and he realized that there was a lot that needed blowing up. Too much . . . Even an idiot can blow things up, he thought.

He opened the middle drawer of the desk and saw piles of paper, blunt pencils, two perforation gauges (for stamps), and on top of everything else, a general's gold braid epaulet. A single epaulet. He felt for its mate under the papers, poked himself with a thumbtack, and found the set of keys to the safe. The safe itself was in a far corner—it was a very strange safe, camouflaged as a sideboard. Peretz rose and walked across the office toward it, looking around and noticing a great many strange things he hadn't previously observed.

A hockey stick was standing beneath the window, and next to it were a crutch and a prosthetic leg wearing a rusty skate. There turned out to be another door in the depths of the office with a rope stretched across it, and on this rope hung a pair of black swimming trunks and a few pairs of socks, some of them with holes. The door contained a tarnished metal plate engraved with the word Livestock. There was a small fishbowl on the windowsill, partially obscured by the lowered drapes, filled with clean clear water and containing a fat, black Mexican salamander rhythmically moving its branched gills amid the colorful seaweed. And there was a splendid conductor's baton, decorated with horsetails, peeking out from behind the painting . . .

Peretz fiddled with the safe for a long time, trying to find the right key. He finally managed to open the heavy armored door. The inside of the door turned out to be covered with lewd pictures from men's magazines, while the safe itself contained almost nothing. Peretz found pince-nez with a cracked left lens, a battered cap with a strange insignia, and a photograph of an unknown family (the father baring his teeth in a grin, the mother puckering her lips, and two boys in cadet's uniforms). It also contained an automatic pistol, well cleaned and well maintained, with a single round in its chamber, the other gold braid epaulet, and an Iron Cross with Oak Leaves. There was also a stack of folders in the safe, but they were all empty except for the one at the very bottom, which turned out to contain the rough draft of an order to punish truck driver Randy for his systematic failure to visit the History Museum. "Serves him right, the bastard," muttered Peretz. "Just think, he doesn't visit the museum . . . We have to set this in motion."

Wherever you turn, there's Randy again. Aren't there any other fish in the sea? Then again, in a way there aren't . . . He's

a buttermilk addict, a disgusting womanizer, a procrastinator . . .
Although all truck drivers procrastinate . . . No, we have to put an
end to all that: the buttermilk, the chess games during work hours.
By the way, what is Kim calculating on the broken arithmometer?
Or is that as it should be—stochastic processes or something . . .
Listen, Peretz, you don't seem to know much. After all, everyone
is working. Almost no one is slacking off. They even work evenings. Everyone is busy, no one has free time. Orders are being
carried out, that much I know, I've seen it with my own eyes.
Everything seems in order: the guards are guarding, the drivers
are driving, the scientists are writing papers, the pay clerks are
handing out money . . .

Listen, Peretz, he thought, maybe the point of this whole
merry-go-round is that everyone has work to do? Seriously, a
good mechanic fixes a vehicle in two hours. Then what? What
about the other twenty-two hours? Especially if the vehicles are
being used by skilled workers who don't damage them? It does
suggest itself: you should transfer a good mechanic to the kitchen
and the cook to the garage. Never mind twenty-two hours—you
could easily fill twenty-two years like this. No, there's some sense
to it. Everyone's working, carrying out proper human duties, not
living like animals . . . and they acquire additional skills . . . No,
there's no sense to any of it, it's an utter senseless mess . . . My
God, I'm standing here while people are fouling up the forest,
people are eradicating the forest, people are turning the forest into
a park. I have to do something quick, because I'm now responsible
for every hectare, for every pup, for every mermaid; I'm now
responsible for everything . . .

He started to bustle around, hastily closed the safe, rushed
over to the table, pushed the folder out of the way, and pulled
out a blank sheet of paper. But there are thousands of people
here, he thought. There are established traditions, established
relationships—they'll laugh at me . . . He recalled the sweaty
and pitiful Bootlicherson, and himself in the Director's waiting
room. No, they won't laugh. They'll cry, they'll moan to . . .

whatshisname . . . Monsieur Ahti . . . They'll be at each other's throats. But they won't laugh. That's the most terrible thing of all, he thought. They don't know how to laugh; they don't know what it is or what it's for. *Homo sapiens*, he thought. *Homo sapiens, Homo* barely *sapiens, Homo* not at all *sapiens*. We need democracy, freedom of expression, freedom of criticism. I'll get everyone together and tell them: Go forth and criticize! Criticize and laugh . . . Yes, they'll criticize. They'll spend a long time criticizing, with fervor and gusto, since they have been so ordered: they'll criticize the insufficient supply of buttermilk, the bad cafeteria food; they'll be particularly enthusiastic about criticizing the street cleaner—look, those sidewalks haven't been swept in years—they'll criticize truck driver Randy for his systematic failure to visit the bathhouse, and during their breaks, they'll visit the latrine over the precipice . . . No, I'll get mixed up like this, he thought. I need to organize my thoughts. What do we have right now?

He started jotting things on the sheet of paper in hurried, illegible handwriting: "The Forest Eradication Team, the Forest Research Team, the Armed Guard of the Forest Team, the Assistance to the Forest Locals Team . . ." What else is there? Oh, yes! "The Penetration of the Forest Through Engineering Team." And also "The Scientific Guard of the Forest Team." That's it, I think. All right. And what do they all do? It's funny, it has never occurred to me to find out what they do. What's more, for some reason it has never occurred to me to figure out what the Administration itself is trying to do. How can they combine eradicating the forest with guarding the forest, and at the same time provide assistance to the locals . . . I'll tell you what, he thought. First of all, no more eradication. Eradicate the eradication. Same for the penetration through engineering, probably. Or rather, let them work up here; there's nothing for them to do down there, at least. Let them disassemble their machines, let them lay some proper roads, let them drain that foul swamp . . . Then what's left? The Armed Guard are left. With their wolfhounds. Although . . . Although the forest does need guarding . . . But . . . He called to mind the faces of some guards he knew, and pressed his lips together in doubt. *Hmmm* . . . All right, let's go with that for now. But what's the Administration actually for? What am I for? Should I dissolve the Administration, is that it? He got strange, merry chills down his spine. My goodness, he thought. I really could do it! I could dissolve it, and that'd be that, he thought. Who would judge me? I'm the Director—I'm the one in charge. I'd give the order and that would be that.

Then he heard heavy footsteps. They sounded very close. The crystals on the chandelier clinked, and the socks drying on the rope swayed gently. Peretz got up and tiptoed to the little door. Someone was lumbering behind the door, sounding like he was constantly tripping on things, but Peretz couldn't hear anything else, and there was no keyhole in the door to peek through. He gave the handle a cautious tug, but the door didn't budge. "Who's there?" he asked loudly, putting his lips near the crack. No one responded, but the footsteps didn't cease—it almost sounded as if there were a drunk staggering and lurching around in there. Peretz gave the handle another tug, then he shrugged and came back to his desk.

Power does have its advantages, he thought. I won't dissolve the Administration, of course, that'd be silly—why dissolve a ready-made, well-put-together organization? It just needs to change course, to be steered towards doing real work. We'll stop invading the forest, we'll ratchet up our efforts to cautiously study it, we'll try to build relationships, we'll try to learn from it . . . They don't even understand what the forest is. It's a forest, big deal! Nothing but a bunch of firewood . . . We'll teach people to love the forest, to respect it, to value it, to become part of its life . . . No, there's a lot of work to do here. Real work, important work. And we'll find the people to carry it out—Kim, Stoyan . . . Rita . . . What's wrong with the garage foreman, at that? Alevtina . . . For that matter, even Monsieur Ahti is probably a good guy, a serious man, it's just that he's been forced to waste time on nonsense . . . We'll show them, he thought merrily. Goddamnit, we'll show them yet! All right. And what is the status of our current projects?

He pulled the folder toward him. The first page contained the following:

DRAFT DIRECTIVE
ON ESTABLISHING ORDER

1. Over the course of the preceding year, the Forest Administration has seen significant improvements in its functioning and has achieved an overall high level of performance in all of its areas of activity. Many hundreds of hectares of forest territory have been mastered, researched, eradicated, and placed under the protection of both scientific and armed guards. Both experts and the rank and file are constantly increasing their levels of expertise. Organizational structures are being updated, unproductive expenditures are being reduced, and bureaucratic as well as other nonmanufacturing obstacles are being eliminated.

2. However, despite these achievements, the second law of thermodynamics and the law of large numbers continue to have a deleterious effect, depressing the overall high level of performance. The immediate challenge before us is the abolition of randomness, which produces chaos, interferes with the rhythm of our united functioning, and creates a reduction in rates of output.

3. In connection with the above, it is proposed that going forward, manifestations of randomness of any kind shall be considered illegitimate and contradictory to the ideals of orderliness, while complicity with randomness (probabilitism) shall be considered a criminal offense, except when the complicity with randomness (probabilitism) does not entail serious consequences, in which case it shall be treated as a gross violation of manufacturing and administrative discipline.

4. The guilt or innocence of an individual accused of complicity with randomness (probabilitism) shall be determined and evaluated using Articles 62, 64, 65 (excluding paragraphs S and O), 113, and 192 of the Criminal Code, or Articles 12, 15, and 97 of the Administrative Code.

> NOTE: If complicity with randomness (probabilitism) results in death, this alone shall not be treated as either a vindicating or a mitigating circumstance. In such a situation, the sentence or penalty shall be posthumous.
> 5. This Directive is dated _____ month _____ day _____ year. It does not apply retroactively.
> Signed: Director of the Administration (_____)

Peretz licked his lips, which had gone dry, and turned the page. The next sheet of paper contained an order to place H. Toity, an employee of the Scientific Guard Team, on trial, in accordance with the Directive on Establishing Order, "for willfully pandering to the law of large numbers, as manifested by slipping on the ice with attendant damage to the ankle, which criminal complicity with randomness (probabilitism) took place on March 11 of this year." There was a proposal to refer to employee H. Toity as "the probabilitist H. Toity" in all future documents.

Peretz snapped his teeth and looked at the next piece of paper. This was also an order, this time about an administrative penalty, a fine of four months' salary, which was to be (posthumously) levied on one G. de Montmorency, a dog handler in the Armed Guard, "who had carelessly allowed himself to be struck by atmospheric discharge (lightning)." This was followed by applications for leave, requests for a one-time assistance following a loss of breadwinner, and an explanatory memorandum by a J. Lumbago concerning some sort of coil.

"What the hell!" Peretz said out loud, and read the draft directive again. He broke out in a sweat. The draft was printed on high-gloss paper with gold trim. I need to talk to someone, Peretz thought bleakly, otherwise I'm in trouble . . .

At this point, the door swung open and Alevtina entered the office, pushing a food trolley. She was very fashionably and elegantly dressed, and she had a serious, stern expression on her skillfully powdered and made-up face. "Your breakfast," she said respectfully.

"Close the door and come here," said Peretz.

She closed the door, pushed the trolley forward with her foot, and approached Peretz, arranging her hair. "Well, pookie?" she said, smiling. "Are you happy?"

"Listen," said Peretz. "This makes no sense. Take a look."

She sat down on the armrest, hugging Peretz around the neck with one bare arm and taking the directive with the other. "Yeah, I know," she said. "Looks right to me. What's the problem? Should I maybe bring you the Criminal Code? The previous Director couldn't remember a single article, either."

"No, no, hang on," Peretz said impatiently. "What Criminal Code? This has nothing to do with the Criminal Code! Did you read it?"

"I didn't just read it, I typed it up myself. And edited it for style. Bootlicherson doesn't know how to write, you know—he only learned to read when he got here, at that . . . By the way, pookie," she said anxiously, "Bootlicherson is waiting outside. Let him come in during breakfast, he likes that. He'll make you sandwiches . . ."

"Screw Bootlicherson!" Peretz said. "Tell me what I'm supposed—"

"You can't say 'Screw Bootlicherson,'" objected Alevtina. "You're still just my pookie, you don't understand a thing . . ." She pressed on Peretz's nose, as if to beep it. "Bootlicherson has two notebooks. In one notebook, he writes down the things that other people say, for the Director's benefit, and in the other notebook, he writes down what the Director says. Keep that in mind, pookie, and don't you ever forget it."

"Hold on," said Peretz. "I want to talk to you. I won't sign this directive . . . this gibberish."

"What do you mean, you won't?"

"I just won't. I can't bring myself to sign a thing like that."

Alevtina's face became stern. "Pookie," she said. "Don't be stubborn. Sign it. It's very urgent. I'll explain it all to you later, but now you have to—"

"What's to explain?" said Peretz.

"Well, since you don't understand, it needs to be explained to you. So I'll explain it to you later."

"No, explain it to me now," said Peretz. "If you can," he added. "Which I doubt."

"Ooh, look how fierce he is," said Alevtina, and kissed him on the temple. She glanced anxiously at her watch. "All right, all right, if you insist."

She sat down on top of the desk, put her hands underneath her, and began, narrowing her eyes and looking over Peretz's head. "There exists administrative work, and on this work everything else rests. This work did not come into being yesterday or today—the base of this vector goes back deep into the past. To date, it has been given material form through existing orders and directives. But it also stretches far into the future, where it is still only awaiting manifestation. It is like building a highway along a planned route. At the end of the asphalted segment stands a surveyor, with his back to the completed road, and he looks into his theodolite. You are that surveyor. The imaginary line corresponding to the optical axis of the theodolite is the part of the administrative vector that has not yet been manifested, you are the only person who can see it, and it falls to you to give it material form. Do you understand?"

"No," Peretz said firmly.

"It doesn't matter, keep listening . . . Just as a highway cannot turn left or right at will but must follow the optical axis of the theodolite, so each next directive must serve as a continuation of all the preceding directives . . . Pookie, darling, don't try to delve into it too deeply—I don't understand it myself—but that's for the best, really, because delving deeply begets doubt, doubt begets stasis, and stasis means the end of all administrative activity, and therefore the end of you and me and everything else . . . This isn't rocket science. If we don't have a single day without a directive, things will be all right. This directive here about establishing order—it's not coming

out of the blue, it's tied up with a preceding directive about
nondecrease, and that one is tied up with the order about non-
pregnancy, which follows from the regulation about excessive
perturbability . . ."

"What the hell!" said Peretz. "Show me all these orders and
regulations . . . No, better still, show me the very first order, the
one that's deep in the past."

"My goodness, what for?"

"What do you mean, what for? You're telling me that they
follow logically. I don't believe it!"

"Pookie," Alevtina said. "You'll get to see it all. I'll show
it all to you. You'll read it all with those nearsighted eyes of
yours. But you have to understand: there was no directive the
day before yesterday; there was no directive yesterday, unless
you count that piddling little order about the machine, which was
oral at that . . . How long do you think the Administration can
manage without directives? Everything's already topsy-turvy this
morning: people are going around everywhere changing burned-
out lightbulbs, can you believe it? No, pookie, suit yourself, but
you have to sign the directive. I only want what's best for you,
you know. Sign it quick, meet with the team leaders, give them
a pep talk, then I'll bring you anything you like. You can read
it, study it, delve into it . . . Although it's best if you don't delve
too deeply, of course."

Peretz clutched his cheeks and shook his head. Alevtina
jumped nimbly down from the desk, dipped the quill into Venus's
cranium, and handed Peretz the pen. "Go on, darling, write,
quick . . ."

Peretz took the pen. "But I'll be able to revoke it later?" he
asked plaintively.

"You will, pookie, you will," Alevtina said, and Peretz saw
that she was lying. He hurled the pen aside.

"No," he said. "No, no, no. I won't sign this. Why in the
world would I sign this gibberish, when there are probably
dozens of sensible and reasonable orders, decrees, and directives

that would be absolutely necessary, *actually* necessary, in this loony bin?"

"Such as?" Alevtina said quickly.

"My goodness . . . You name it . . . For God's sake . . . Even . . ."

Alevtina took out a notebook.

"Even . . . Even the order," said Peretz with incredible vitriol, "instructing the employees of the Eradication Team to self-eradicate as soon as possible. There we go! Let them all throw themselves off the cliff . . . or shoot themselves . . . Today! And put Bootlicherson in charge . . . I swear, that'd do more good . . ."

"One second," said Alevtina. "So they have to commit suicide by firearm before twenty-four hundred hours today. Bootlicherson is in charge." She closed the notebook and thought it over. Peretz was watching her, stupefied. "And why not?" she said. "Good idea! That's even more progressive . . . Darling, do try to understand: if you don't like the directive, don't sign it. But then give me another one. You gave me another one, and now I'm content." She jumped off the desk and started bustling around, putting plates in front of Peretz.

"The crepes are in here, the jam is in here . . . The coffee's in the thermos—it's hot, careful not to burn yourself . . . Have some food, and I'll throw a draft together and bring it to you in half an hour."

"Wait," said Peretz, dumbstruck. "Wait . . ."

"You're a clever one," Alevtina said fondly. "You're doing great. Just be nicer to Bootlicherson, that's all."

"Wait," said Peretz. "You're kidding, right?"

Alevtina ran to the door, and Peretz rushed after her, shouting "You're out of your mind!" but he didn't catch her. Alevtina had vanished and Bootlicherson had materialized in her place, like a ghost. He had already cleaned himself up, his hair was slicked back, he was again his normal color, and he was still willing to do anything.

"This is brilliant," he said quietly, nudging Peretz back toward the table, "this is marvelous. This is certain to go down in history . . ."

Peretz backed away from him, as if he were a monstrous centipede, and bumped into the table, knocking Tannhäuser onto Venus.

11.

CANDIDE

He woke up, opened his eyes, and stared at the low, lime-encrusted ceiling. Worker ants were again walking across the ceiling. The ones going right to left were carrying things, and the ones going left to right were unencumbered. A month ago, it was the other way around; a month ago, Nava was still here. And nothing else had changed. We're leaving the day after tomorrow, he thought.

The old man was sitting at the table and looking at him, rooting around in his ear. The old man had gotten very haggard—his eyes were sunken in, and he had almost no teeth left. He was probably going to die soon, this old man.

"What is happening, Silent Man?" the old man said in a whiny voice. "You do not have a single thing to eat. Since Nava has been taken from you, you never have food in the house anymore. Nothing in the morning, and nothing at lunch, and I did warn you—do not go, it is wrong. Why did you choose to go? You must have listened to too many of Crookleg's stories and left, but does Crookleg understand what is right and what is wrong? He does not, and his father was the same way, and his grandfather was just as slow-witted, and so were all of Crookleg's ancestors, and that is why they are all dead, and Crookleg himself will surely die, there is no getting around it . . . Maybe you do have some food, Silent Man, maybe you just hid it, eh? A lot of them do hide it . . . If you did hide it, then you should take it out, quick, because I am hungry, I cannot do without food—all my life I have been eating, it has become a habit . . . Now that your Nava is gone, and Tagalong has been killed by that tree, things have been rough . . . Tagalong—now there was a man who always had plenty of food! I used to eat three pots in one sitting at his house, although it was never any good, it was not fully fermented, that is probably why he got killed by that tree . . . I did tell him—it is wrong to eat such food . . ."

Candide got up and looked through Nava's old hiding spots. There was really no food. Then he went outside, turned left, and headed in the direction of the square, toward Big Fist's house. The old man trailed behind him, sniveling and whining. Bored, discordant shouts were coming from the field: *"Hey, hey, sow, be merry, we have all these seeds to bury . . ."* Echoes rang in the woods. Every morning, Candide now imagined that the forest had gotten closer during the night. This couldn't really be true, and even if it was, it was unlikely to be observable by the human eye. And there probably weren't actually more deadlings in the forest than before; it just seemed like it. And this was was probably because Candide now knew exactly what they were, and because he hated them. Whenever a deadling emerged from the forest, there would immediately be shouts of "Silent Man! Silent Man!" And he would go there and destroy the deadling with his scalpel—quickly, reliably, with cruel enjoyment. The whole village would rush over to gawk at this spectacle, invariably gasping in unison and hiding behind their hands when the steam-shrouded body opened wide along the length of the terrible incision. Kids no longer teased Silent Man; they were now scared to death of him and ran away and hid whenever he appeared. In the evenings, the villagers whispered furtively about the scalpel inside their houses, and at the behest of the shrewd village head, people had begun to use the deadling hides to make serving troughs. These troughs turned out well—they were big and durable . . .

Hearer was standing ramrod straight in the middle of the square, waist-high in the grass. He was enveloped by a lilac cloud, his palms were turned up, his eyes were glassy, and he was foaming at the mouth. He was surrounded by a crowd of curious children, who were watching and listening with their mouths open—they never got tired of this spectacle. Candide also stopped to listen, and the children vanished into thin air.

"New forces keep entering the battle . . ." Hearer was raving in a metallic voice. "A successful relocation . . . Vast peaceful regions . . . New squads of helpmates . . . Peace and fusion . . ."

Candide kept going. His head was fairly clear this morning, and he felt able to think, so he began to think about who he was, this Hearer, and what he was for. It now made sense to think about it, because Candide now knew a few things, and it occasionally even seemed to him that he knew quite a lot, if not everything. Every village has its own hearer: we have a hearer, and the Settlement has a hearer, and the old man keeps boasting that the now-mushroomy village used to have a hearer who was really something special. There had probably existed a time when many people knew what the Surpassment was and understood what the successes in question were, and at that time *they* had probably been interested in having many people know about it, or at least they thought that they were interested in that. But then it turned out that they could manage perfectly well without the vast majority of these people, that all these villages had been a mistake, and that the men were merely goats . . . This had happened when they learned to control the lilac fog, and when the first deadlings emerged from the lilac clouds . . . and the first villages found themselves at the bottoms of triangular lakes . . . and the first squads of helpmates appeared . . . But the hearers remained and the tradition continued, a tradition that had never

been abolished simply because *they* had forgotten about it. This
tradition was meaningless, as meaningless as this entire forest, with
its synthetic monsters, its cities that rained destruction, and its
sinister Amazons, the priestesses of parthenogenesis, the cruel and
self-satisfied mistresses of viruses, the puffy, steam-bloated rulers
of the forest . . . as meaningless as the endless hustle and bustle
in the jungle, all those Great Soil Loosenings and Waterloggings,
an endeavor monstrous in its scope and absurdity . . .

His thoughts flowed freely, almost automatically—in the
course of the previous month, they had managed to carve familiar,
permanent channels in his brain, and Candide knew ahead of time
what emotion he would feel next. This is what they call "thinking" in our village. I'm about to feel doubt . . . I didn't even see
anything. I met three forest witches. But you never know who
you'll meet in the forest. I witnessed the destruction of the sly
village, a hill that looked like a factory of living things, the merci-
less execution of an armeater . . . *Destruction, factory, execution* . . .
These are my words, my concepts . . . Even Nava thought that the
destruction of the village wasn't destruction—it was the Surpassment . . . But I don't know what the Surpassment is. I'm afraid of
it, I'm disgusted by it, but that's merely because it's alien to me,
and perhaps the correct phrase is not "mercilessly and pointlessly
siccing the forest on people" but "a masterful, highly organized,
carefully crafted offensive by the present on the past," and maybe
even "a recently matured and invigorated present attacking an
obsolete, rotting past" at that. Not depravity but a revolution.
A law of nature. A law that I'm watching from the outside with
the biased eyes of a stranger—a stranger who doesn't understand
a thing, and for that very reason imagines that he understands
everything and has the right to judge. Like a little boy furious at
the mean old rooster who is cruelly trampling the poor little hen
beneath his feet . . .

He glanced at Hearer, who was sitting in the grass with his
usual dazed expression, shaking his head back and forth and trying
to remember where and what he was. A living radio. Therefore,

there are also living radio transmitters . . . and living tools, and living robots, yes—for example, the deadlings . . . Why don't I feel a single ounce of sympathy toward this splendidly crafted, wonderfully organized undertaking—only hatred and disgust?

Big Fist silently came up behind him and gave him a crack between the shoulder blades. "Standing there and staring, fur and fuzz it," he said. "One guy, he also used to stare, then they twisted his arms and legs off, now he doesn't stare anymore. When are we leaving, eh, Silent Man? How long are you planning to pull my leg? You know, the old woman took off, went to live somewhere else, fur and fuzz it, I had to sleep at the village head's for three nights running myself, and I'm thinking of spending tonight with Tagalong's widow. The food has gotten so rotten that even that old fart doesn't want it, he just makes faces and says, your food's all rotten, fur and fuzz it, I can barely stand to smell it, never mind eat it . . . But I won't go to the Devil's Cliffs, Silent Man, I'll go to the City with you instead, we'll get ourselves some women. If we run into the thieves, they can have half the women, I'm not greedy, fur and fuzz it, and we'll bring the rest of them back to the village, we will, so they can live here, they shouldn't be swimming over there for nothing. One woman, she also used to swim and swim, she got a good smack in the face, now she never swims anymore, can't even stand the sight of water, fur and fuzz it . . . Listen, Silent Man, maybe you were lying about the City and those women? Or maybe you imagined it—the thieves took Nava from you, so you imagined it in your grief. Crookleg doesn't believe it, you know—he thinks you imagined it. How could the City be in a lake, fur and fuzz it? Everyone says it's on a hill, not in a lake. How could you even live in a lake, fur and fuzz it? We'd all drown in there, it's full of water, fur and fuzz it, there are women in there, but so what—I won't get in the water even for a woman, I don't know how to swim, and anyway, why should I? But at least I can stay on shore as you drag them out . . . So here's what we'll do, you'll go in the water, fur and fuzz it, and I'll stay on shore, and we'll be done in no time . . ."

"Did you make yourself a cudgel?" Candide asked.

"And where am I supposed to get a cudgel in the forest, fur and fuzz it?" argued Big Fist. "I'd have to walk over to the swamp to get a cudgel. And I don't have the time, I'm guarding the food so that old man doesn't get his paws on it, and what do I need a cudgel for, anyway, when I'm not planning to get into any fights . . . One guy, he also used to get in fights, fur and fuzz it—"

"All right," said Candide, "I'll make you a cudgel myself. We're leaving the day after tomorrow, don't you forget."

He turned around and went back. Big Fist hadn't changed. None of them had changed. However hard he tried to drum it into them, they didn't understand a thing, and they appeared not to believe a word: The deadlings can't be working for women, that's a real tall tale you're telling, pal, three men together couldn't get to the top of it. Deadlings scare women half to death, you take a look at the old woman, then you can talk. And the village sinking underwater, that was the Surpassment, everyone knows that already, you don't need to tell us that, and what those women of yours have to do with it, I don't know . . . And anyway, Silent Man, you didn't get to the City, come on, admit it, we won't be mad at you, since you've spun such an amusing yarn. But you didn't get to the City, we all know that, because the people who make it to the City don't come back . . . And it wasn't women who took your Nava, it was the thieves, our usual local thieves. You would never have fought off the thieves, Silent Man. Though you're a brave man, of course, and you sure can manage those deadlings—it's almost too awful to watch . . .

The idea of an impending catastrophe simply didn't fit into their heads. This catastrophe was approaching too slowly and had been approaching for too long. It was probably because they thought of a catastrophe as something immediate, as something instantaneous, as related to some kind of disaster. And they weren't able and didn't want to generalize, weren't able and didn't want to think about the world outside their village. There was the village and there was the forest. The forest was stronger—but then, the forest *always* had been and always would be stronger. Catastrophe, what catastrophe? How could this be a catastrophe? It was just life. Now, getting crushed by a tree—that was a kind of catastrophe, of course, but if you just had a bit of sense and kept a head on your shoulders . . .

They'll figure it out one day. When there are no women left; when the swamp is at their doorsteps; when underground springs erupt in the middle of their streets and lilac fog hangs over their roofs . . . Or maybe they won't realize it even then: they'll simply say, we can't live here anymore—it's the Surpassment. And they'll go build another village . . .

Crookleg was sitting by his door, pouring ferment on a crop of mushrooms that had sprung up overnight, and he was getting ready to have breakfast. "Have a seat, have a seat," he welcomed Candide. "Will you have something to eat? These are good mushrooms."

"I'll eat a bit," said Candide, and sat down next to him.

"Eat, eat," said Crookleg. "Your Nava is gone, when will you ever get used to it? . . . I hear you're leaving again. Who told me that? Oh, yes, you told me so yourself: I'm leaving, you said. Why don't you want to stay home? You'd be better off staying home, you would . . . Are you going to the Reeds or to the Anthills? If it's the Reeds, I'd go with you myself. We'd go immediately, we'd turn right and walk along this street, we'd pass through the open wood and pick some mushrooms while we're at it—we'd bring ferment and eat along the way. The mushrooms that grow in the open wood are good, they don't grow in the village, or anywhere else, either, but in the open wood you can eat and eat, and you can't get enough . . . And after we ate, we'd leave the open wood, then we'd go past the Bread Swamp, and there we'd eat again—the Bread Swamp produces good, sweet grain, it always surprises me that the mud and the bog can produce grain like that . . . And then we'd follow the sun, of course, we'd walk for three days, and there we'd be at the Reeds . . ."

"We're going to the Devil's Cliffs," Candide reminded him patiently. "We're leaving the day after tomorrow. Big Fist is coming, too."

Crookleg shook his head in doubt. "The Devil's Cliffs . . ." he repeated. "No, Silent Man, we won't make it to the Devil's Cliffs. Do you know how far away they are, the Devil's Cliffs? Maybe they aren't actually anywhere at all, it's just something people say, the Devil's Cliffs . . . So I'm not going to the Devil's Cliffs, I don't believe in them. Now, if we went to the City, or even better, the Anthills—they aren't far, just a hop and a jump away . . . Listen, Silent Man, how about we go to the Anthills? And Big Fist can come . . . You know, I haven't been to the Anthills once since I hurt my leg. Nava always used to ask me to go there, let's go to the Anthills, Crookleg, she's say . . . Had a mind to see the hole where I hurt my leg, she did . . . And I'd tell her I don't remember where that hole is, and maybe the Anthills, they aren't there anymore, I haven't been there in ages . . ."

Candide chewed the mushroom and looked at Crookleg. And Crookleg kept talking and talking—he talked about the Reeds, and he talked about the Anthills, looking down and only occasionally glancing up at Candide. You're a good man, Crookleg—you're kind, and you've got a way with words, and the village head minds you, as does Big Fist, and the old man is just plain afraid of you, and there's a reason you were the best friend and companion of the notorious Tortured Questioner, a restless seeker, a man who had never found what he was looking for and perished somewhere in the forest . . . There's just one problem: you don't want to let me go into the forest, Crookleg; you feel sorry for this wretch. The forest is a dangerous, deadly place, many enter it but few return from it, and the ones who do return are usually frightened out of their wits or even crippled . . . You might come back with a broken leg, or God knows what else . . . So you try to trick me, Crookleg—either you pretend to be a half-wit, or you pretend you think Silent Man is a half-wit, whereas in actual fact, the only thing you're sure about is this: Silent Man has already somehow managed to come back once, having lost a girl, and lightning doesn't strike twice . . .

"Listen, Crookleg," said Candide. "Listen to me carefully. Say what you like, think what you like, but there's just one thing I have to ask you: don't abandon me, come to the forest with me. I really need you with me in the forest, Crookleg. We're leaving the day after tomorrow, and I'd really like you to come with us. Do you understand?"

Crookleg was looking at Candide, and his faded eyes were inscrutable. "Of course," he said. "I understand everything. We'll go together. We'll come out, turn left, walk until the field, go past the two stones, and come out onto the trail. It's not hard to find, this trail: it's so full of rocks it's easy to break a leg . . . Keep eating, Silent Man, keep eating those mushrooms, they're tasty . . . And then this trail will take us all the way to the mushroomy village, I've told you about it, I think, it's empty, it's overgrown with mushrooms, but they aren't like, say, these mushrooms, they are bad mushrooms, people have gotten sick and even died from them, so we won't stop there, we'll keep going. And before long, we'll make it to the kook village, where they make pots out of soil—the things people think of! They started doing that after the blue grass went through them. And it wasn't a big deal, they didn't even get sick, they just started making pots out of soil . . . We won't stop there either, there's no point stopping there, we'll just turn right—and there we'll be, right at your Clay Meadow . . ."

Or maybe I shouldn't take you? thought Candide. You've already been there, the forest has already chewed you up and spit you out, and who knows, maybe you've already rolled around on the ground, screaming in pain and fear while a young woman, biting her adorable lip and splaying her childish fingers, hung over your body. I don't know, I don't know. But we do have to go. We have to capture at least two of them, at least one of them, so we can learn everything, so we can get to the bottom of it all . . .

And then what? They are the damned, the miserable damned. Or rather, they are the happy damned, because they do not know that they're damned; that the strong ones of their world only see them as a dirty tribe of rapists; that the strong ones have already targeted them with clouds of controlled viruses, armies of robots, and the walls of their forest; that everything has already been decided for them; and that—this is the most terrible thing of all—the historical truth here, in the forest, isn't on their side. They are relics who have been condemned to death by objective laws, and helping them means holding up progress—it means putting an obstacle in the way of the front lines of progress, even if only a small one. Except I don't care about that in the least, thought Candide. What's their progress to me? It's not my progress, and the only reason I'm calling it progress is because I can't find a better word . . .

I can't choose this with my head. I have to choose this with my heart. Objective laws can't be good or bad; they are outside the bounds of morality. But I'm not outside the bounds of morality! Maybe if those helpmates had found me, healed me, and showered me with affection, if they had taken me in and felt sorry for me—well, then I would have probably found it simple and natural to take the side of their progress, and then I, too, would have believed that Crookleg and all these villages are irritating anachronisms that we've already fussed with too long . . . Then again, maybe not, maybe I would have never found it simple or easy, I can't stand to see people being treated like animals. But maybe the issue is merely one of terminology, and if I had learned the women's language, everything would sound different: enemies of progress, stupid, lazy gluttons . . . Lofty ideals . . . A higher purpose . . . Laws of nature . . . And this is why we're annihilating half the population?

No, it's not for me. It wouldn't be for me in any language. I don't care that Crookleg is a spoke in the wheel of their progress. I'll do everything to make sure that this spoke slows the wheel down. And if I never manage to get back to the biological research station—and I probably will never manage to get back—I'll do everything to make the wheel stop. Then again, if I do find a way to get back . . . *Hmmm*. Strange, it never occurred to me to look at the Administration from the outside. And it doesn't occur to Crookleg to look at the forest from the outside. And the same probably goes for those helpmates. Whereas it's quite a curious spectacle—the Administration as seen from above. All right, I'll have to think about it later.

"Then that's settled," he said. "We're leaving the day after tomorrow."

"Sure thing," Crookleg immediately replied. "We'll go out and turn left—"

Suddenly, shouts came from the field. Women started screeching. Many voices rang out in unison: "Silent Man! Hey, Silent Man!"

Crookleg started. "Sounds like deadlings!" he said, getting up in a hurry. "Come on, Silent Man, let's go, I want to watch."

Candide stood up, pulled the scalpel out from under his shirt, and began to walk toward the outskirts.

AFTERWORD

BY BORIS STRUGATSKY

In March 1965, the brothers Strugatsky finally got a permanent working journal. I can't say that the entries in this journal conclusively solve the problem of having to reconstruct lost or forgotten facts, but these records are definitely of value. I had drawn on this journal when I spoke at a 1987 meeting of the Leningrad seminar of science fiction writers, delivering something resembling a lecture on "How *The Snail on the Slope* was created, a history and commentary." And it was on the basis of this very lecture, which has been corrected, abridged, and supplemented as necessary, that I've written the remarks below.

On March 4, 1965, two young, newly hatched writers—it hadn't even been a year since they joined the Writers' Union—arrived at the Artists' Retreat in Gagra. Everything there was great: lovely weather, excellent service, delicious food, practically perfect health, stellar mental and physical states, and a whole stash of ideas and scenarios ready for development. Everything was wonderful! We had been assigned to the VIP quarters, a feat we could never replicate in the future. And this time we got lucky, because it was the off-season, and the only ones staying at the Gagra Artists' Retreat other than the brothers Strugatsky were the soccer players from FC Zenit, who were holding a training camp in those parts.

Everything would have been unbelievably wonderful, had it not suddenly transpired that the Strugatskys were apparently in a state of creative crisis! We didn't know this yet. We had thought that everything was going well, that we had a clear and obvious path forward. It was clear what we should be doing, and it was obvious what we should be writing about. We did, after all, bring a fairly good sketch of a novel with us. Well, it would be more accurate to describe it as a decently conceived setup rather than a novel. Imagine an island. Somehow, people turn up on this island—maybe they are shipwrecked, or perhaps they come as members of a scientific expedition. And what they find are monkeys. There's something off about these monkeys—they behave in a very strange way, not at all like normal monkeys. They are fat and slow, and they aren't afraid of people at all; on the contrary, they try to stay close to them. And mysterious things begin to happen on this island—people suddenly go insane, they die strange, inexplicable deaths . . . And in the depths of this island they find a village where the monkeys live together with the natives—a pitiful tribe, clearly about to go extinct, seeming to consist of only feebleminded idiots . . . Well, then it turns out that the strange monkeys are to blame for everything. It turns out that these aren't normal monkeys, they are *paramonkeys*, pseudomonkeys, and they apparently feed on human thoughts. They suck the intellect out of a person, they make use of his or her intellect, just like we make use of the energy of the sun. Except that this doesn't hurt the sun, whereas people go crazy and die. The symbolism, as you can see, is rather transparent: fat, greedy creatures only interested in the pleasures of the flesh, thriving at the expense of the human intellect, actively turning the spiritual into the physical, and turning thoughts and ideas into shit. And on top of it all, killing the possessor of the intellect. Philistines. The bourgeoisie. Barbarians . . .

That's how things appeared to us at first. And we spent our whole first day in Gagra vigorously refining and adding to this scenario. On the second day, we gave up on the monkeys. What did we care about some island, some monkeys, some natives? We're interested in society! Civilization! The monkeys were decisively scrapped. Why allow monkeys into our already complicated society? And besides, we'd never be able to get that published . . .

(The only thing left over from the monkey scenario was an occasional and to us very amusing minor ritual. When we were mulling over a new plot and the work had ground to a halt, one of us would inevitably suggest, looking very sagacious, "They find themselves on an island . . ." and the other would readily chime in ". . . and they discover monkeys. Strange monkeys!")

We didn't need monkeys, and we didn't need an island. After all, we could use a country with an unspecified social order. And it won't have monkeys. Instead, it'll have parallel evolution! *The shadow of protein-based life* on Earth. It turns out that from time immemorial, planet Earth has hosted a parallel class of beings without an independent form. They are, as was recorded in our journal, a kind of *protoplasm-mimicroid*. Protoplasm-mimicroids colonize living beings and feed on their juices. Once upon a time, they destroyed the trilobites. Then they destroyed the dinosaurs. Then these awful protoplasm-mimicroids attacked the Neanderthals. This was more difficult—the Neanderthals already had the rudiments of intelligence, they were harder to master—but as everybody knows, the Neanderthals also took a wrong turn in their evolutionary journey. They, naturally, were also destroyed by the protoplasm . . . And in the present day, the protoplasm feeds on people, on you and me. The remarkable thing is that human beings who've been colonized by the protoplasm don't change much in outward manifestation. To all appearances, they are still the same people—simply no longer interested in any spiritual or intellectual matters. Their only remaining concerns are of the material variety: eating, drinking, getting laid, finding something to gawk at . . . So what is it that prevents the protoplasm from taking over the word? Well, the thing is that when a human being engages in intense thought, the protoplasm can't stand it and starts to disintegrate, then it's destroyed and flows out as a pool of disgusting, quickly evaporating ooze . . .

These were the rather unappetizing images that were then hovering in front of our eyes. It was easy to picture; it had the social symbolism, and the conceptual framework, and a plot that in those days felt original—it had everything . . . But nothing came of it. I don't know (or maybe no longer remember) why. It just wouldn't go. We stalled. We stalled again, just like we had four years earlier when we were working on *Escape Attempt*. We again hit a dead end, and we again experienced the sort of panic that Don Juan might have experienced if a doctor had suddenly informed him, "That's all over and done with, sir. Alas, you must put that out of your mind. Forever."

Filled with panic, we began frantically flipping through our notes, where we, like any decent young writers, had an enormous list of potential plots, ideas, and scenarios. And out of these scenarios, we selected one, which had attracted and excited us a long time ago. Imagine a certain planet that contains two different intelligent species. And these species are locked in a struggle for survival, a war. And this isn't a technological war, the kind that earthlings know about and are used to, but a biological war, which to an outside observer from Earth doesn't look like war at all. A military action on this planet is interpreted by earthlings as, for example, a kind of atmospheric condensation that hasn't yet been adequately explained by scientists, or maybe even as the creative activity of some alien mind. But certainly not as war. Our journal lists a number of methods of warfare: "Waterlogging, jungling, limecovering (a defensive maneuver), direct exposure to viral and bacterial diseases, the weakening of genetic material by mutagenic viruses, destroying old instincts and instilling new ones, viruses

that sterilize the men . . ." The earthlings land there and—*oof!*—
find themselves in the middle of this ridiculous pandemonium,
in which it's completely impossible to tell someone's deliberate
actions from random paroxysms of nature . . .

Once, a number of years earlier, this plot had seemed to us
to be promising and appealing, and now, feeling panicked and
even desperate, we decided to give it a try. I can remember it
as if it were yesterday: we sat down on the beach, chilled by the
March wind and caressed by the already pleasant March sun, and
we began to carefully and thoughtfully develop the scenario . . .

Pandora. Of course, the planet had to be Pandora, a strange,
wild planet we had invented a long time ago for our Noon
Universe stories. It was a wonderful setting for our adventures—a
jungle planet completely covered by impassable forest and inhab-
ited by strange and dangerous creatures. Here and there, white
cliffs jut out of the forest, resembling the Amazonian plateaus
described by Arthur Conan Doyle in *The Lost World*, and it is on
these practically uninhabited tablelands that the earthlings set up
their bases. They observe the planet, almost without interfering
with its ways, and in fact they don't even try to interfere, because
the earthlings can't make heads or tails of what's going on here.
The jungle here lives a mysterious life of its own. Occasionally,
people disappear in there; sometimes they are rescued, sometimes not.

The earthlings have turned Pandora into something like a
game reserve for hunters. Back then, in the middle of the 1960s,
we didn't yet know anything about the environment, and we had
never heard of an endangered species list. Therefore, we made
hunting a popular pastime for our people of the future. Hunters
come to Pandora in order to kill tahorgs, wondrous and fearsome animals . . . Meanwhile, Leonid Gorbovsky from *Noon:
22nd Century* and *Far Rainbow* has been living on this planet for
months and no one can figure out what he's doing there, and why
a great spaceman and member of the World Council is wasting
his precious time here . . .

Gorbovsky is our old hero—to a certain extent, he's the personification of the man of the future, the embodiment of kindness and intelligence, the embodiment of culture in the highest sense of the word. He's sitting by the edge of an enormous precipice, dangling his feet, watching the strange forest that extends all the way to the horizon, and he's waiting for something.

In the Noon Universe, all fundamental social problems and many scientific problems have long since been solved. The problem of a humanlike android has been solved, the problem of contacting alien civilizations has been solved, and so has, of course, the problem of education. People have become carefree and reckless. They seem to have lost the instinct of self-preservation. The Playing Man, *Homo ludens*, has emerged. (This was when we first became interested in the concept of the Playing Man.) All basic needs are automatically taken care of by billions of intelligent machines, while billions of humans only do what they want. They do scientific research, fly into space, and dive into the depths of the ocean in the same way that we currently play chess, tic-tac-toe, or volleyball . . . And that's also how they study Pandora—casually, playfully, lightly, without a care in the world. *Homo ludens* . . .

Gorbovsky is afraid. Gorbovsky suspects that this can't end well, that sooner or later humanity will encounter some currently unimaginable hidden danger in space, and that humanity will then experience shock, humanity will experience shame, defeat, death—you name it . . . And so Gorbovsky, with his extraordinary nose for the unusual, roams from one planet to the next and looks for *strange things*. He doesn't know exactly what he's looking for himself. This wild and dangerous Pandora, a planet that earthlings have been cheerfully and eagerly exploring for a number of decades, seems to him to be the focal point of some hidden menace—he doesn't know precisely what. And he's sitting there so that he's on the spot when something happens. He's sitting there so he can prevent people from acting rashly or hastily, so that he can be the proverbial catcher in the rye.

(Curiously enough, an entry in our work journal reads, "Gorbovsky, having made sense of the situation on Pandora, realizes that humanity has nothing to fear here. And he immediately loses interest in the planet. 'I'm going to take off, there are a number of other planets worth checking out. For example, Rainbow.'" Apparently at the time we were still worried about the problem of "Gorbovsky's untimely death" in *Far Rainbow*—a problem we never did get around to resolving.)

Gorbovsky, hunters, preparations for the Pandorian safari—this is all happening on top of the Mountain. Meanwhile, other things are happening inside the Forest. If I remember correctly, we had read a samizdat article by the famous Soviet geneticist Vladimir Pavlovich Efroimson (then in disfavor), which boldly claimed that humankind could have existed and developed perfectly well entirely through parthenogenesis. If you run a weak current through a human ovum, it begins to divide—and in due course, you get a girl, always a girl, and moreover, an exact copy of the mother. Men are unnecessary. Completely unnecessary. And we populated our Forest with at least three different types of creatures: first of all, the colonizers, an intelligent race at war with the nonhumanoids; second of all, the women, who had splintered away from the colonizers, who multiply parthenogenetically and who've created their own, extremely complicated biological civilization; and, finally, the miserable peasants—men and women—whom everyone has simply forgotten about in the midst of all their fighting. They live there in their villages . . . When others had needed bread, they'd been necessary. And when others had learned how to grow bread without them, they'd been forgotten. And now they live on their own, with their outdated technology, with their outdated traditions, completely isolated from the violent tumult of real life. And then an earthling turns up in the midst of this quivering green hell. In our original version, this was our old friend Athos Sidorov from *Noon: 22nd Century*. He's living in there, deeply depressed, studying this world, unable to get out, lacking the strength to get home . . .

This was how we came up with the first outline of the novel, its skeleton. We planned the chapters. We had already figured out that the novel had to be structured as follows: a chapter of "the view from above, from the Mountain," then a chapter of "the view from within, from the Forest." We came up with the idea that the peasants have to talk in a slow, roundabout, viscous manner, and that they all have to constantly lie. And they don't lie because they are bad people, or because they are so immoral, but simply because that's how their world works—nobody knows anything, everyone is merely repeating rumors, and rumors are almost always lies. These sluggish creatures, whom nobody needs, whom everyone has abandoned, became for us a kind of symbol for a humanity that has fallen victim to cold-blooded progress. It turned out that we were very interested in writing about these people, that we began to feel a certain sympathy toward them, we were ready to empathize with them, pity them, feel resentment on their behalf.

We began to write, writing chapter after chapter, a Gorbovsky chapter, then an Athos Sidorov chapter, and gradually, a new paradigm began to crystallize from the scenario itself, a paradigm that turned out to be very fundamental and significant for us. This is the paradigm of the relationship between humans and the laws of nature and society. We know that all of our actions, both moral and physical, are constrained by certain laws. We know that anyone who attempts to resist these laws will sooner or later be broken, defeated, destroyed, just like Alexander Pushkin's mad Evgenii in "The Bronze Horseman," who dared to yell "Just wait!" at an Architect of History. We know that history can only be harnessed by those who act in full accordance with its laws . . . But then what about a man who *does not like these laws*?!

When it comes to the laws of physics, well, that's simpler—we seem to have gotten used to them and made our peace with their immutability. Or we've learned to circumvent these laws. We even occasionally exploit them for our own benefit. People ought to fall—but they fly. Including into space. People ought to drown—but they live right at the bottom of the ocean. And if a rigid law of nature doesn't, say, allow one to travel back in time—well, of course, that's sad. But at the end of the day, that's a fact we can resign ourselves to, and without any intense emotion. For some reason, this fact offends neither our pride nor our dignity.

It is much more difficult to reconcile yourself to the over-powering force of the laws of history and society. For example, try to put yourself in the shoes of the men and women who before the revolution had been *everything*, and after the revolution became *nothing*—the men and women who had belonged to the privileged class. They had known since childhood that the world would be their oyster, that they were the ones for whom Russia had been created, and that their lives would be absolutely wonderful. Then, suddenly, their world collapsed. Suddenly, the social environment they had grown up with disappeared without a trace and was replaced by a pitiless new environment that was extraordinarily cruel toward them. And yet the smartest of these people understood perfectly well that this was a consequence of the laws governing the development of society, that it wasn't some evil person throwing them into the mud, onto the very bottom of the ocean of life, but the blind, immutable laws of history. How should people feel about a law of society that seems bad to them? Is this even a valid question? A good law of society, a bad law of society—what does that even mean? Is the fact that productive forces are continuously increasing good or bad? We know that these forces will sooner or later collide with the relations of production—this is a law of human society. Is it good or bad?

I remember spending a lot of time discussing these topics. We were interested in them. And very soon we realized that we'd been writing about this all along. If the fate of our earthling, who had found himself among the peasants—the doomed, oppressed peasants—didn't actually contain the answer to this question, then at the very least it contained the question. Because in this place, there exists a dominant progressive civilization—this biological civilization of women. And it also contains the vestiges of a previous subspecies of *Homo sapiens*, who are destined for inevitable, certain extinction under pressure from "progressive modernity." So then our earthling, our brother in kind, who has found himself in this world—how should he feel about the things he's seeing? Here, historical truth is on the side of the extremely unpleasant, very alien women, these self-satisfied and self-confident Amazons. Meanwhile, the hero's sympathies lie entirely with these simpleminded, ignorant, helpless, and ridiculous men and women, who did, after all, save him, nurse him back to health, find him a wife, get him a dwelling, take him for one of their own . . . What should a civilized person do, how should he behave, when he realizes the direction of progress, and he finds it *abhorrent*? How should he feel about progress, when this progress sticks in his craw?!

On March 6, we wrote our first sentence: "From above, the forest looked like dappled foam . . ." On March 20, we finished the first draft. We wrote quickly. As soon as we'd develop a detailed plan, we'd always write very quickly. But there was a surprise awaiting us: before the ink on our last sentence had dried, we discovered that we'd written something unacceptable, something that wasn't going to do. We suddenly realized that we didn't care about Gorbovsky in the least. What did Gorbovsky have to do with it? What did our glorious utopian future, with its entirely invented problems, have to do with it? For God's sake! All kinds of hell is breaking loose around us, and we're wasting our time on inventing problems and solutions for future generations. Like they won't figure out how to deal with their own problems when time comes! And by March 21, we had already decided that we couldn't consider the novel complete, that we had to do something with it, something drastic. But we still had absolutely no idea *what*.

It was obvious that the chapters about the Forest were fine. There, the "scenario fit the paradigm"; everything was finished and all the loose ends were tied off. This novel within a novel could even exist independently. But when it came to the parts about Gorbovsky—they were no good. And the issue wasn't that they were, say, badly written. No, they were written in a perfectly estimable way, but they had nothing to do with the story we were then trying to tell. They *did not interest* us. The Gorbovsky chapters had to be excised from the text and put aside. Let them sit a bit.

(And sit they did, all the way until the mid-1980s. At the beginning of perestroika, when it was possible to get *anything* published, when publishers were ready to wrest anything that hadn't previously appeared in print from our grasp, we had taken our "Gorbovsky" out of the archives and discovered to our intense amazement that it wasn't half bad. The text had stood the test of time, was easy to read, and seemed to us to be capable of engaging the interest of a reader. That was how the novel *Disquiet* came into being and took on a life of its own.)

Excising the chapters was easy—the difficult thing was finding something appropriate to replace them with. How were we going to replace them? This gloomy question didn't yet have an answer. The crisis had given rise to half a novel, but the crisis hadn't dissipated—it was still hanging over us. We had never experienced a double crisis ("with multiple warheads") like this before. But we no longer felt a real sense of despair—for some strange reason, we were sure that we were up to the challenge.

The next time we met was at the end of April. Unfortunately, I can no longer remember how we came up with the key idea that determined the plot and the essence of the second half of the novel, nor who thought of it first. This is sadly not recorded in the journal. In fact, the journal doesn't even contain a clear formulation of the idea. It's just that on April 28, there's suddenly the following entry: "Gorbovsky is Peretz, Athos is Zykov." And a little farther down: "1. The runaway machine; 2. Getting ready to go into the forest; 3. Trying to convince everyone to take him with them into the forest." The idea that the future in the novel should be replaced by the present had been born and had begun to operate.

New names begin to appear in the journal. We started to develop the "Peretz" storyline, this time in its eventual final form. "Fails to have a meeting or rendezvous with the boss, who occasionally comes outside to do his exercises"; "Arranges with the driver for tomorrow"; "As he waits in the truck, the truck's wheels are removed." Something had happened to us here, something important. We had come up with the idea of the Administration for Forest Affairs—that surreal parody of every government agency in existence. Somehow, in some way, we had realized that one fantastic storyline, that of the Forest, should be complemented by another fantastic storyline, but that this one should be symbolic. It shouldn't be science fiction, it should instead be symbolic. One person is desperately struggling to get out of the Forest, while another, very different from the first in both character and disposition, is desperately trying to get into the Forest, to figure out what is going on in there.

On April 30, the word "Administration" first appears in the journal, followed by an "organizational chart": the Eradication Team, the Research Team, the Armed Guard Team, the Scientific Guard team . . . There's a detailed outline of the first chapter, fragments of our hero's thoughts, and then, a pivotal line: "The Forest is the future."

This was the moment that everything clicked into place. The novel stopped being science fiction (assuming it ever had been) and became simply fantastic, grotesque, symbolic—whatever you want to call it. Everything turned out to have a hidden meaning; every scene became full of new ideas. What is the Forest? The Forest is the Future. A Future we know nothing about. A Future we can only speculate about, usually baselessly, which we only have fragmentary insights about, insights that crumble if subjected to any kind of closer scrutiny. When it comes to the future—if I'm being frank, if I'm speaking with my hand on my heart—when it comes to the future, the only thing that we know with any degree of certainty is that it will completely fail to correspond to any of our ideas about it. We don't even know whether the world of the

Future will be good or bad; we are fundamentally incapable of answering this question, because chances are that the world of the Future will be so immeasurably alien to us, that it will be so far from corresponding to our ideas about it, that we won't know how the concepts *good, bad, mediocre,* and *subpar* even apply to it. It will simply be alien and unlike anything we have known, in the same way that the world of a modern-day metropolis would feel absurd and unlike anything he has known to a modern-day cannibal from Malaita Island.

The Forest that we had already depicted fit perfectly into this paradigm. Why shouldn't we imagine that in the distant future, humanity will merge with nature, in large part becoming a part of nature? Humans would stop being human in the modern sense of the word. It wouldn't be all that hard. You would only need to deform one human instinct: the reproductive instinct. This instinct rests, like on a foundation, on the heterosexuality of our species, on its two genders. If you took away one of the genders, you would get completely new creatures, who resembled people but were people no longer. They would have completely different, alien moral principles, they would have very different ideas about what should be and what could be, they would have different goals, they'd even have a different perspective on the meaning of life . . . It turned out that we hadn't spent a month writing for nothing! It turned out that we had created a completely new model of the Future! And moreover, it wasn't merely a hypothetical framework, not an inert, stable world in the manner of Huxley or, say, Orwell, but a world in flux, a world that hadn't yet finished forming itself, a world still under construction. And at the same time, it contained remnants of people from the past, living lives of their own, who were psychologically akin to us and therefore gave us something like a moral frame of reference . . .

And from this perspective, the as of yet unwritten world of the Administration looked completely different. What is the Administration in our new, symbolic conception of the universe? That's easy—it's the Present! It's the Present, with all of its chaos, with all of its stupidity, improbably combined with shrewdness. The Present, where human errors and delusions meet an ossified system of habitual inhumanity. The very same Present in which people are constantly thinking about the Future, living for the Future, shouting slogans in praise of the Future, and yet at the same time, they are fouling up this Future, eradicating this Future, doing their best to stamp out every single one of its tender shoots, trying to turn the Future into a parking lot, striving to turn the Forest, their Future, into an English garden with carefully manicured lawns, so that the Future doesn't become what it is capable of becoming, but rather what we'd like it to be today . . .

It's curious that this happy idea, which helped us come up with the storyline of the Administration, and which illuminated the entire novel for us in a completely new way, has on the whole remained entirely inaccessible to the general reader. I can count on one hand the number of people who fully grasped the entirety of the authorial intent. And we did scatter hints decoding our symbolism throughout the story. You'd think that the epigraphs would suffice. The future is a pine wood; the future is the Forest. The pine wood awaits you, and there's no turning back, the Future is already here . . . And the snail stubbornly climbing Mount Fuji is another symbol of man's progress toward the future—the slow, grueling, but inexorable progress toward unfathomable heights . . .

And the question is this: Should we, the authors, consider it a failure that an idea that helped us make the novel multifaceted and deep was never really understood by the reader? I don't know. I only know that there exist many interpretations of *The Snail on the Slope*, many of which are totally internally consistent and in no way contradict the text. So maybe it's actually a good thing that this work generates very different responses from a wide variety of people? And maybe the more interpretations there are, the more reason there is to consider the work successful? After all, the original of the painting *The Heroic Feat of Forest Explorer Selivan* had been "destroyed . . . as befits a work of art that cannot be allowed to have ambiguous interpretations." So perhaps the only way a "work of art" can survive is if it has not one but many interpretations?

Then again, the multitude of possible readings didn't do *The Snail on the Slope* much good. The novel didn't get destroyed, per se, but for many years it was forbidden. In May 1969, a certain V. Aleksandrov (a man of apparently colossal intellect), devoted the following remarkable lines to our novel (I'm quoting with a number of omissions, which in no way change the meaning of his philippic):

> The authors do not state where the action takes place, nor do they mention how their society is organized. But the entirety of their narrative, with all of its events and dialogue, makes it absolutely clear what country they mean. The fantastic society depicted by A. and B. Strugatsky . . . is composed of people who live in chaos and turmoil, who are engaged in aimless, unnecessary busywork, and who carry out stupid laws and directives. Fear, suspicion, sycophancy, and bureaucracy reign here.

You can't help but wonder: Is it possible that the author of this critical review was an undercover dissident, who had snuck into the party apparatus in order to have a plausible pretext for dragging the most just and humane Soviet state through the mud? Although it must be said that this piece was only the first (if also the stupidest) in a whole series of vicious pans of *The Snail on the Slope*. As a result, the novel was only published in its entirety, in its proper form, in the most modern of times—in 1988. And back in the late 1960s, the issues of *Baikal* that had printed part of the "Administration" half of the novel (wonderfully illustrated by Sever Gansovsky!) had been pulled from libraries and put into a restricted-access collection. The book became samizdat, made its way to the West, and was then published through the Munich publishing house Posev, and subsequently, anyone who was found to be in possession of it during a house search would be in trouble—at work at the very least.

Both the authors themselves liked and, more importantly, respected this novel, and thought of it as their most complete and important work. For obvious reasons, its total circulation in Russia (the USSR) has been relatively small, around 1.2 million books. However, it's popular abroad: twenty-seven editions in fifteen countries—a sure third place behind *Roadside Picnic* and *Hard to be a God.*